SURF
SMUGGLERS

Center Point
Large Print

Also by Melody Carlson and available from
Center Point Large Print:

As Time Goes By
We'll Meet Again
Harbor Secrets
Riptide Rumors

THE LEGACY OF SUNSET COVE

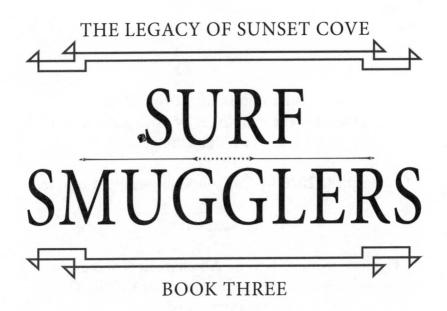

SURF
SMUGGLERS

BOOK THREE

MELODY CARLSON

CENTER POINT LARGE PRINT
THORNDIKE, MAINE

This Center Point Large Print edition
is published in the year 2020 by arrangement with
WhiteFire Publishing.

The text of this Large Print edition is unabridged.
In other aspects, this book may vary
from the original edition.
Printed in the United States of America
on permanent paper.
Set in 16-point Times New Roman type.

ISBN: 978-1-64358-702-8

The Library of Congress has cataloged this record under
Library of Congress Control Number: 2020942114

CHAPTER 1

May 1917

Anna could tell by Jim's expression that the news was not good. But it was the end of the day and the end of the week, and tomorrow's newspaper had already been finished. The clanking of metal told her the press was just starting.

"What is it?" She set her hat on her desk and braced herself for whatever it was her managing editor had to say. Hopefully not another tragedy for the Allied troops battling tyranny in Europe. Not when it already sounded nearly hopeless over there.

Jim glumly shook his head, fingering the strip of paper that must've just come over the telegraph. "Well, as you know, the Nivelle Offensive failed."

"Yes, a huge loss for France and Britain. But that's not news, Jim."

"And you know how Robert Nivelle raised Allied hopes, predicting such a *brilliant* victory." His tone was sullen. "Pride before the fall."

Anna was well aware of the recent French and

British bloodbath. "I suppose American troops will be needed more than ever now." She sighed to consider all the young men about to ship overseas. Even their office boy Willy had just signed up.

"Thanks to Nivelle." Jim frowned. "What a mess."

"War is a mess. But we covered Nivelle's story last week." She reached for her hat again.

"The news is that he's been replaced by Pétain. But the bigger news is that battlefield statistics have been released." Jim waved the strip of paper. "An effort to prove that Nivelle was inept and deserved to be removed. The count's not fully in, but it's been leaked that France suffered more than a hundred-fifty thousand casualties."

"One-hundred-fifty thousand soldiers injured?" Anna gasped.

"And as many as thirty thousand dead."

"Oh, my." She sank back into her chair. "I can't even grasp that number. It's obscene."

"And that was only the French statistics. The Brits aren't talking."

"What about the Germans?" she asked in a flat tone. "What kind of losses do you suppose they suffered?"

"Hard to say. Kaiser Wilhelm isn't exactly communicating with the US."

She rolled her eyes. "Who would trust him anyway?"

"Anyway, I thought you should know about this. If you like, I'll stop the press and run this story."

She pursed her lips, considering those huge numbers blown up across the front page of Saturday's paper. As editor in chief, it was her decision. But Sunset Cove was a small town, and lately the war news had been so very grim. "Do you think it's really necessary for tomorrow's paper? It's not that I want to keep our readers in the dark, but those numbers are so disturbing. And, really, it's just one piece of a much greater picture. I can understand the French wanting this information released—it gives them good reason to can Nivelle. But I think we should save it until our next edition. Maybe more information will be available by then and make for a bigger story."

"Good point." Jim looked relieved.

"And then I can do an op-ed on it as well."

He brightened. "Great. I guess we can call it a day then."

She stood, putting on her hat. "And the good people of Sunset Cove won't be slammed with another hard-hitting war headline with their Saturday morning coffee. It's like a small reprieve."

"I like how you think, boss."

She glanced at the clock. "I'm sure you're relieved not to work late. Especially since I know you're going to the dance tonight." Anna's

7

daughter Katy had already mentioned that Jim was escorting her to the Spring Fling. Even though Anna was aware of Jim's interest in her daughter, she was still getting used to the idea.

"But I wouldn't use a silly dance as an excuse to shirk my responsibilities here at the paper."

"Nor would I." She walked with him through the newspaper office, which, besides the noisy pressroom, was mostly vacant. "As it turns out, I have plans for tonight as well."

"The dance?" he asked.

"Perhaps." She smiled coyly.

"Oh . . . ?" His brows lifted with typical reporter curiosity, but Anna didn't offer any more information. Jim might have a nose for news, but he didn't need to know everything about her and her family. Not yet, anyway. It was one thing for Jim to take Katy to a dance, but Anna felt certain her daughter wasn't taking his attentions too seriously. And that was just fine with Anna.

Because Katy had a bright future ahead. At seventeen, she'd attained her high school diploma and, though not yet eighteen, she was part-owner and head designer of Kathleen's Dress Shop. As Anna walked home, she felt grateful her daughter was independent and strong-willed. Jim was a good man, but Katy was a modern young woman with a mind of her own.

Before going into the house, Anna paused in front of the tall stone mansion that overlooked the sea. The historic McDowell house had been her home as a child and then, after twenty years of absence, had become her home again. She could hardly believe that nearly a year had passed since she and Katy had left Portland to move back here. Did she regret giving up her job as the first female editor at the *Oregonian*? Not a bit.

Anna went inside, stopping by Mac's sitting room like she usually did after work. Even though Mac wasn't fully recovered from last spring's stroke and was still coping with a paralyzed arm and clumsy leg, his speech had improved greatly.

"Good afternoon, Anna." His pale blue eyes lit up. "I just asked Bernice to bring some tea. Care to join me?"

"I'd love to." Anna removed her hat and jacket, laying them on a side chair.

"Get the paper finished?" he asked with his usual interest.

"In the hands of the pressmen." She smiled. Poor Mac. It had been hard on him to let her take over his newspaper. For that reason, she tried to include him in the daily goings on . . . and to ask his advice. So she explained about Nivelle's dismissal and the French army's dismaying statistics.

He slowly shook his head. "That's too bad. But France was right to get rid of Nivelle. Bad for morale."

"The news only just came. So I decided to hold

off on the story until next week. Hopefully, we'll get more information by then."

He rubbed his chin with a creased brow. "Well, I suppose that's a good call."

"Hello, Anna." Bernice set down the tea things. "I just made the shortbread this afternoon. And that's my huckleberry jam."

"Thank you." Anna watched Bernice fill a teacup. "Looks delicious."

"I brought in enough for Katy too. In case she joins you. And since no one's home for dinner tonight, Mickey and I plan to enjoy a nice quiet evening to ourselves."

"Not going to the Spring Fling?" Anna teased.

Bernice chuckled as she straightened her apron. "All I want is to put my feet up, and I expect Mickey will be sound asleep before eight."

"Sounds like a good plan," Mac told her. "If Lucille hadn't talked me into going, I'd do the same." Anna winked at Bernice. They both got a kick out of the way Mac and his previously estranged wife got along so congenially these days. Handy since Lucille now lived only two doors down.

"Well, I hope you all have a good time." Bernice looked at Mac. "And Mickey'll be along around six to help you into your evening duds."

After Bernice left, Anna turned to Mac with concern. "Do you think Bernice is working too hard?" she asked quietly. "I know she's older

10

than you are. Mickey is too. Do you ever wonder if they're getting too old? Should you consider letting them retire?"

Mac frowned. "I guess I never gave it much thought."

"It would be different if they were only caring for you. But with Katy and me . . . and the additional social activities we all enjoy, well, I sometimes worry the workload might be too much for them. But every time I offer to help with housekeeping, Bernice practically throws a fit."

"Well, she's always saying she likes to stay busy." He shrugged. "I wouldn't be too concerned."

"Hello in the house," Katy called out.

"In here," Anna replied. "Tea and fresh shortbread."

"Lovely." Katy entered the room, greeting them with her usual flair. Her shell-pink layered satin skirt rustled as she unpinned her oversized hat, laying it on Anna's things before she took the chair next to Mac. "I'm famished."

"Here you go." Anna handed her a fresh cup of tea.

"What a day." For the next few minutes, Katy amused them both with the latest comings and goings at Kathleen's Dress Shop. She always made it sound so exciting and dramatic, but Katy was like that about everything.

"Such an interesting place to work." Anna

sipped her tea. "Far more entertaining than the newspaper office."

"Hmm?" Mac's brow creased.

"Well, we certainly get more than our fair share of tittle-tattle." Katy giggled. "If we wanted, I suppose we could publish our own newspaper."

"Or at least a gossip column," Anna teased.

"Speaking of columns." Mac pointed to Katy. "Did you finish your fashion column for tomorrow's edition?"

"Of course. I turned it in to Jim days ago." Katy set her teacup in the saucer and stood. "And now, if you'll both excuse me, I need to get ready for tonight's festivities."

Mac glanced up at his mantle clock. "It takes you more than two hours?"

"Grandmother left the shop at two o'clock so she could take four hours!" Katy glanced at Anna. "And you should come up and try on that new dress I brought home for you, to make sure it fits right. Although I'm fairly certain it's perfect."

"Three generations of McDowell women." Mac smiled with pride. "You'll all be the belles of the ball."

"Come on, Mother." Katy reached for Anna's hand. "I have something special to show you upstairs."

Anna excused herself and followed Katy up to her room. "I received a letter from Portland this morning," Katy said mysteriously.

12

"From one of your old school friends?"

"From Sarah." Katy extracted a small white envelope from her soft leather handbag, holding it up like a prize.

"Sarah? Do you mean *Sarah Rose?*" Anna looked at the letter with interest. She hadn't heard from their old friend and housekeeper in several years—not since Katy was old enough to be left home unsupervised.

"That's right." Katy removed two neatly folded pages.

"I can't believe it." Anna peered down at the letter, recognizing the neat penmanship and remembering how Sarah's mother had been a teacher before they'd moved from Connecticut. "I haven't seen our Sarah in ages."

"It's been nearly seven years," Katy said. "I remember because I'd just turned eleven when she married Abe. And I was so upset about her leaving us."

"How is she?"

"Unfortunately, she's not doing very well." Katy handed over the letter. "See for yourself while I run my bath."

Concerned for her old friend, Anna began to read.

Dear sweet Katy,

Thank you for the birthday package you sent me care of the Portland Hotel. It took two months to reach me because Abe no longer works at the hotel, but a neighbor woman got it to me. The scarf is very beautiful. I think of you whenever I wear it.

Abe left the hotel last winter to work in the shipyard. Not long afterward, he met his fate in a terrible accident. I am now a widow. I wish I had better news to share, but times are hard.

I am happy to hear of your new dress shop, Katy. You were always a good seamstress. I wish I could find a good job like I had at the hotel, but jobs here are scarce as hen's teeth. Newcomers keep coming. They take our jobs and push us from our homes. I now rent a room from a family, but each month it's harder to pay my share.

Portland is not the same as when my parents brought me here as a child. There is hardness and hatred all around. Sometimes I wish I could join Abe and my parents and my baby too. But the Good Lord knows best. I can only trust Him. Please give your sweet mother my love. She is a good woman, and you are too.

Warmest regards,
Sarah Rose Lewis

Anna slid the sad little letter back into the envelope and sighed. "Poor dear Sarah Rose. I wonder if there's some way we could help."

"I agree, Mother. I read her letter this morning, and my heart's been aching for her all day long. Think of it—Sarah Rose was part of our family . . . From as early as I can remember, she took really good care of me and helped us around the house. Right up until she married Abe."

"I just assumed life would go well for her." Anna handed back the letter. "And to think she's lost a baby too."

"What do you think she means about hardness and hatred everywhere?" Katy set the letter on her bureau.

"I'm afraid it has to do with the color of her skin, Katy. Just a year ago, while working at the *Oregonian*, I covered some stories regarding the numerous immigrants flocking to Portland. Despite the fact that many colored families had been there for decades, the immigrants started to displace them from jobs and homes and neighborhoods. I was concerned then, and I'm afraid it's grown worse thanks to the European war. Unfortunately, the immigrants from solely Caucasian countries might be unfamiliar with people of African descent . . . and perhaps feel superior." Anna knew this was an understatement.

"I remember being out with Sarah Rose, going to the market or the park . . . and occasionally someone would treat Sarah Rose like she was inferior." Katy headed back to the bathroom. "But I just thought they were stupid."

"Yes, but stupidity . . . or ignorance . . . can be dangerous when it evolves into prejudice."

"Do you think that's why Abe left the hotel, Mother? Because he was colored and a white immigrant took his job?"

"It's possible . . . but we don't know this."

"Maybe that's why Sarah can't find work now."

Anna simply nodded, following Katy to the bathroom as she turned off the bathtub tap. "It's all very sad."

"And unfair. Sarah is a darling. She's like family. And that makes me even more certain that I've done the right thing."

"The right thing?" Anna unbuttoned the back of Katy's dress.

"I sent Sarah a telegram."

"A telegram?"

"Yes. This afternoon." Katy turned to face her. "I invited Sarah to come work for me in the dress shop. She is an excellent seamstress, and I've needed more help ever since Ellen ran off to get married—which from what I hear isn't working out so well. Anyway, I offered Sarah a job and a train ticket and a place to live."

Anna didn't know what to say, but she suspected her horrified expression said it all. Naturally, Katy had no idea what she'd done by inviting Sarah Rose to come live and work in Sunset Cove. How could she understand? Katy had known Sarah since infancy, and she'd accepted her without the slightest concern over the color of her skin. For that matter, Anna had as well. She loved Sarah Rose and wanted nothing but the best for her. But Anna also knew Oregon's history, especially in small isolated towns like Sunset Cove. And as much as she loved her home state, she did not love its history when it came to fair treatment of all races.

CHAPTER 2

"Wasn't that the right thing to do, Mother?" Katy demanded as she dumped a generous portion of bath salts into the steaming tub. "Aren't we *supposed* to love our neighbors? And Sarah is much more than a mere neighbor." She set the jar down so hard, Anna thought it might break. "Sarah is like family!"

"You don't understand me, Katy. And I'm afraid you didn't think this through. Your telegram put Sarah in a very precarious—"

"Sarah was like a second mother to me. She taught me to sew and took care of me while you were at work. And I never mentioned this before, but I was pretty brokenhearted when she left us to marry Abe. Oh, I tried to act happy for her sake, but I felt like I lost part of my family." Katy peeled off her dress, handing it to Anna with a hopeful smile. "But now we can have her back with us. That is, if Sarah says yes—and I just know she will."

Anna took in a deep breath. "I sincerely hope she says no."

"Mother!" Katy glared at her. "How dare you say that about our Sarah Rose? I thought you loved her."

"I do love her, Katy. That's exactly why I said that." Anna carried the dress into Katy's bedroom, laying it over a chair with a long sigh. How to make Katy see this from all sides? When she returned to the bathroom, Katy was in the tub—and it looked like they were both steaming.

"This probably isn't the time for a history lesson. But I suspect what I need to explain to you was not taught in your school."

"Well, I'm not going anywhere. Why don't you give me a quick lesson?"

Anna knew that Katy was seriously aggravated at her and might argue over every point but decided to take advantage of her captive pupil anyway. She pulled a straight-backed chair next to the tub. "I'm not going to go into all the dark details of Oregon's history. But take my word for it, when it comes to fair treatment of anyone who is not white, our laws have been very backward and discriminatory. More so than most of the country. And, unfortunately, our laws are still backward."

Anna quickly relayed facts about Oregon's exclusion laws in regard to other races, explaining how although slavery was illegal before the Civil War, it was also illegal for colored people to live in their state. "A colored person could be severely whipped if they didn't leave." Anna cringed. "These were things I read up on while working for the *Oregonian*," she explained, "in order to write some pieces for the paper."

"But that was *then*, Mother. This is the twentieth century. Times are changing. People are modern. You're talking about old history."

"Some of those old laws are still on the books, Katy. And some people would still adhere to them if given the chance. The trouble with history is that it sometimes repeats itself." Anna explained about how people of color were still discriminated against in Portland. "Not only in housing and jobs but in theaters and restaurants and churches and—"

"But think about it, Mother. I remember going to visit Sarah in the Albina District—you know, after she was married. She and Abe lived in a sweet little house. And they seemed so happy. And Sarah and I took a walk and all their neighbors seemed happy. And they had businesses and several churches nearby. It was all quite nice."

"And did you notice that everyone living in Albina was colored?"

Katy shrugged, reaching for the soap.

"And you read what Sarah wrote about the newcomers . . . and hatred."

"Yes, yes, but I do not see what any of this

has to do with Sarah coming to Sunset Cove." Katy turned to scowl at her mother. "It feels like you don't want her here. Is it because you're embarrassed by her race?"

"No. It's because I'm worried about her. If Sarah comes here, she will be the only colored person in town. And I don't like to prejudge people here in Sunset Cove, but we've known some pretty bad apples this past year. Think about how Clint Collins or Cal Snyder may treat someone like Sarah."

"But those thugs are long gone, Mother."

"Don't be so sure of that." Anna didn't want to worry Katy, but at the same time she didn't want her daughter to go around with a false sense of security. According to Chief Rollins, rum-running was still alive and well along the Oregon coast. Some boats came up from California, and some came down from Canada. "Collins and Snyder may appear to be gone. But there's still a criminal element in these parts. I don't care to name names but don't assume that our town is squeaky clean now."

"Are you suggesting Sarah would be in danger in Sunset Cove?"

"I don't know for sure."

"Because we can protect her." Katy dredged a washcloth out of the water. "We'd keep her safe. And she sounds so unhappy in Portland. If what you're saying about immigrants treating colored people so badly is true, how could it be safe for Sarah to remain there?"

"I honestly don't know the answers, Katy. But at least Sarah would have her community in Portland. She wouldn't be the only person of color in an all-white town."

"Then perhaps we should ask Sarah Rose to bring a whole bunch of her friends with her." Katy threw the washcloth into the tub, causing a splash that made Anna jump.

"That's an interesting idea." Anna stood, shaking the water droplets from her skirt. "And, personally, I wouldn't mind a bit. But based on what I know about Oregon history and Oregon law . . . it could create some serious problems for Sarah and her friends if they did come."

"Well, I think it's high time that Oregon laws and Oregon history change for the better." Katy reached for a towel. "Women got the vote here, and the power of females at the polls brought prohibition. That was a big change. And I'll bet women voters will change those stupid old discrimination laws too."

"I sincerely hope that's true, Katy. And maybe it's up to you and the next generation to ensure that it happens. But it may not be easy." She handed Katy her bathrobe.

"Didn't you always tell me that most good things don't come easily?" Katy pulled on her robe, cinching it around her waist.

Anna leaned over to kiss Katy's flushed cheek. "And that is what I love about you, darling daughter. You can come across as flibbertigibbet clothes-horse, but underneath all that style and fashion, you're an intelligent woman who's passionately determined to make this world a better place. Thank you."

Katy pointed to Anna. "And to make this world a better place, I must insist you go clean yourself up and don your new evening dress. We don't want our dear Dr. Dan to arrive only to discover you're not ready."

Anna checked her watch. "Yes, you're right. We will continue this conversation later."

But as she hurried to her room, Anna still felt concerned. What if poor Sarah didn't understand? What if she accepted Katy's offer and came to Sunset Cove with high hopes only to learn it was a mistake?

As Anna prepared for the evening, she ran this dilemma round and round through her mind. Finally, she decided that, at the very least, Sarah would enjoy a train ride to the Oregon coast. She would be reunited with her old friends and have a nice holiday. And then Anna would explain the challenges in their small town and offer to send her back to Portland with enough money to help sustain her until she found some sort of work or a gainfully employed husband. Certainly, Anna wished they lived in a different world, more like the one Katy was imagining. But reality could be cold and harsh sometimes. And history did not change itself overnight.

"Well, look at you." Katy came into Anna's room, nodding with approval. "The dress is perfect."

"Are you sure this shade of turquoise isn't too vivid for a woman my age?" Anna studied her reflection in the mirror.

"Look how it matches your eyes and makes your skin tone glow." Katy began to brush, curl, and pin Anna's auburn curls on top of her head. "And I've seen women twenty years older than you wearing this same color. But I must say, it looks much better on you."

Katy fussed a bit more with Anna, but the sound of male voices downstairs reminded them that it was seven. "I hope the buffet dinner is good tonight." Katy did a final check of her own image, smiling when the layers of soft pink fabric swirled as she swung around. "Because I plan to dance the night away, but I don't want to perish from hunger. I want to eat first."

Anna chuckled. "I'll just warn everyone to make way for you at the buffet table," she teased. "Step aside, people, Katy McDowell is starving!"

"Mother." Katy wrinkled her nose. "You wouldn't dare."

Katy slowly led the way downstairs. As usual,

Anna marveled at her graceful and composed daughter. Where did she get that from? Well, other than her grandmother Lucille. In many ways, they were like two peas in a pod. And yet, they were different too.

"Louise and Mac already left," Jim informed them. "Meanwhile, my chariot awaits."

"Why don't you go on ahead without us?" Daniel sent Jim a tired smile. "I want a chance to speak to Anna for a moment."

Katy's brows arched with interest at this, but fortunately she didn't say anything as Jim helped her with her wrap. "See you later," she called as Jim escorted her out the front door.

"I'm glad we don't have to hurry," Anna told Daniel. "I feel like I've been hurrying all day."

"I was hoping we could talk," he said solemnly.

"Sure." She nodded nervously. "Of course." She pointed him toward the living room, and soon they were seated on the settee. She waited for him to begin. Judging by his expression, whatever it was he had to say was not good. Perhaps he'd been rethinking spending time with her like they'd been doing the past few weeks. Maybe he'd decided to take the chief of staff position in that Boston hospital after all. Whatever it was, she wished he'd get on with it.

"I had a busy day too," he began slowly. "And a disappointing one."

"I'm sorry," she said gently. "May I ask what happened?"

"Do you remember how I told you about the young man I treated earlier this week?"

"Oh, yes. The fellow on the dairy farm. Wasn't his name Caleb? Katy said he was a classmate and that they took their diploma test together. She said he's very nice and she planned to pray for his quick recovery. Were you able to save his leg?" She suspected that based on his expression, he wasn't.

"Caleb is dead." Daniel leaned forward, his elbows on his knees, dejected.

"Dead?"

"The boy wasn't even eighteen. His parents are devastated." Daniel looked down at his hands. "Their only son. He'd gotten his diploma and quit school to help them run the dairy farm. And now he's gone."

"Oh, Daniel." She placed a hand on his shoulder. "I'm so sorry."

He glumly shook his head. "I told his parents that Caleb needed to be in a hospital to receive proper care. I explained how serious it was and how the infection had already set in before I was called. But his mother assured me she could clean the wound and re-bandage it daily."

"Yes, I remember you saying that. And you even sent your nurse to help her with it for the first day."

"My nurse." He looked up at her with angry eyes. "I've discovered that Norma's so-called nursing training was a correspondence first aid class. And she never even took a test."

"Oh." Anna didn't want to admit that she'd never liked Norma . . . didn't trust her.

"I fired her about an hour ago."

"Was it her fault Caleb died?"

"No, I must take that responsibility. But I did learn she did a poor job of helping Caleb's mother. Norma made it seem that the daily cleaning of the wound and applying a new bandage was unnecessary."

"Oh, dear."

"You don't have any medical training, Anna, but I know you'd make a far better nurse than Norma. I remember how you helped me when Jim was hurt." He ran his fingers through his hair. "But like I said, I can't blame this all on Norma."

"And you can't blame it all on yourself either, Daniel."

"It's just so frustrating . . . and sad."

"I'm sure it is." She sighed. "And I can completely understand how you may prefer not to go to the dance tonight."

"Thank you. I'm not in a celebratory mood."

"Are you hungry?"

"Not exactly." He sighed. "Although I haven't eaten since breakfast."

"Well, Bernice and Mickey have the night off,

but I'm sure I can rustle us up some leftovers." She stood.

"That'd be good. Mind if I join you?"

"Of course not." Anna led the way, turning on the lights in the kitchen. Then, realizing that Katy would throw a fit if she ruined this pretty dress, she put one of Bernice's old aprons over it. As she foraged through the icebox, Daniel sat at the worn kitchen table without saying anything. So Anna went into reporter mode and proceeded to gently probe him with some questions. But his answers were brief and flat—and not very revealing.

"How do you feel about beef stew?" Anna decided to change topics. "We had it last night and it was delicious, but it's even better on the second day."

His countenance brightened a bit. "My mom used to make a tasty stew. Sounds good to me."

As she poured the stew into a cast iron pot, Daniel seemed to open up. But as she began to slice the hearty rye bread that Bernice had baked yesterday, it became clear that Daniel was severely questioning himself, having second thoughts about a lot of things. He seemed to be shaken to the core over the young farm boy.

"I can understand how Caleb's death is very upsetting." She set out the butter and huckleberry jam. "Especially since it's so fresh in your mind. But if you give yourself some time to—"

"Time?" His tone grew sharper. "How much time do I give it, Anna? Will time improve the conditions here? Will time improve my practice? Do you know that I will turn forty in a few weeks? *Forty!* That means my professional career is half over—"

"Maybe the best is yet to come," she said meekly.

"I don't think so." He softened. "I don't like complaining like this, but it's as if my life is off track. As if I took the wrong turn at some junction."

Anna knew his story of losing his wife in child-birth . . . his discouragement in medicine . . . and how he'd transplanted his life from the East Coast to the West in an effort to find purpose and a fresh start. "I've felt like that before," she said quietly, turning from the stove to gaze at him. Dismayed to see he appeared even more downhearted than earlier, she didn't know what to say. He was obviously questioning everything, perhaps even her. And, really, other than a few random kisses, it wasn't as if they'd made any real commitments . . . except in her heart, which now ached for him.

"Maybe my father was right. Maybe Sunset Cove really is too remote."

"You mean this backwater, one-horse town," she supplied, remembering how the senior Dr. Hollister had disdained their small community.

"I don't really feel like that, Anna, but perhaps Sunset Cove doesn't need a doctor like me."

"You mean we only need a country bumpkin doctor." She tried to keep the cynicism out of her voice but knew she'd failed.

"I'm not trying to criticize this town. You know how much I love Sunset Cove." His expression was genuine. "It's just that my medical training was meant for, well, something more . . ."

"Something like a large, well-equipped Boston hospital with a professional medical staff and other physicians who—"

"Yes," he said suddenly. "Maybe that's where I really belong."

"But consider the people you've helped right here, Daniel. The lives you've saved. Think about Mac and his stroke. And how you helped Jim when he was shot." She began to list others, including the survivors from the recent explosion at Charlie's Chowder House. "Where would they be without you?"

"It's true that I was able to help them. But don't forget that many of those burn victims had to be shipped out for better medical care." He pounded a fist onto the old pine table. "Because I was unable to properly deal with them in my limited facilities here." He looked into her eyes. "Am I a fool for trying to establish a practice here, Anna? Especially when I could be chief of staff in one of the premiere hospitals in the country. Perhaps the world. Have I been blind?"

"I . . . I don't know." She smelled something burning and turned back to the stove. "Oh, drat!"

"What's wrong? Did you burn yourself?" He rushed over to see.

"No. I scorched the stew." She started to move the heavy pot, but Daniel intervened, doing it for her.

He peeked into the pot. "Well, there's plenty stew on top that looks just fine. We'll eat that." He took the ladle from her and started to fill the bowls she'd set out.

"Do you mind eating in the kitchen, or should I set up the dining room?"

"It's cozier in here." He handed her a bowl.

"Yes, I think so too." She moved the teakettle onto the hot part of the stove to have for later, and before long they were seated across from each other at the old work table. But now she didn't feel hungry . . . and didn't particularly want to talk.

"Shall I ask the blessing?" Daniel said quietly.

"Yes, thanks," she murmured. But as he prayed, all she could think was that she was losing him. Daniel wanted out of Sunset Cove and there was nothing she could do—or *would* do—to stop him. And, really, why shouldn't he return to Boston and take his place as chief of staff? Wasn't that exactly what his father wanted? What a wonderful opportunity that would be for Daniel to become the very best in his field. Perhaps he would be instrumental in the future of medicine. If she really did love him—and she knew that she did—she wouldn't stand in his way.

CHAPTER 3

As usual, Anna, Katy, and Mac sat down to a leisurely breakfast on Saturday. But Anna didn't feel like visiting this morning. Fortunately, Katy and Mac had plenty to say in regards to the previous evening's festivities.

"Why didn't you and Daniel come?" Mac finally said to Anna. Katy had already asked about this, but Anna had kept her answer evasive.

"Everyone was speculating that Daniel proposed to you last night," Katy told her. "And that you two had eloped."

"You couldn't be further from the truth," Anna said crisply.

"What does that mean?" Mac demanded.

Anna picked up the newspaper she'd already read and pretended to be absorbed with the classified section.

"Yes, Mother, what does that mean?" Katy asked. "Are you and Daniel parting ways? And if so, don't we have the right to know?"

"Yes," Mac agreed. "If you and Daniel had a row, you could at least tell us."

"No, no." She laid down the newspaper. "Nothing like that." She suddenly remembered what had initially set Daniel off. "In fact, Daniel was very discouraged over some bad news." She turned to Katy. "Remember your school chum Caleb? I told you about his accident with the plow and how Daniel was worried the boy may lose his leg?"

"Oh, dear." Katy nodded solemnly. "Did he lose his leg?"

"The poor boy died." Anna gave them both time for that to sink in before she explained how it had happened. "And, naturally, Daniel took it quite hard."

"Of course." Mac shook his head. "That's a hard blow."

"Poor, poor Caleb." Katy wiped a tear with her napkin. "He was such a really nice young man."

"That's what Daniel said too." Anna felt a lump in her throat now. "We should all be praying for Caleb's family."

They discussed this for a bit longer then Anna confided to them about Daniel's interest in returning to Boston.

"You mean for good?" Mac asked with a frown. "Or just a visit?"

"I don't really know," Anna said stiffly. "I guess you'll have to ask him."

"But what about you, Mother?" Katy's eyes

34

grew big. "Does that mean you'd go to Boston too?"

"No, no, of course not." Anna firmly shook her head.

"But I thought you two were—"

"We are good friends," Anna told her. "And as Daniel's friend, I will be supportive of whatever decision he makes."

"But what about—"

"I understand how he feels," Anna continued. "Sunset Cove is a small, remote town, and Daniel gets frustrated when he can't offer the medical treatment that his patients need. He knows what it's like to have a modern, well-equipped medical facility and what a difference that makes for his patients. Can you blame him for that?"

"Then we should get a modern hospital," Katy suggested.

Mac slapped the table so hard the dishes clattered. "You are right, Katy. We should get a hospital."

"A hospital?" Anna considered this.

"Sunset Cove is growing and will continue to grow," Mac declared. "Why *don't* we have a hospital?"

"Because hospitals cost money?" Anna didn't know much one would cost, but she estimated it would be a lot.

"Money can be raised," Katy said with confidence. "Remember the fundraisers I had for

Mayor Wally's campaign. I could do that again."

"And the city could help. Perhaps voters could approve a bond," Mac added. "And business owners could contribute their share."

"You're right," Anna told him. "The Chamber of Commerce should get involved. And the police and fire departments too."

"This is turning into a great idea," Katy said with enthusiasm.

"But great ideas can slip through the cracks if left unattended." Anna pointed to Mac. "We need a well-respected citizen to take this bull by the horns. Someone who's well-connected and savvy and with time on his hands. I nominate you."

"I *second* the nomination!" Katy shouted.

Mac pursed his lips, rubbed his chin, and nodded. "I accept the nomination."

They were just congratulating him when the front doorbell rang, and Mickey went to answer it. "A telegram," he announced as he came to the dining room. "For Miss Katy McDowell."

"Oh, dear." Mac frowned as Bernice handed it to Katy. "Who died?"

Katy eagerly opened it then let out a happy shriek. "Sarah Rose is coming."

"Sarah Rose?" Mac asked her. "A school friend?"

"Not exactly," Anna muttered.

"Better than a school friend." Katy beamed

at him. "Sarah is like family. She was like my second mother when I was growing up. Then she got married, but her husband tragically died, and she lost her baby too."

"Oh, my. Poor woman." Mac shook his head. "Did you invite her here for a visit?"

"I invited her to come here and work for me in the dress shop." Katy refolded the telegram. "I hope it's all right for her to live here for a while. Or I could ask Grandmother."

"No, no, invite your friend to stay here," Mac said. "We've plenty of room."

"Oh, thank you, thank you!" Katy jumped to her feet, kissing Mac on the cheek. "I've got to go write Sarah a letter right now."

After Katy left, Anna took in a deep breath. "There's something you should know about Sarah Rose, Mac."

"Yes?" He picked up his coffee cup.

"Sarah Rose is colored."

His cup clattered down into the saucer. *"What?"*

"That's right."

Mac blinked. "Oh."

"And although Katy and I dearly love Sarah Rose, I am well aware that not everyone shares our sentiments. Not even in the modern metropolis of Portland. Right now, there are new immigrants attempting to squeeze out the colored population. And certainly not here in Sunset

Cove where the population has always been whiter than white."

"That's not exactly true."

"What do you mean?" She frowned. "I've never seen a single—"

"There was a colored man here once, Anna. About ten years ago. Jumped a fishing boat after suffering a bad bout of sea sickness. His name was Ben Smith, and I'm sorry to say he didn't receive a very warm welcome when he came into town."

"I can imagine that, and I assume he's not here now. What happened?"

"I hired Ben to work in the pressroom. He was a big, strong guy, and I figured he'd be a good asset at the paper. I called him Big Ben. He was smart and a hard worker. I let him sleep in the storage room, just until he could save enough money to rent a place." Mac's face seemed to pale.

"And . . . ?"

"Well, some folks didn't like Ben. Not because he ever did anything wrong. He never did. It was because of the color of his skin. I knew about it, but I thought Ben would be okay. I thought if they gave him enough time, people would get used to him and realize he was a good guy. I even wrote a couple of editorials about it." Mac let out a long, weary sigh. "Ben went missing one night. Some people acted like he'd left on his own volition, but I didn't believe it . . . because some of his personal items as well as the rent money he'd been saving—and kept hidden—was still there. I went out looking for him." Mac shook his head. "His beaten body washed up on the shore a couple weeks later. Chief Rollins thought it looked like he'd been murdered and even investigated it, but without any witnesses or suspects . . . well, that was the end of it."

Anna felt sick inside. "Mac, do you think anyone would hurt Sarah Rose?"

He picked up his coffee, shaking his head. "I don't know. I'd like to say no, that because she's a woman, she'd be safe." He took a sip. "But truth be told, I just don't know."

"I already warned Katy that it could be a problem. But you know how stubborn she can be. She thinks it's going to be wonderful, and that Sarah can work at the dress shop, and that we can all protect her. She believes the world is changing."

"Yes, but it may not be changing fast enough."

Anna stood. "I probably can't convince her not to bring Sarah out here, but I can write to Sarah and tell her exactly what she'll be coming to."

"Out of the frying pan and into the fire?"

Anna cringed. "Do you really think so?"

"No, probably not." Something about his expression seemed to say more.

"I'd like to believe that Sunset Cove is a good place, Mac, and that it—"

"It *is* a good place," he declared. "Unfortunately, it's also a place that attracts some bad apples. I think it's partly due to it being a little remote. Some men think they can give the law the slip out here in the wilds of the Oregon coast."

"Sounds like you've been talking to Chief Rollins." Anna sighed. "He tipped me off that there's been more rum-running nearby."

"Yep. Maybe even here in town again."

"Well, maybe that's why we need to keep building this town up, Mac. We need to push out the bad with the good. And we need to keep publishing the truth in our newspaper and telling good stories about good people doing good things." She laid her napkin by her plate with fresh resolve. "That's just one more reason to push for a hospital."

"Wally and Harvey and I plan to meet for coffee this afternoon. I'll run the hospital idea by them."

"Wonderful. The mayor and police chief are the perfect place to start." Anna put her finger over her lips. "But perhaps you could keep it under wraps for the time being. I'm not sure I want Daniel to hear about it just yet. I hate to get his hopes up . . . in case it all falls apart."

"I don't plan for it to fail. But I'll ask the boys to keep it quiet for now."

"Mac." Anna sat up straighter. "I just thought of something. I heard that the old chowder house property was confiscated by the city."

"I'd sure love to see Cal Snyder's face when he hears about that."

"Seems fair to me. He used it illegally then flew the coop."

"Rumor is he's in South America." Mac rubbed his chin. "But I doubt it."

"Even so, wouldn't the old chowder house be a great location for a hospital?"

Mac's eyes lit up. "You're onto something, Anna. I'll talk to Wally about this."

"Wouldn't it be ironic if the very site where people were injured and killed turned into a place of modern medicine and healing?"

"It seems right." Mac stood, reaching for his cane. "In fact, I think I'll call Wally and see if there are a few other people of influence that we can include in our meeting this afternoon."

"And tell them to keep it under their hats," Anna reminded him. "You know, Daniel's fortieth birthday is a few weeks from now. I'm not sure what day yet, but wouldn't it be wonderful if we could have something nailed down by then?"

"Do you think it would entice him to stay here?"

Anna shrugged. "Probably not. But it may encourage him to think we're trying to emerge from the Dark Ages."

"You sound like you've been talking to Daniel's father." Mac growled.

"Well, compared to Boston, we probably do

seem a bit backward." She forced a smile. "Now, if you'll excuse me, I need to write a letter to Sarah Rose."

Anna didn't see Daniel for the next few days, but she was grateful for this little reprieve because she felt certain that the next time their paths crossed, he would be informing her of his plans to shut down his practice and take the next train east. And she wasn't sure how she would react. She needed time to get her heart and her head ready.

By midweek, she felt perhaps she was ready for what she knew would be a difficult conversation. Her plan was to stop by his office on her way home from work under the pretense of checking on him. But it wasn't until Thursday that she got up the nerve.

She'd left the newspaper office early when she was stopped by Mayor Wally. "Did Mac tell you the good news?" he asked eagerly.

"Good news?" She caught her hat before it sailed away with the wind.

"Let's get inside before we're blown away." He nodded toward Brown's Café across the street. "You have time for a cup of coffee?"

She agreed, and before long they were situated in a booth by the window. "What's your news?" she asked. "We can always use good news these days. I hate filling the paper with nothing but grim and gruesome war stories. Although I don't expect that to change anytime soon."

"Well, this news isn't exactly ready for the newspaper yet." He set his hat on the seat next to him. "It has to do with the hospital plans."

"Oh, yes, Mac mentioned you'd had a couple of planning meetings and were making progress, but he didn't give me details."

"Well, we agreed to keep it under wraps for now. But Mac said it was all right to tell you since you were in on it from the beginning." He grinned. "Well, I just came from an emergency council meeting, and it's been approved."

"What's approved?"

"The old chowder house property is being donated for the new hospital building site."

"Oh, that's wonderful."

"Chief Rollins is delighted." He chuckled. "I sort of wish Cal Snyder were around to hear the news. I'm sure he'd throw a fit."

"If he were around, the chief would probably throw him in jail."

The mayor nodded. "But that's not all, Anna. The council also agreed to put up a bond for the voters' approval. It was decided to hold a special election on the third Tuesday of this month. And hopefully the bond will pass and we can break ground by Decoration Day. I am already preparing a speech that I'd like to deliver at our annual ceremony."

"Oh, Mayor, that's such great news."

"But not a word in the paper yet."

"Why not? Shouldn't we start informing voters?"

"First, we plan to get all the businesspeople and anyone else of influence to give us their endorsements—and donations. Put their money where their mouths are. And, really, who wouldn't agree that a hospital is a good idea? So we'll get that list as big as possible then pass it along to you so that can write a nice big article and print all their names alongside it. I will be reminding them all that it's also some good advertising."

"Excellent plan." She nodded. "I'm impressed with how quickly you fellows are progressing with it. At this rate, we may have a hospital much sooner than I imagined possible."

"I just talked to your industrious daughter. Katy said she wants to plan a fundraiser dinner and ball, as well as something she's calling a fashion show. Although I'm not too sure what that will be, but she said it's for women only anyway." He frowned slightly.

"Well, women are voters too," Anna reminded him.

He smiled. "Good thing for that. I may not have been elected otherwise."

Anna shuddered. "Can you imagine our town if Calvin Snyder had been reelected?"

44

He grimly shook his head. "We're lucky to be rid of that scoundrel."

"But don't you wonder sometimes . . ." She lowered her voice. ". . . what became of him and Clint Collins? Every time I ask around, no one seems to know."

"Well, Chief Rollins feels fairly certain they took that stolen Krauss boat down to Mexico. And I say good riddance."

"I agree." She thanked him for his updates and promised to keep the news under her hat until further notice. And then, although she'd planned to stop by Dr. Daniel Hollister's office, she decided to go straight home. Oh, it wasn't that she didn't want to see the good doctor. She most certainly did. But now that it sounded like a hospital could be in Sunset Cove's future, she felt uneasy about encouraging him to pursue his professional goals in Boston . . . and equally uneasy about enticing him to remain here in Sunset Cove based on the hopes of a new hospital. For the time being, she would simply have to keep her thoughts to herself.

CHAPTER 4

Anna was walking through the newspaper office when she heard excited voices from the vicinity of the telegraph machine. She stuck her head around the corner to see that Ed, the business writer, and Jim were intensely discussing something.

"Can you believe it?" Ed said loudly.

"I knew it was just a matter of time." Jim stared down at the strip in his hand.

"What is it?" Anna asked as she joined them.

"News from Washington," Ed told her.

"Congress passed the Selective Service Act," Jim said.

"You mean the Conscription Act that they started working on late last year?" she asked.

"Well, that's another name for it," Ed agreed. "Means the same thing. President Woodrow Wilson, the man who promised we'd never go to war, now has the power and authority to draft men into the military. There's no stopping it now."

"I'm guessing it will go into effect soon," Jim said glumly.

"What does this mean for you?" Anna asked him.

"Oh, Jim will be exempt," Ed assured her. "It's only for men between the ages of twenty-one and thirty."

Jim grimaced, exchanging glances with Anna.

"How old do you think Jim is?" Anna asked Ed.

Ed shrugged. "Well, mid-thirties or thereabouts."

"I'm twenty-six," Jim confessed.

Ed's graying brows shot up. "You're pulling my leg."

"Nope. I never lied, but I did try to appear older. Even Mac fell for it. He assumed I was thirty when he hired me, but I'd had less than two years of college and wasn't even twenty then."

Ed laughed. "Does Mac know about this?"

"He does now," Anna said. "Jim came clean."

"I guess that helps your case with Anna's daughter." Ed chuckled. "People can stop acting like you're old enough to be Katy's father."

"That's one good thing." Jim smiled stiffly.

"But you're sure to be drafted," Ed told him. "Sorry to hear that, old boy."

"What about signing up to go over as a war correspondent?" Anna asked him. "Some of my friends at the *Oregonian* were talking about doing that."

"Do you really think a reporter from a Podunk

newspaper in Oregon has a chance at that?" Jim asked with skepticism.

Anna frowned. "Probably not."

"Well, maybe you should start honing your rifle skills." Ed slapped a hand to Jim's back.

"Thanks a lot," Jim said dourly. "I'll keep that in mind."

Anna didn't know what to say. She understood Jim's reaction to today's draft news. Many young men would be eager to fight, bravely marching through the streets, waving the flag with admirable patriotism. But here at the news-paper office they were bombarded, almost daily, with horrific war stories and ghastly photos. And as managing editor, Jim usually read them first then presented what he felt newsworthy to Anna. But she would determine that many of the tales were too gruesome to include in their friendly small-town paper. The recounts of French and English soldiers suffering horrible deprivations and diseases while trying to survive the trenches was one thing, but photos of soldiers with lost limbs or suffering the ill effects of poisonous gasses—well, it was too much. For Jim's situation, ignorance would've been bliss. She followed him back to his desk and, placing a hand on his shoulder, attempted to smile bravely.

"You would be a real asset to the US Army," she told him. "Between your intelligence and excellent physical condition, I'm sure you'll be just fine."

He nodded glumly. "Or maybe the war will get wrapped up before our troops land." His expression suggested he did not believe that.

"I won't mention this to Katy," she said. "Unless you want me to."

"Doesn't really matter to me. It'll be in tomorrow's paper anyway." He rolled a blank sheet of paper into his typewriter. "I'll make sure of that."

"Right."

And then, while typing, he started whistling "Yankee Doodle Dandy." Anna couldn't help but smile. Jim Stafford was going to be just fine.

Still, as she walked home, she felt deep concern. Not only for Jim but for all the young men who would soon be drafted and shipped overseas . . . and for those who would come home with injuries . . . and the ones who would never come home at all. God help them all.

On Friday afternoon, Katy felt uneasy as she drove Mac's Runabout to the train station. She wasn't nervous about driving since she was an old hand at that. No, Katy was suddenly uneasy about picking up Sarah Rose. She hadn't told anyone that Sarah was scheduled to arrive at 4:10 today and, despite her earlier bravado, Katy was having second thoughts. Not that she was doing anything wrong. She sincerely wanted to help

Sarah and truly believed that her old friend could be better off in Sunset Cove than in Portland.

Unless she wasn't.

That's what was worrying Katy as she parked in front of the train station. What if Katy's impetuousness put Sarah Rose in some kind of real peril? Since living in Sunset Cove, Katy had witnessed all sorts of dangers that she'd never even considered before. Certainly it was exciting, but it was also a grim reminder that their small town was occasionally lawless and a bit like living in the old Wild West. It could be fun at times, but there'd also been moments when it was downright scary.

The hiss of train brakes made Katy jump as she walked through the terminal. What if Sarah Rose had encountered a problem while traveling from Portland to here? That was probably a real possibility, although Katy had consoled herself with the idea that many train employees were often colored. Surely they would take special care with Sarah's safety. Wouldn't they?

Katy waited as a conductor placed a step outside of the passenger car, helping people off . . . until finally, after it seemed everyone else had disembarked, Sarah Rose slowly stepped down. Unlike the other passengers, Sarah was laden with several bags. Katy rushed toward her, taking the largest carpet bag and a smaller one.

"Welcome to Sunset Cove," Katy told Sarah

as she hurried her into the terminal and then, dropping the bags, embraced her in a warm hug. "How was your trip?"

"It was . . . all right." Sarah smiled, but her voice sounded uncertain.

"No problems at all?" Katy held her at arm's length, looking deeply into Sarah's dark amber eyes.

Sarah shrugged, looking down at her shoes. "Nothing I haven't seen before." She tugged at her glove. "People are people."

Katy suddenly noticed that the few people in the terminal seemed to be blatantly staring at them. "Well, let's get you into the car, and we can talk more on our way home."

"Yes, ma'am, that'd be good."

"Oh, Sarah, you don't need to call me *ma'am*." Katy reached for the big carpet bag, but Sarah stopped her.

"I can carry that."

"Then let me take this one." Katy picked up the midsized bag.

"Yes, Miss Katy." With the other bags in hand, Sarah followed her outside, and they were soon in the car, but Katy could see that people were still watching them.

"Please, Sarah, just call me Katy," Katy said as she started the Runabout.

"Yes . . . Katy."

"I know you've been through some hard times,"

51

Katy said as she drove. "And I can tell you've changed some."

"Hard times can do that to you."

"I'm sure that's true." She paused at the intersection to smile at Sarah. "But I really hope that you'll like it here. Sunset Cove is a very pretty place . . . but I must admit that it's had some troubles too."

"Troubles?" Sarah's forehead creased. "You mean like we've been having in Portland?"

"I'm sure my mother wrote to you about her concerns. . . ."

"Yes, she did write to me. She explained I'll be the only colored person in your town. And that doesn't trouble me too much. As long as I can work to earn my way and, as long as I have you and your mother around, I'll be fine." Sarah seemed to brighten. "And you know, Katy, I always wanted to see the ocean."

"Then you will definitely see the ocean," Katy assured her. "In just a couple minutes too."

"I've seen photographs and paintings of the sea. And I've read about it some. My parents always wanted to make the trip . . . before they passed. I didn't think I'd ever get the chance either."

"Well, you'll get the chance today. My grandfather's house is right next to the ocean, and you'll be staying there with us." Katy grimaced, hoping that no one would object to Sarah occupying a small bedroom on the third floor.

Katy had stayed up late last night getting it ready. "Your room looks right out over the ocean. So you will wake up to see the big blue sea every day."

"Oh my, that sounds wonderful." Sarah sighed. "I must say, Miss Katy, you look all grown up. And so elegant too."

"Thank you." As Katy drove down Main Street, she pointed out her dress shop. "That's where you'll be working." Katy hoped she wasn't mistaken not to tell her other employees—or even her grandmother—about Sarah Rose.

"This is so exciting. I'm so grateful to you, Miss Katy."

Katy was tempted to correct her again but decided to ignore it. After all, some of her employees called her Miss Katy. Maybe Sarah Rose knew best. "Here we are," Katy announced as she slowed down in front of the tall stone house. "My grandfather's family built this house before the Civil War. It's one of the oldest homes in Sunset Cove." As she parked in the carriage house, she explained about the family newspaper.

"So this is where your mother learned the newspaper business," Sarah said as they got out and gathered her bags from the back. Then as they walked toward the house, Sarah got a glimpse of the ocean in the background. "Oh my, is that it? Is that the sound I hear? The waves?"

"Yes. That sound is always there, but it changes

with the tide and the weather. Let's go inside, and you'll have an even better look at the seascape." She led Sarah Rose around to the porch, hoping to avoid Mickey and Bernice in the rear of the house. Then, feeling somewhat sneaky, she quietly opened the front door and led Sarah Rose up two flights of stairs. "This is your room." Katy opened the door to the room she'd prepared for Sarah.

"Oh, this is lovely, Miss Katy." Sarah set her bags on the floor then rushed to the window, pulling open the lace curtains. "And that is the ocean! Oh my—it's so big. And beautiful. Much, much bigger than the river in Portland."

Katy pointed out things in the small room, and Sarah gushed even more. "A room like this all to myself. I can hardly believe it." She paused to admire the small vase of flowers on the dresser. "So pretty." She smoothed her hand over the patchwork quilt that Katy had found in the back of a linen closet. "Very nice." Katy showed her to the third-floor bathroom, which was not as elegant as Katy's but was perfectly adequate.

"And indoor plumbing." Sarah Rose smiled at Katy. "I feel like I've died and gone to heaven."

Katy hugged her. "I hope you'll be at home here."

"I'm so grateful . . . I don't even have the words."

Katy quickly explained about their household,

how Mickey and Bernice worked for Grandfather, and how Katy and her mother's rooms were on the second floor. "Dinner is usually between six and seven, depending on when everyone is home. You take this time to unpack and settle in, and I'll tell Bernice to add a place for you at the table and let you know—"

"Oh, no, no, Miss Katy." Sarah's eyes grew wide. "I can't eat dinner with your family. No, that won't do."

"Why in the world not?"

Sarah held up a hand. "I just can't do that. It won't be—"

"But you always ate with Mother and me."

"That was different, Miss Katy. If you don't mind, I'd prefer to take my meals in my room."

Katy didn't know what to say.

"That is how it must be," Sarah said firmly. "I'll talk to your cook about it. And rest assured, she won't have to lift a finger to take care of me. I'll see to that."

"All right," Katy reluctantly agreed. "But I'll need to talk to Bernice."

"And would you please tell Miss Bernice that I'm more'n happy to lend a hand in the kitchen or around the house? It'll be my way to repay you kind folks for my room and board. I may be poor, but I'm no freeloader." Sarah bent down to open a bag.

Katy excused herself to discuss this with

Bernice and went downstairs. She had no idea how Bernice would react to their new houseguest or Sarah's offer to help in the kitchen. Bernice could be pretty persnickety about her kitchen and housekeeping. Once again, Katy felt uneasy. What if she'd taken on too much this time, over-stepped some invisible boundary?

Well, it wouldn't be the first time, would it? Besides, wasn't that who she was and what life was all about for her? Take chances and make changes. Why go a different route now? But instead of heading straight for Bernice like she'd planned, Katy decided to stop by Grand-father's sitting room first. If she could convince anyone to understand her dilemma and back her up, it was her devoted grandfather. Her mother sometimes teased that Katy had the old sweet-heart wrapped around her baby finger, and maybe that was partly true, but Katy also knew that her grandfather had a stubborn streak that was even broader than her own. And if he shot her down now, she would probably be driving Sarah back to the train station tomorrow.

As usual, she cheerfully greeted him with a kiss on his cheek. "Do I have news for you, Grand-father." She flopped down on the chair adjacent from him, smoothing her moiré satin skirt and composing herself.

His pale blue eyes lit up. "Tell me everything, dear girl. You know I love news."

And so she poured out her story, in detail. Of course, he was already aware she'd invited Sarah Rose to work in her dress shop, but he seemed quite surprised to learn Sarah was, right this minute, in his house and upstairs unpacking.

"I hope you don't mind, Grandfather." She smiled sweetly. "I'll take full responsibility for her in your house. I got her room ready without bothering Bernice at all. And I don't want Bernice to be burdened with a single thing while Sarah is here. And Sarah wishes to manage her own meals and take them to her room." Katy paused for a breath. "Although I don't see why that's necessary. I told Sarah that she's welcome to join us in the dining room."

"You did?" His expression was impossible to read.

"That's what she did with Mother and me in Portland—I mean, taking meals with us. Although, to be fair, our apartment was so small there wasn't any other alternative. But just the same, we thought of Sarah as family. And I still do, Grandfather. She truly was a second mother to me. I hope you'll welcome her into your house too." She waited, almost holding her breath.

"Well, well . . ." He scratched his white wooly head with his good hand. "Not sure what to make of all this, Katy. Do you think you may have bitten off more than you can chew this time?"

She frowned. "Well, Grandfather, if you're

57

unwilling to have Sarah Rose, a woman who helped to raise me, under your roof, I'll just go talk to my grandmother and see what she thinks. She has a couple of spare rooms, and I'm sure she wouldn't mind showing hospitality to my old friend. Besides that, Grandmother is a modern sort of woman who's lived in a big city."

"I'm not sure that city folk are any better than small town folk, Katy." Grandfather cleared his throat. "Seems to me that wherever you go, you get folks on both sides. Some are understanding . . . and some are not."

"That may be true." She remembered what Mother had told her about Portland. "But which are you?" She locked eyes with him, ready for a showdown.

"As it turns out, I'm on the understanding side."

Relief washed over her as she jumped up from her chair to hug him. "Oh, I'm so glad to hear it. I just knew you wouldn't mind that she's here. Thank you so much, Grandfather. You really are a dear!"

"I'm not finished," he said after she'd sat down again.

"Oh . . . ?"

And now he told her a sad story about how he'd helped a colored man called Big Ben . . . and how it had ended badly.

Katy's stomach grew tight. "Are you saying

that Sarah Rose may be in some kind of danger here, Grandfather? And if so, shouldn't we contact Chief Rollins and seek protection for her? After all, unless I'm mistaken, anyone who would attempt to hurt Sarah would be pressed with criminal charges. Right? So the chief should be able to help."

"You're right about the law, but right doesn't always win, Katy. Not at first anyway. You've already seen that in this town. Laws get broken . . . and people get hurt." His eyes grew sad. "Sometimes things change . . . and sometimes it just takes time."

She folded her arms in front of her, releasing a long, loud discouraged sigh. "I'm sure you're right. But what do I do now? I don't want Sarah Rose to be in any sort of danger. She was so happy to be here, Grandfather. You should've seen her. She compared this place to being in heaven."

His countenance softened. "I don't want to squelch your enthusiasm," he said gently. "In fact, I applaud you, Katy. I'm proud of you for taking your stand . . . and I give you my word, I'll stand by you."

She brightened. "You mean it's all right if Sarah stays here with us?"

"Of course it's all right."

She hugged him again. "Thank you!"

"But we've got to be smart about it. I remember

my mother used to quote a Bible verse. She'd say we should be as *smart as serpents but as innocent as doves*."

"Yes, I've heard that before."

"In this situation, you should keep that in mind, Katy. And now you need to talk to Bernice about your houseguest. I'll leave all that up to you." His eyes twinkled with amusement. "Can't wait to hear how that goes."

Despite having lived in this house for nearly a year, Katy still wasn't completely sure about Bernice. Sometimes she came down on Katy for being too impetuous and reckless. She'd chastise Katie for walking alone on the beach or sneaking down to the kitchen to get a snack after everyone was in bed, or for designing dresses late into the night. But at other times, Bernice seemed so caring and loving and protective, it was like having another grandmother. Katy could never be exactly certain where she stood with the opinionated old woman. But hopefully Bernice wouldn't have anything against Sarah Rose . . . or the color of her skin.

CHAPTER 5

A nna immediately knew that something was
up. She'd just gotten home from work and
was about to change out of her office clothes
when she was met by her daughter on the second-
floor landing. Well acquainted with Katy's
expressions, it was clear that her daughter had
some sort of new plan up her pretty sleeve.

"How was your day?" Anna cautiously asked
Katy as she removed her hat and gloves.

"Just wonderful." Katy smiled brightly. Perhaps a bit too brightly. "Business at the shop
has been better than ever this week. Orders for
summer dresses come in almost faster than we
can take them—and much faster than we can
make them. At this rate, my seamstresses and I
will be working around the clock before long."

"Maybe it's time to hire some extra hands."

Katy's eyes lit up. "Precisely what I've been
thinking." And just like that she confessed that
Sarah Rose was upstairs, right this minute,
getting settled in and planning to stay.

"Oh, my goodness." Anna weighed her words.

"Well, I'll be happy to see Sarah Rose. But I just hope that she'll be equally happy to be here in Sunset Cove. More than that, I hope she'll be safe."

Katy's eyes looked uncertain, but she waved a dismissive hand, clearly trying to appear more confident than she felt. "Sarah will be just fine, Mother. She'll go to and from work with Grandmother and me, and we'll be with her throughout the day. And anyplace else she goes, we'll be sure to accompany her or have someone else go."

"Similar to a captive prisoner," Anna suggested.

"No, it's not like that at all, Mother." Katy glanced up the second flight of stairs. "You'll see. And just so you know, Sarah Rose is very glad to be here."

"Where's she staying?"

Katy explained about how she'd set up a small room on the third floor. "With an ocean view too. Sarah loves it."

"I'm glad you've made her comfortable." Anna nodded approval. "And if this turns out to be nothing more than a pleasant seaside vacation, well, I suppose no one could complain."

"Grandfather approves," Katy assured her. "And I just explained the situation to Bernice . . . and that Sarah wants to take meals in her room."

"Really? And is Bernice expected to deliver those meals?"

"No, of course not. Sarah will take care of all that. I was just on my way to get her now, so I can introduce them before dinnertime."

"Well, that's a relief. You know, Bernice is getting on in years. I've been thinking we all should be making her work lighter these days."

Now Katy patted Anna's back in a slightly placating way. "Yes, Mother dear, I'm well aware of that. Don't worry, this will not add to Bernice's workload. In fact, Sarah Rose has offered to help with housekeeping and kitchen work. Won't that be nice?"

"As long as Bernice appreciates it."

"I told her all about how Sarah took care of me and our household. It took some convincing, but I think Bernice may actually be looking forward to some help."

"And you explained to her—" She lowered her voice—"about Sarah?"

"I did." Katy nodded eagerly. "And Bernice assured me that as long as Sarah pulls her weight, she doesn't care if she's green or pink or purple. Those were her exact words."

"Oh, good." Anna squeezed Katy's hand. "Don't get me wrong, I do love that you're such a kindhearted and generous young lady. It's just that I feel protective of Sarah Rose. You understand, don't you?"

Katy's features softened. "Believe me, Mother, I do." She looked up the stairs. "But since I encouraged her to come, I plan to take full responsibility for her now that she's here. So don't worry."

"Fine, I won't." Anna touched her daughter's cheek. "But please feel free to ask if you need any help or run into any problems. And ask Sarah Rose to come to my room to visit me after you're done introducing her to Bernice. I can't wait to see her again."

As Anna went to her room, she still felt uncertain. Although she wanted to support Katy in her efforts to help Sarah Rose, she knew that her daughter's benevolent plan could easily backfire. But as long as no one got hurt, Anna would remain supportive.

She had just changed from her work suit into a comfortable dress when Sarah Rose knocked on her door. "Come in, come in." Anna embraced Sarah. "I'm so happy to see you."

Sarah Rose actually had misty eyes. "Thank you for letting me come, Miss Anna. Everyone has been so kind, and it's so pretty here. Do you know, I can see the ocean from my room?"

Anna invited her to sit. "I was so sad to hear about Abe. He was such a good man. I'm terribly sorry for your loss. You've been through so much . . . especially after losing your parents and your baby. I'm just so sorry."

"I know you've been through hard times too, Miss Anna."

"Please, Sarah, you always called me Anna before."

"That was before." Sarah sniffed as if she were about to cry.

Anna removed a lace-trimmed linen handkerchief from her bureau. "Here, I want you to keep this, *Miss* Sarah Rose." Anna winked at her.

Sarah almost smiled as she wiped her eyes. "It has been hard . . . Anna. I've lost so much that, well, I almost didn't want to live anymore. But I know that's wrong. I have to trust the Good Lord for my days here on earth. He knows best."

"Yes. And you're a brave woman. I've always believed that."

"I've been praying for the Lord to make a way for me, but until Miss Katy invited me to come work for her, I'd almost given up. Times are hard in Portland these days. Getting harder and harder for folks like me."

"In the year before we left, I'd covered some of those stories at the paper. I knew things were taking a turn—and I was worried."

"I don't like to talk bad about people, but these newcomers . . . they don't speak English or understand our ways, yet they shove us aside just as if we are nothing, as if their skin color makes it right."

"Well, it's not right," Anna declared. "I'm sorry it's happening. And it's not right."

They talked awhile longer and then Katy

knocked on her door, reminding Sarah that it was time for her to go down and get her dinner. When Sarah made her exit, Anna exchanged glances with Katy. "I wish she could just sit down at the table with us," Anna said. "It seems wrong to have her eating alone in her room."

"It's what she wants," Katy pointed out. "She was pretty adamant about it."

"Yes . . . I suppose she would be. But it just feels awkward."

"Maybe in time, she'll want to eat with us," Katy suggested. "Maybe she just needs to settle in a little first. We should give her time."

"You're probably right."

"And it's probably a good thing because Jim had mentioned stopping by after dinner tonight. We were going to take a little evening stroll on the beach."

"Oh, yes . . . Jim." Anna suddenly remembered the president's new authority. "When did you last talk to him?"

"Just this morning."

"So you haven't heard the latest news?"

"News?" Katy's brow creased with concern. "Is something wrong? Did Jim get hurt or—"

"No, no, dear. Nothing like that."

"Oh, good." Katy sighed. "You know, I still remember that night, Mother, when the old chowder house blew up and Jim was hurt so badly. I was so scared when I thought he could die."

A chill went through Anna. How would Katy feel to learn Jim would soon be facing life and death battles overseas? "But you were so brave in taking care of him. I know how much he appreciated how calm you remained and how well you handled everything. That's probably the night when you really grew up in his eyes."

Katy smiled. "We both changed that night."

Anna stood to gaze out the window. "Looks like clouds rolling in. It may be a good sunset."

"But what were you saying, Mother? About the latest news? For some reason, I thought it had to do with Jim."

"Some news came in this afternoon," Anna said absently. "Over the wire."

"What was it?" Katy came over to stand next to her by the window.

"Congress passed a bill." Anna turned to look at Katy. "A bill that allows President Wilson to draft American men into military service."

Katy didn't respond but continued to look out the window.

"We knew it was in the works, but I suppose it still felt surprising. It makes it feel even more real that our country is truly going to war." Anna didn't want to mention what a horrible sort of war was raging on the other side of the world.

"What does that mean exactly? Will all American men be called out to be soldiers?"

"Only young men between the ages of twenty and thirty."

"Jim is twenty-six," Katy said quietly.

"Yes, I know."

"So he will have to go?"

"Most likely."

"When will this happen?" Katy's voice was barely more than a whisper. "How soon until he has to go into battle?"

"I don't think anyone knows exact dates, Katy, but the way things are going over there . . . Well, I'm sure it won't be long before our soldiers are shipped over."

"Oh . . ."

"But from what I've heard, the young men will be examined by doctors, to be sure they're physically fit. Not all young men will be sent into active service."

"I'm sure Jim is fit enough." Katy sighed.

"After that, the draftees will go to training camps to learn to be soldiers, and then they'll be sent overseas."

"When? Do you know *when?*"

"No one knows for sure yet. I read somewhere that soldiers will receive at least six weeks of training . . . so my best guess is they won't ship out before midsummer." Anna didn't want to admit that she wouldn't be surprised if it were sooner.

"Oh, Mother." Katy began to cry, and Anna

wrapped her arms around her, trying to comfort her but unsure of what to say. So she just held her until Katy stopped crying.

"You know what Jim did this afternoon?" Anna said, pausing to wipe her own teary eyes. "After we heard the news?"

"What?" Katy blew her nose.

"He sat down at his typewriter, just like this." Anna held her hands like she was merrily typing. "And he began whistling 'Yankee Doodle Dandy' as if he didn't have a care in the world."

Katy broke into a little smile. "That sounds just like him. I can actually imagine him doing that."

"He'll be all right. Jim's a tough cookie. He's a survivor. He's smart and quick and keen-witted. He'll make a fine soldier. In fact, I bet they'll make him an officer before long."

"I think you're right." Katy nodded. "And I'll be brave about it tonight, Mother. Although I'm glad you told me, so I could cry on your shoulder instead of his. I don't want him to think I'm a big baby."

"Don't worry." Anna pushed an auburn curl away from Katy's forehead. "I don't think he'll ever think of you like that." Bernice's dinner bell interrupted them, and as they went down the stairs, Katy began humming "Yankee Doodle Dandy."

CHAPTER 6

Katy was determined to present a brave front to Jim as they strolled down the beach after dinner. She could tell that he was keeping their conversation even more positive and upbeat than usual. But she sensed seriousness just below the surface. And finally, when they paused to sit on a big driftwood log, she decided to speak out.

"Mother told me about the bill that was passed today," she announced.

"Yes, well, it's not much of a surprise." He picked up a stick, hurling it toward the surf's edge. "It'd been just a matter of time. The US needs more troops."

"Haven't a lot of men signed up already?" She thought of how AJ Krauss had chosen the army instead of jail and of several other local fellows who'd eagerly enlisted. "But apparently they need more?"

"It'll take a lot more boots on the ground to end this war."

"How many?" She didn't really expect an answer.

"Well, I've been doing some research for the paper, and right now there are about a hundred thousand enlistees."

She blinked. "Goodness, that's probably more than the population of Portland."

"Compared to other countries' armed forces—especially on the enemies' side—the United States Army is minuscule."

"Oh."

"So, you see, selective service was inevitable."

"How does it actually work?" She studied the sky where a streak of orange was just starting to glow on the far western horizon.

"Men between the ages of twenty-one and thirty are required to register for the draft. Sounds like that will begin soon, probably within the next few weeks. Then the men will be classified."

"Classified?"

"Yes, I was just reading about the five classifications. I plan to write a piece on this for next week's paper. The first class will be men sent directly to army camps around the country, where they'll be trained and—bing, bang, boom—shipped overseas and into battle."

"So that's first class?" She frowned. "Doesn't sound very posh to me."

He chuckled. "Yes, it's not quite like traveling by ship or train."

"How do they decide who is first class?"

"Those lucky fellows must be unmarried and have no children—"

"What if they're married?" she asked a bit too quickly. Her cheeks grew warm, and she hoped he didn't think she was dropping hints. She certainly wasn't!

"Well, it all depends. If a draftee's wife is of independent means, or if his children are old enough to work and help at home, they still have to serve."

"So married men with young children *don't* have to serve in the army?"

"Not exactly. But if a married man has too many children and insufficient income, he can be exempt due to what is called extreme hardship."

"So . . . if you got yourself a dependent little housewife and a passel of small children and a crummy job . . . you'd be exempt too?"

He laughed. "Thanks, Katy, but I think I'd rather go straight to the battlefront."

She giggled too. "Can't say that I blame you."

"There are other reasons for exemption. Men studying for the clergy or who are in college are ineligible. And, of course, if there's a physical problem, that's automatic exemption. And the rest of the married fellows—the ones with wives and kids that need them—they are temporarily deferred, which means they can be called up later if necessary."

"Oh." She sighed sadly. "So it's pretty much a certainty that you'll be going."

"That's right." He nodded firmly.

"How do you feel about that?" she asked tentatively.

He looked at her. "Quite honestly, I wasn't too pleased. Oh, I knew it was coming, but I also know what's been going on over there." He turned away, gazing toward the horizon, which was getting more colorful.

"Is it really bad?" she asked quietly.

He blew out a slow sigh. "It's war, Katy."

She felt silly now. Of course it was bad. Men were dying. How could that be anything but bad?

"But you know what?" His tone sounded more positive. "I'm actually starting to look forward to it."

"Really?" She glanced at him and could see that his countenance appeared brighter. Unless it was just the warm amber light from the sunset. "Why's that?"

He picked up another smooth stick of driftwood, spinning it around in his hands. "While I was doing research, I read about Camp Lewis up in Washington state. It sounds like a really amazing place. I'd actually like to see it."

"What is Camp Lewis?"

He told her about a beautiful place near a lake. "It's the biggest army training camp in the country. Set in the forest, with a camp that's been recently built and all set up for soldiers. It's fairly certain that I'll be sent there." He grinned. "Have you ever heard of the Boy Scouts?"

"Sure. They started a program in Portland a few years ago and some boys from my school were members. They'd go camping and fishing and lots of fun stuff." She frowned. "But it was *boys only.*"

He chuckled. "Well, I was obviously too old for the Boy Scouts, but I'm not too old for this. May be fun to camp with a bunch of fellows my age." He stuck his stick into the sand like a flag-pole.

Katy wasn't so sure about that but decided to contain her thoughts. "So how soon until you head off to your big Boy Scout camp?"

"That's a very good question." He ran his fingers through his sandy brown hair. "I've been giving it some serious thought today. You see, I could wait and register with the draft, which buys me a few more weeks, maybe even a month . . . or I could enlist right now."

"Right now?" Katy grimaced.

"If I enlist now, I may be able to get an officer's commission."

"Oh . . . that makes sense. And I'm sure you'd make a fine officer, Jim."

He smiled at her. "I suppose I'd rather lead than follow."

She forced a smile. "I understand . . . but I will miss you."

"You've been a good friend, Katy. I hope our friendship continues to grow . . . despite the miles between us."

"Well, I'm a fairly good letter writer," she said with a lump in her throat. "And I know you're a good writer, Jim."

Jim leaned toward her, gazing into her eyes, and for a brief instance, she thought they actually were going to kiss . . . and she really hoped that they would. But he landed a kiss on her forehead. "So is it a deal?" He looked hopeful. "We'll both write regularly?"

She nodded. "Yes. It's a deal."

He pointed toward the ocean. "Just look at that sunset. What a beauty."

She turned to see, but the scene looked slightly blurry to her. Fortunately, it was dusky enough that Jim couldn't see her tear-filled eyes. And for a long moment, they just sat there in silence, watching the sky changing from shifting shades of orange and red and purple, as tears rolled down her cheeks.

On Saturday morning, Katy felt she'd handled the previous evening as well as possible . . . but she still felt gloomy to think that Jim was about to enlist in the army. But instead of dwelling on it, she focused her attention on Sarah Rose. She started by giving her a full tour of the house, even introducing her to Mac. Finally, they stopped in the library.

"I know you like to read," Katy told Sarah. "And Grandfather already said it was all right for you to borrow books."

"That's very kind of him." Sarah's eyes grew wide as she looked at the tall shelves of books. "My goodness."

"Why don't you pick out a couple of books now?" Katy pointed out some titles she thought Sarah might enjoy.

"You know how many people assume that I am unable to read and write? Just because of my color." Sarah removed a history book. "Even when I explain that my mother was a teacher back in Connecticut, before we moved out west when my father took a job with the railroad. But I don't think they believed me about that either." She selected another book. "Of course, my mother wasn't allowed to teach here in Oregon. Well, except for me. I'm so grateful she taught me."

"Your mother always sounded like a fine woman." Katy glanced at the clock. "I need to go to my dress shop in order to open at nine o'clock."

"Oh, I'll hurry then." Sarah put the books under her arm. "Just let me run and get my hat and—"

"I thought you should stay home today, Sarah."

Katy had already rehearsed this. "You see, on Saturdays I'm usually quite busy with shoppers and fittings and such. So I won't have time to train you."

"But you don't need to train me, Miss Katy. I already know how to sew."

"Believe me, I know you're a fine seamstress. But I still think today is a good day for you to just relax here at home." She pointed to the books. "Read if you like. Or just enjoy the ocean view from your window."

"But I'm here to work and—"

"I know. But for today, just enjoy some free time."

Sarah's brow creased. "Well, maybe I can be of help to Miss Bernice."

"If you'd like." Katy paused. "But I must ask one thing of you."

"Yes, of course, anything."

"Please, don't go outside . . . alone."

Sarah tipped her head to one side. "And why is that, Miss Katy?"

"My grandfather recommended it. Unless Mother or I or someone else is with you, for the time being, it would be better if you stayed indoors." Katy felt a heaviness to have to say this. As if she were making Sarah a prisoner. It felt awful. "But when I get home this afternoon, we could go walk on the beach together. If you want."

Sarah brightened. "I would love that."

"So you do understand?"

Sarah gazed down at the floor. "Yes, I under-stand, Miss Katy."

"And don't worry, Sarah. I'll be keeping you so busy at the dress shop that you'll look back on this day of leisure and hope to have another." Katy laughed as she pinned on her hat. "Of course, you'll always have Sundays off." She pulled on her gloves. "Now, I wish you a good day, and I'll see you around four o'clock."

Sarah thanked her, and Katy let herself out of the house. She'd planned to walk to work, but since she was running late and the sky was growing cloudy, she decided to take the Run-about. Her grandfather's stroke had made it impossible for him to drive his sweet little car, but to her delight, he was happy for her to use it whenever she liked.

As she drove the short distance to her dress shop, she thought about Jim. Was he possibly enlisting in the army today? Or would he have to wait until Monday? And how quickly would they take him after he enlisted? Would it be immediately? Or would they give him a chance to tell his friends and loved ones goodbye? These were questions she hadn't thought to ask last night.

Thinking about last night was frustrating . . . and confusing. As much as she'd been enjoying

Jim's company of late, she'd always been relieved that their relationship had remained that of two good friends. Oh, she had no doubt that Jim might have a romantic interest in her. She knew enough about those things to suspect it. Yet he'd always remained a perfect gentleman. And she appreciated that. At least she used to. But last night, she had really hoped that he would kiss her. She wasn't even sure why. Was the urgency related to him going into the army? Or was it something more?

She'd always assumed that his hesitancy to make a romantic gesture was simply because her mother and her grandfather were his bosses. One wrong move on his part could be risky. And up until recently, they had both assumed he was much older than Katy. Although Katy had known the truth for some time, it had been her secret.

Katy asked herself why she'd been so hopeful for that kiss. Why had she closed her eyes and leaned toward him like that, only to feel like a silly schoolgirl later when he'd simply kissed her forehead? She realized that she'd truly wanted that kiss. And she'd been severely disappointed not to get it. Despite knowing that a kiss like that could change—and possibly ruin—everything, she'd wanted it! Was it because she'd wanted to change everything? As she parked behind the dress shop, she felt more confused than ever. But as she went in through the back door, she knew it was time to place thoughts of Jim behind her.

Besides having a busy day ahead of her, Katy needed to prepare the women for the news about Sarah Rose. Oh, Grandmother and Clara, who were essentially partners in the dress shop, already knew that a new seamstress would be joining them on Monday. But they didn't know anything more than that. And somehow Katy had to convey details about Sarah in a way that would help everyone to fully accept her and make her feel at home.

She turned on the lights and did some quick shop-keeping, tidying the shelf of scarves, straightening the boxes of lingerie, arranging the hat counter to look enticing, and just making sure everything about the upscale dress shop was pure perfection. And then she unlocked the front door. Since it was still a bit early for customers, she returned to the back room to put some finishing touches on a couple of new summer hats she'd been working on.

"Good morning, darling." Lucille bustled into the back room with her usual flourish of silk skirts and the aroma of rose perfume. "I see you drove today. I should've called you for a ride."

"I'm sorry, Grandmother. I didn't even think." Katy set down the ostrich feather. "But I'll give you a ride home."

"Thank you." Lucille unpinned her hat and looked around. "Clara not in yet?"

"Here I am." Clara came down the stairs from the apartment above. In her hands was a plate of baked goods. "I thought you would forgive me being a bit tardy if I came bearing gifts. These cinnamon rolls just came out of the oven."

"I have some news," Katy said as they nibbled on the cinnamon rolls. "My friend Sarah Rose is here. She's an excellent seamstress, and she'll be in to work on Monday."

"That's the woman who taught you to sew?" Clara asked.

"Yes, and she took care of me while my mother went to work." Katy took in a breath. "And she is a colored woman."

The back room went quiet.

"Oh?" Lucille nodded with a hard-to-read expression.

"I realize I probably should've mentioned this," Katy said nervously. "But Sarah Rose is such a good friend—like family really." She glanced at Clara. "I hope you don't mind."

"I've never known a colored person before," Clara admitted. "But my folks came from up north, and we were antislavery."

"So you'll both be all right with Sarah Rose?" Katy asked anxiously.

"As long as she's your good friend, I have no complaints." Still, Lucille looked a little concerned.

"As long as she can sew, I don't mind," Clara added.

"Oh, I'm so glad." Katy hugged them both. "Grandfather and Mother said a few things that made me feel worried about Sunset Cove. I was afraid Sarah may not be accepted here."

Clara frowned. "Well, just because we accept her doesn't mean everyone else in town will, Katy. I know for a fact that my late husband was not kind or generous to people who were, uh, different. But for that matter he was not kind or generous to his own wife."

"And we have some customers," Lucille pointed out, "who are not always kind and generous."

"Yes, I know." Katy sighed to think of certain ladies who didn't hesitate to speak their minds, even if their opinions were narrow-minded and mean-spirited. "Grandfather has suggested that we don't let Sarah go anywhere unaccompanied. But I plan to take full responsibility for that."

"We will help too," Lucille assured her.

Katy heard the bell in front. "A customer." She wiped her sticky fingers on a napkin. "I'll see to her."

But instead of a customer, it was Jim Stafford. "I'm sorry to interrupt you at work." He twisted his hat in his hands. "But I'm on my way to enlist, and I just wanted you to know."

"Where are you going? I mean to enlist?"

"Salem." He pursed his lips. "And I'm taking a bag with me . . . just in case."

"You mean you could be gone for good?" she asked with wide eyes.

"It's a possibility. I already informed your grandfather and . . . I just wanted you to know."

"But this is so fast." She wanted to do something to put on the brakes. "Why such a hurry, Jim?"

"I got to thinking last night—after we talked on the beach—that a lot of men are probably thinking just like I am. Fellows who will be eager to enlist in the hopes of getting an officer's commission. I thought I should jump on it. Mac agreed." Jim checked his watch. "And the train leaves at ten forty, so I should be going."

"I'll drive you to the station," she said eagerly. "Just give me a moment." She hurried to the back room, quickly explaining the situation as she grabbed her hat and things. "I'll be back before noon."

Then, as she drove Jim to the station, he explained how he'd spent the whole night packing his personal items. "I haven't slept at all, not a wink, but I don't feel tired. My landlady was very understanding this morning. She even returned next month's rent money and let me store my boxes in her basement. And then I called Mac, and he promised to convey the news to your mother." He sighed. "It's all happened so quickly, yet it feels right."

It didn't feel right to her, but as they neared the train station, she tried to gather her thoughts. Was this the last time she would see Jim before he headed off to war? Or would she have another chance? And if he did go off to war . . . would she ever see him again *at all?* Finally, she parked in front of the small terminal building, where they talked for a while longer. Katy knew she was doing everything she could to keep him here in the car with her, possibly thinking that if she stalled long enough the train would come and go and he would be stuck in Sunset Cove until the next train came, which probably wouldn't be until Monday.

"I better go inside and get my ticket," he finally said. "But thanks for the ride, Katy."

"I'll go in with you." She hopped out of the car, following him into the terminal and waiting as he purchased his ticket. And then, still unwilling to part ways, she walked him out to the platform.

"It's starting to rain," he told her. "You should go inside."

"That's all right." She pointed down the track. "I think I can hear it coming."

"But your pretty hat, Katy. It'll be ruined."

"I don't care," she said in a husky voice that was choked with tears. "I'm not leaving until I see you onto the train, Jim."

He peered curiously down at her, touching

her cheek. "Katy? Are you crying or is that a raindrop?"

"Maybe it's both," she retorted with a sniff.

"Oh, dear Katy." He grasped her hand. "That is so sweet."

"And you'd think that a fellow heading off to war . . . would want to kiss his sweetheart good-bye." She waited stubbornly. "That is, if I *am* your sweetheart, Jim Stafford."

He dropped his bag and swept her into his arms, landing the sweetest, most romantic kiss imaginable on her lips. So lovely that she felt slightly dizzy and lighthearted when he finally let her go, but the sound of the train whistle made her jump, jerking her back to reality.

"Do you think you're my sweetheart now?" he asked with a happy grin.

She just smiled, nodding eagerly, and he hugged her again.

"I'll write you as soon as I can," he assured her as the train's brakes hissed.

"Yes, and send me an address so I can write back," she said loudly enough to be heard over the rumble of the train stopped right next to them.

"I will." He kissed her again. "Thank you for coming here with me."

"Thank you for letting me." She reached for her handkerchief but knew it would be useless since she was completely drenched by the rain now. And so she handed it to him. "Something to remember me with."

He tucked it into his coat pocket then picked up his bag, still looking deeply into her eyes. "I'll be back for you," he declared. "Count on it."

"I'll be waiting."

He waved as he climbed onto the train, and she waited, watching through the pelting rain as he hurried to a window to wave down to her. And then with rain and tears falling, she waved back, watching as the train chugged away from the station. "God go with you," she said quietly. "And keep you safe."

Chapter 7

Anna was shocked to learn that Jim Stafford had quit the paper. Oh, she knew it was inevitable, but good grief, Congress had passed that bill only yesterday.

"He hopes to ensure an officer's commission," Mac explained over coffee, pointing to the article Jim had squeezed onto the front page of Saturday's paper. "And I don't blame him at all. Jim is officer material."

"And you don't think he'll return to Sunset Cove before he goes to army training camp?"

Mac slowly spread blackberry jam over his toast. "Hard to say. Jim felt it was likely he wouldn't be back. He spent all last night packing his belongings for storage—arranged everything with his landlady—so he could clear out."

"Seems he could've waited until at least Monday. We could've given him a little send-off at the paper." She frowned at the thought of not being able to say goodbye to her good friend. And what would Katy think? She didn't want to think about that.

"His reasoning makes sense to me. Right now thousands of young men must be preparing to do the same thing. Good for Jim for getting a jump on it."

"I suppose you're right."

"He did feel bad about not getting a chance to tell you goodbye, Anna. But you weren't down yet when he called. And Katy had just left for the dress shop."

"I wonder how she'll take this. You know that she and Jim were pretty good friends."

Mac nodded. "Yes, well, Jim assured me he planned to stop by her shop to explain things to her."

"Oh, that's good." She reached for a piece of bacon. "Do you know if Katy took Sarah Rose to work with her?"

"She didn't. Although she did bring in Sarah to meet me." He lowered his voice. "I was impressed. She seems like a good woman." His brow creased. "But I'm still concerned for her welfare, Anna. I don't want to frighten her, but when I think about Ben . . . Well, I hope Katy will be cautious."

"I know, Mac. I understand."

"I told Katy, privately, that I don't think Sarah should go anywhere in town on her own. At least to begin with."

"Katy already assured me that she would do that." Worried that Sarah might be somewhere within hearing distance, Anna changed the subject. "I'd asked Jim to write a piece for the midweek paper about the upcoming hospital building project, but it looks like I'll have to do that myself now."

"Unless you'd like me to take a stab at it." His pale eyes brightened. "I realize with Jim gone, you'll be shorthanded. Maybe I could step in some."

"That'd be wonderful, Mac." Then she paused to consider this. "I mean, do you feel up to working again?"

"I feel the best I've felt since my stroke. It's been almost a year now. My speech is almost back to normal, and I've gotten rather adept at one-handed typing."

"Should you consult with Dr. Hollister about working, to make sure it won't set you back on your recovery?" She didn't want the stress of working to risk Mac's health, and she knew another stroke could be the end.

"Dr. Hollister?" Mac's brows rose. "Since when are you on such formal terms with Daniel?"

She shrugged. "I don't know. I suppose I'm preparing myself . . . thinking about when he'll be leaving."

"Leaving? But if we get the hospital building started, do you really think he'll abandon us? Wasn't that part of the reason for this plan?"

"We have to face reality. Even if Sunset Cove

builds a perfectly lovely hospital, it won't begin to compete with that big modern one in Boston— or of Daniel being chief of staff there. And I suspect he wants to be near his father as well."

"His father." Mac huffed. "Why would he want to be near that argumentative, arrogant old man?"

"*Old* man?" Anna teased. "He's not much older than you, Mac." She knew Mac's intense dislike of Daniel's father had more to do with the attention the older gentleman had bestowed on Anna's mother. Mac had been greatly relieved to see his competition leave, and since then, unless Anna had imagined it, Mac had been even more attentive to Lucille. But whenever Anna pressed her father about the chances of her parents remarrying, he brushed her off. And perhaps that was for the best.

"Well, back to that hospital article for the newspaper," Mac said. "How about if you and I go over it this morning, and I'll start working on it today? I'm not as fast as I used to be. May take me a day or two to get it just right."

Anna got a notepad, and they began to go over the announcement of the donated land and listing the names of all those who were backing the project as well as the upcoming fundraisers.

"And we can't forget the bond measure on the May ballot," he reminded her.

"Wally is feeling quite positive about it." She noted this.

"Just think, Anna, by this time next year, Sunset Cove will probably have a real hospital." He sighed. "Our town is really coming along nicely."

"I hope the building will have plenty of windows to take full advantage of the ocean view up there. Patients may recover more quickly if their rooms look out on it."

"I agree. Did I tell you Randall Douglas already recommended an architect? He has a college chum who's been working down in San Francisco. Randall invited him here for a visit."

"That's wonderful." Anna handed her notes to Mac. "So if we announce this in the midweek paper, it may be time for me to mention it to Daniel."

"Yes, the committee wants to get Daniel involved." Mac held up the page of notes. "We should include him with the rest of the backers. After all, he's our only doctor. At least for now."

Anna finished her coffee. "In fact, I think I'll pay Daniel a little visit this morning . . . and share the good news."

Mac grinned. "Maybe it'll encourage him to forget about Boston and that obnoxious father of his."

"I wouldn't count on it."

"While you're there, find out his birthday," Mac said as she stood. "I mentioned to the committee he'd soon turn forty. And Wally suggested we schedule the groundbreaking ceremony to coincide with a birthday celebration."

"What a wonderful idea."

"But don't tell Daniel about that. It'd be fun to keep it a surprise."

Before heading to town, Anna went upstairs to check on Sarah Rose. Peeking through Sarah's opened door, she found her sitting by the window reading. "You look cozy up here," Anna said.

"Oh, Miss Anna." Sarah set her book aside and stood. "Good morning."

They exchanged pleasantries, and Sarah explained how she'd offered to help Bernice with kitchen chores but had been turned down. "Everyone seems to think I need to rest." Sarah looked frustrated as she paced back and forth in the small room. "But I feel so full of energy. I think it must be from the ocean. Or perhaps the clean, fresh air. It makes me feel different. Younger and stronger." She gazed out the window. "Even though it's raining, I would love to go outside."

"How would you like to walk to town with me?" Anna said suddenly.

"Oh, Miss Anna, that'd be wonderful."

"Well, put on something to keep off the rain, and I will give you a quick, albeit somewhat damp, tour of our little town. And if you don't mind, we'll stop by the doctor's office on our way."

"Oh, dear, are you sick?" Sarah asked with concern.

"No, not at all. The doctor is a friend. It will be a social visit."

With hats and coats and gloves and sturdy shoes, they set off for town. Anna was actually grateful for the inhospitable weather because town was somewhat deserted. She used the opportunity to show Sarah the various businesses, finally ducking into the building where the doctor's office was located.

They peeled off their damp outer clothes, giving them a shake, and hung them on the hall tree by the door. Then they went upstairs to find Daniel in the reception area, where Norma used to work, sorting through a stack of papers.

"Hello," Anna called out. "Can we interrupt you for a moment?"

"Oh, hello, Anna." Daniel looked up from a pile of papers. "Please, come in."

Anna quickly introduced him to Sarah, explaining how she'd been an integral part of their Portland family. "And now she'll be working at Katy's dress shop." To Anna's relief, Daniel didn't act the least bit surprised as he politely greeted Sarah Rose.

"Welcome to town," he said with a pleasant smile.

"Thank you. Miss Anna just gave me a tour."

"Dr. Hollister is a relative newcomer too," Anna told Sarah. "He's from Boston. How long have you been in Sunset Cove now?" she asked him.

"Not even three years."

"My family came from Connecticut," Sarah eagerly told him. "That's not too far from where you're from."

"That's right . . . but it's a long way from here." He glanced at the window, now being pelted with sheets of rain. "I'm sorry our weather isn't more accommodating."

"I don't mind the rain a bit," Sarah assured him. "It's the first time I've seen the ocean, and I must say, it's just wonderful. I was reading a book this morning, but the big blue sea kept distracting me from it. I would stop to stare out the window and nearly had to pinch myself to think I was really here."

He smiled. "It certainly is a beautiful stretch of beach out there. Much nicer than the beach my family and I used to visit in Massachusetts. It was so rocky there, you could barely walk, let alone swim. If you went for a swim and the tide was coming in, you had to be careful not to get slammed into the rocks."

"You actually swam in the ocean?" Sarah looked impressed.

"Occasionally." He turned to Anna now. "So to what do I owe the pleasure of this visit?"

He pointed to the messy desk behind him. "Or perhaps you've come to help me dig out."

"Looks like you could use a shovel," Anna said.

"I know I needed to let Norma go. And going through the files and paperwork, I'm even more certain that was the right thing to do. But now I can't seem to find anyone to replace her. I felt certain I'd have someone by now. Even if just temporarily."

"Have you let people know?" Anna asked.

"I put an ad in your midweek classifieds and today's paper too. And I've put a note on the Mercantile bulletin board. I don't even expect to get a trained nurse right now. Just someone with enough know-how to mind this desk, answer the telephone, and maybe sort out this mess so I don't have to. I even spoke to the high school principal on Wednesday, hoping one of the older girls may want work. But so far no one's called. I don't even care if the person has actual office experience. I just need them to read and write and operate a telephone."

"I have office experience," Sarah Rose said quietly.

"You do?" Anna's brows lifted.

"Yes." Sarah shyly nodded.

"I didn't know that," Anna said. "I knew you'd worked as a seamstress, but I hadn't heard about office work."

"I worked as a seamstress at the Portland Hotel

to start with. That was back when they still hired mostly colored folks. My husband Abe helped me get the job. When the hotel manager found out I could read and write and do arithmetic, he asked me to help in the office. The secretary trained me, and I worked there for four years." She sighed. "But then they replaced me . . . and my husband too . . . and lots of the colored staff . . . when the new immigrants began pouring in. It all began to change."

"That's why Sarah came to Sunset Cove," Anna told Daniel. "Work was hard to find in Portland, and Sarah's husband passed away." She placed a hand on Sarah's shoulder. "And Portland has turned into a rather rough place."

"That's true." Sarah nodded somberly.

"But I can imagine you were a valuable office worker," Anna told her. "Your penmanship is beautiful, you're a good reader, and I still remember how you helped Katy with her math schoolwork. We were both so grateful."

"Thank you, Miss Anna."

"I wish you could work for me," Daniel told Sarah.

Her eyes opened wide. "Truly? You would hire . . . *me* to work for you?"

"I certainly would. But Katy may not like it if I snatched her new employee away from her."

For a moment no one spoke. Anna wasn't sure if Daniel's offer was sincere, but she couldn't imagine he'd say something like that in jest. "That's very interesting," Anna finally said carefully. "What would you think about working in a doctor's office, Sarah?"

Sarah still looked dumbfounded. "Oh, dear, well, I don't know. Miss Katy brought me out here to sew for her."

"But which would you prefer?" Daniel asked eagerly.

"I don't mind sewing at all," she admitted, "but I did enjoy office work." She tapped the side of her head. "It made me use my brain. I liked that."

Anna told Daniel about how Sarah's mother had been a teacher in Connecticut and how Sarah had profited from her mother's education. "But teaching opportunities were, uh, more limited here in Oregon."

"I see." He turned to Sarah. "Do you think you'd be comfortable working in a doctor's office?"

Sarah's forehead creased. "Perhaps I should ask you . . . would your patients be comfortable with me?"

He folded his arms in front, seeming to consider this. "I'm not sure I particularly care."

Sarah's brows arched. "Oh?"

"I'm sorry. That didn't sound right. It's not that I don't care about my patients' feelings," he said slowly. "But I'm the only doctor in town. Folks don't have much choice when they need my help.

And, to put it mildly, they're not always grateful for it. To be honest, as a newcomer from back East, I've experienced some resentment myself. Even Anna's father questioned me—until he had his stroke. Then Mac was forced to accept my professional help."

"And now my father has the utmost respect for Dr. Hollister," Anna told Sarah.

"So, if I determine you're qualified to work for me, then why should anyone question that?" He seemed to study Sarah Rose.

"I appreciate that." Still, Sarah's smile seemed uneasy.

"How about if you take some time to think about this?" Anna told Sarah. "Meanwhile, I'd like to have a private word with Dr. Hollister."

"Yes." Sarah nodded eagerly. "That's a wise counsel, Miss Anna. I think I'd like to pray about this decision. That is, if you're truly certain, Dr. Hollister, that your offer of employment is genuine."

"It is definitely genuine," he assured Sarah, opening the door to his private office. "But you go ahead and pray about it. I'll respect your decision."

As Anna walked into his office, she felt unsure. What if they were putting Sarah Rose in jeopardy by encouraging her to work here? After all, Daniel was well aware of how people could become difficult or contrary when seeking medical help. What if they resented having Sarah Rose the first one to greet them upon arrival? What if they decided she had overstepped her social bounds by being here? Even worse, what if someone tried to hurt this dear woman?

CHAPTER 8

Concerns for Sarah Rose continued to plague Anna as she sat in Daniel's consulting office. "Well, I sure wasn't expecting that," she confessed as Daniel took a seat behind his desk. "I don't think Sarah was either. Do you really think it's a good idea?"

"I'm happy to employ her." He sat behind his desk. "She seems intelligent, well-spoken, and fully qualified. More so than Norma. Good grief, you should see the messes that woman left behind. I had no idea she was such a poor manager. It's no wonder some of my patients have neglected to pay me."

"I understand that. But Sarah could be right, Daniel—your patients may not approve of her. They may be unkind."

"Do you think my patients would be any ruder than Katy's customers? Think about someone like Mrs. Elliott Stone."

Anna pursed her lips to consider that outspoken old biddy. He had a valid point. "I just don't want Sarah to be hurt."

"Nor do I. And, don't get me wrong, I'm as aware as anyone that Sunset Cove can be rather, well . . ." He shrugged.

"Backward?" She locked eyes with him, prepared to defend her small hometown.

"No, I wasn't going to say *that,* Anna. But some of the folks here, well, they can be a bit set in their ways."

She sighed. "I'd have to agree with you there."

"Anyway, I don't think that's what brought you here to see me today." He folded his hands, leaning forward with a sincere expression. "All week long I'd been meaning to talk to you. I feel bad about our last conversation. I was upset over Caleb, and I'm afraid I said some things that I—"

"It's all right, Daniel. I understand. You had every right to be distraught."

"But I shouldn't have laid my troubles on you like that."

"I'm your friend," she reminded him.

"Well, thank you. I appreciate your graciousness."

"So did you mean what you said about wanting to go back to Boston?" She wasn't sure she really wanted to hear his answer . . . and yet she had to know.

"I probably meant it at the time. Admittedly, there's reason to long for a modern facility and properly trained staff." He sighed. "Yet, to be honest, I sometimes enjoy the challenges of practicing frontier medicine here."

"Is that how you see Sunset Cove? *A frontier?*"

"I'm sorry. I didn't mean to sound like a snob, but you have to admit, my practice has been trying at times."

She softened. "Yes, you're right about the challenges. I've seen it myself."

"And it's not that I don't read the latest medical journals, and I realize I can order new and improved medical equipment and supplies. In fact, I was just reminding myself that practicing in a remote location probably keeps me on my toes."

"How would you feel if Sunset Cove had its own hospital? Not a fancy one like in Boston. But a facility that was big enough to serve our town and outlying areas. One that was well-located and equipped with some modern equipment and a budget sufficient to support an adequate staff. What would you think about that, Dr. Hollister?"

"I'd think you were pulling my leg."

She laughed and began to explain the past week's activities. "It's been incredible. Everyone in town is getting on board with the idea." She listed names and plans and timelines. "And even the location—I'll bet you can't guess where it will be."

He scratched his head. "I'm too stunned to even think."

"Charlie's Chowder House," she proclaimed. "The city had confiscated that property and wasn't sure what to do with it. Wally presented the idea to the council, and they unanimously voted to donate it for a hospital."

"That'd be a nice site." He rubbed his chin.

She continued to tell him details, explaining about the upcoming bond measure, the architect soon coming to town, and all the other pieces falling into place. "Mac and Wally have worked so hard to pull it together, keeping it under wraps at first. But we all felt it was time that the general public heard about it. Naturally, that meant we needed to tell you. I hope you're pleased."

"I don't even know what to say. This is great news. A hospital right here in town. Will marvels never cease?"

"I know Mac would like you to begin participating with the hospital committee. Especially as they get into the actual planning stages— you know, things like building size and design, budget expectations—as well as the nuts and bolts of running a hospital. Your expertise will be invaluable."

"I'm happy to do that."

"And I hope you don't think this was simply a ploy to keep you in Sunset Cove." She looked down at her gloved hands, hoping he couldn't see right through her.

"I want to stay here," he assured her. "I was just having a bad day, Anna."

"I know . . . and hopefully nothing like that will happen again." She sighed. "I'm sure if Caleb had been cared for in a real hospital, he'd still be alive."

"That's probably true."

For a moment, neither of them spoke. And then Anna stood, glancing toward the door. "I don't want to leave Sarah Rose out there too long. She'll think we've abandoned her." She lowered her voice. "So if she accepts this job . . . can you be certain it won't present problems?"

"I'm certain it *will* present problems. But that's usually the cost of progress. It almost always comes with challenges." He smiled, but his eyes looked sad. "But I think I can handle it—and probably better than Kathleen's Dress Shop."

"You may be right."

He stood. "Perhaps after folks get more comfortable seeing Sarah Rose here, and around town a bit, she'll want to work at both places. If she spent three days a week here, I'm sure I could get caught up. Then she could still work for Katy if she liked."

"That's not a bad idea." She waited for him to open the door, noticing how he took his time, how he let his arm brush against hers, gazing into her eyes with something more than just friendship. Perhaps she'd been wrong to give up on him so easily. Maybe there still was hope for them after all.

When they returned to the reception area, Sarah Rose was already sorting through the paperwork. "I hope you don't mind, Dr. Hollister," she told him. "But I thought it may help me to make my decision if I saw what I'd be working with."

"And what do you think?"

"I think it's similar to working at the hotel. Mostly about organizing—keeping files tidy and tracking expenses and billing. From what I can see, it shouldn't be very complicated."

"So, do you want to work here?" Anna asked.

"I'd be proud to work here." She extended her hand to Daniel, and he clasped and shook it. "When do I start?" she asked.

"Anytime you like."

"What about now?" Her eyes lit up.

He grinned. "That'd be wonderful."

"How about if I break the news to Katy?" Anna asked Sarah.

"I'd appreciate that." Sarah moved some papers to another pile.

Now Daniel mentioned the idea about Sarah working part-time at both places. "Although, if no one minded, I'd like to have you here full-time to begin with. Until we get the place organized. But after that, three days a week—or five mornings—would probably be sufficient. The woman before you was only here part-time."

"Oh, yes, I like that idea. Then I could be with Miss Katy too."

Anna promised to relay this news to Katy, but before she left, she asked Daniel to walk her downstairs. "We don't think Sarah Rose should be walking by herself through town," she said as she pulled on her still-damp coat. She quietly told him what Mac had said about his friend, Big Ben. Although Daniel looked somewhat taken aback, he seemed to understand the insinuation and promised to escort Sarah Rose directly home after work.

"And if it's around dinnertime, perhaps you could stay," she suggested. "I know Mac can't wait to talk to you about the hospital plans."

"I gratefully accept." He smiled. "I've missed you, Anna."

Her heart warmed. "I've missed you too. And I'm very glad to hear you're not leaving us for Boston."

"I'm glad too." He opened the front door and stuck his head out. "Hey, it's stopped raining."

She pinned on her hat. "Great. I'll run over to Kathleen's and tell her about Sarah's new position."

"Give Katy my apologies. But, really, I think it may be in Sarah Rose's best interest. Speaking of Sarah Rose, what should I call her? Norma always insisted I use her first name, but quite frankly, it felt unprofessional to me."

"You can call her Mrs. Lewis," Anna stepped outside, taking a deep breath of the freshly washed air. "It's turning into a nice day."

He nodded. "And it's nice that you brought me both good news about the hospital and some real help. Thank you, Anna. I feel like Mrs. Lewis will be a real treasure."

"A treasure we all need to protect," Anna reminded him before saying goodbye. Still, feeling a bit concerned, she hurried down Main Street to Kathleen's Dress Shop. Her concerns weren't for Katy. Finding a seamstress in Sunset Cove shouldn't be that difficult. And Katy would probably be happy for Sarah Rose. Hopefully Sarah Rose wouldn't regret coming to Sunset Cove. And even if Daniel hadn't called it "backward," Anna knew in her heart that it was partly true.

As Anna entered the dress shop, she spotted her mother at the hat counter, waiting on a couple of ladies that Anna knew were difficult customers. They were, in fact, the very sort of customers who could make someone like Sarah Rose feel very uncomfortable. Anna made a little finger wave at Lucille, tossing a sympathetic smile her way as she nodded toward the door to the backroom. "I'm here to see Katy," she said quietly.

"Just a moment." Lucille quickly excused herself from the hat counter ladies, coming over to Anna. "A word of warning," she whispered. "It was getting a little hot in there."

"Hot?"

"Heated," Lucille hissed as she led Anna toward the fitting rooms. "Ellen is back."

"Ellen?" Anna blinked. "But I thought she and Lawrence Bouchard were in San Francisco."

"From what little I heard, Lawrence is no longer in the family business," Lucille confided. "And I'm not surprised. The Bouchards are good people, and they've been good friends to me, but from what I can see, Lawrence isn't much like them."

"Really? I thought you liked the young man," Anna reminded her. "Didn't you hope at one time that Katy would marry him?"

"Pish-posh. That was then, Anna. I'm ever so grateful Katy had the good sense to refuse him. Especially since I believe the young man is a bit of a scoundrel."

"So, did Ellen come here to see her mother?"

Lucille frowned. "Poor Clara. As happy as she was to see her prodigal daughter, it wasn't long before she realized Ellen was here for money."

"Oh, dear." Anna cringed.

"When Clara said no, Ellen asked if we'd take her back into the dress shop business, but Katy told her she'd already hired Sarah Rose."

"Well, I have some news for Katy. And thank you for the heads up." She nodded to where the two ladies both stared with open curiosity.

"It seems your customers are getting restless."

"Yes, of course." Lucille smoothed her hair and smiled. "If you'll excuse me, dear."

Anna was grateful to know the situation before she went into the backroom where it appeared that Ellen, Katy, and Clara were having something of a standoff. "Well, Ellen," Anna tried to sound friendlier than she felt. "It's good to see you back in town."

"I'm glad *someone* thinks so." Ellen's tone was terse.

"I told you I was happy to see you," Clara reassured her daughter. "I was just surprised. You never wrote or anything."

"I didn't know one needed to inform one's own family if one wanted to come home." Ellen's eyes flashed in anger at her mother.

"So, Ellen, I hope married life has been treating you well." Anna removed her gloves, trying to think of a way to smooth Ellen's feathers. "I must say you are looking quite elegant."

"Thank you." Ellen held her chin higher.

"And how is your husband?" Anna asked. "I assume Mr. Bouchard came here with you."

"Lawrence is just fine. He's at the hotel." Ellen turned back to Clara. "But we can't afford to stay there more than a couple more nights."

"Ellen came to see about getting her job back," Katy told Anna. "But I explained to her about Sarah Rose and how—"

"That's why I'm here." Anna quickly told them about Sarah's new job. "Dr. Hollister was in desperate need of office help, and it seems Sarah Rose has the right sort of experience."

"Yes, Sarah told me she'd done office work in the hotel." Katy frowned. "But I was looking forward to having her work—"

"That means you can hire me back," Ellen declared victoriously. "It's perfect."

"But I need a *seamstress*," Katy told Ellen. "You just told me that you hate sewing."

"That's right," Clara agreed. "You said you wanted to work in front, Ellen. That you only wanted to wait on customers in the shop."

"Well, I can do both." Ellen pointed at Katy. "After all, that's what you do. And Lucille does too. Even my mother helps customers in front sometimes."

"But I prefer being back here," Clara told her.

"And I prefer being out front," Ellen insisted. And suddenly the three of them were arguing again.

"What sort of work does your husband plan to do?" Anna suddenly asked Ellen in an attempt to derail the squabble.

"We don't know yet." Ellen frowned. "Say, do you happen to have any openings at your newspaper?"

"As a matter of fact, I will be looking for an

editor. Does Lawrence have newspaper experience?"

"No, but I'm sure he could—"

"I'm sorry, but I'll need someone with experience. My managing editor, Jim Stafford, just left to join the army and—"

"Jim Stafford's going into the army?" Ellen looked shocked and dismayed.

"Yes, I dropped him at the train this morning." Katy's tone was solemn.

Ellen frowned. "Well, that's a shame. Lawrence was just saying how lucky he is not to be called up."

"Why wouldn't he be called up?" Clara asked. "He's of the right age."

"He's got a physical condition." Ellen sounded defensive.

"He seemed perfectly fit to me," Katy said.

"Maybe so, but he's got flat feet, and according to his father, the army won't take anyone with flat feet. Lawrence is exempt."

Clara frowned. "Sounds pretty convenient to me."

And suddenly the mother and daughter were arguing again. Anna nodded to Katy, pointing to the rear door, and soon they were standing outside in the alley. "I didn't really want to get embroiled in all that," Anna said. "Although I must admit it's somewhat interesting—and I'm ever so thankful you were too sensible to fall for

111

Lawrence Bouchard's tricks. But I really came here to tell you about Sarah." So she went into more detail. "She's so thrilled about working there, Katy. Her face completely lit up when Daniel offered her the position."

Katy sighed. "Well, as much as I hate to lose her—or that we've lost our excuse to send Ellen packing—I'm glad Sarah is happy. And I'm proud of Daniel for offering her the job." She smiled at Anna. "He really is a good man, Mother. You should marry him!"

Anna felt her cheeks warm as she waved a dismissive hand. "Let's not push things. I'm just relieved he's not headed for Boston right now. Not yet anyway." She described how pleased he was about the hospital news and then, realizing that Katy looked a bit gloomy, she remembered about Jim. "Oh, Katy," Anna said gently. "How do you feel about Jim leaving so unexpectedly? I'm glad you were able to take him to the train."

Katy brightened slightly. "And it was a sweet goodbye, Mother. But I'm still sad. It was so sudden. But I do understand."

"Mac thought Jim may be able to come back here for a bit, you know, before he heads out to training, but I suppose we can't know anything for sure."

"He mentioned that possibility to me. But I must admit, it felt like he was leaving for good." Katy sighed. "He gave up his room at the boarding house and packed and stored all of his things."

Anna nodded. "Well, I'm sure you'll stay in touch with him no matter where he goes."

"Of course." Katy pursed her lips. "Mother?"

"Yes."

"Do you think I'm too young to be married?"

Anna didn't know what to say. After all, she'd been Katy's age when she'd married. Not that it had worked out well. And Katy's friend Ellen was even younger, but that already looked a bit shaky. "Katy, you're probably the only person who can answer that question."

"Yes, but what do you think? I respect your opinion."

"I think you're very grown up for only seventeen—*seventeen and a half*." She winked. "But I also think you're an independent young woman with big dreams. I wouldn't want to see you married in haste simply because your young man was marching off to war."

Katy sighed. "Yes, that's pretty much what I thought you'd say."

"Well, despite that, I think Jim Stafford is a fine young man," Anna declared.

"Far superior and much preferable to Mr. Lawrence Bouchard?" Katy had a mischievous twinkle in her eyes.

"Yes, but no one had to tell you that, Katy. You figured it out yourself."

"Too bad Ellen didn't." Katy shook her head. "I'm afraid she's headed for heartache."

"I guess time will tell." They both stepped out of the way as a delivery truck went down the alley, jumping to avoid being splashed by a mud puddle.

"Speaking of time, I should probably get back to work." Katy reached for the door. "I have a customer coming in for a fitting at two."

"You have a good afternoon," Anna said. "I think I'll just head out the alley."

"Afraid of the Krauss women?" Katy teased.

"I suppose I am too. Especially after hearing that Sarah Rose has taken other employment."

"I'm sorry, but I know you understand."

Katy wrinkled her nose. "I do understand, but now we have no excuse not to hire Ellen back. And I'm afraid she intends to make us all miserable."

Anna hugged her. "You'll figure a way to make it work, Katy. You always do."

As Anna walked back through town, she wondered about Katy's mention of marriage. First to Anna regarding Daniel. Where had that come from? But perhaps more concerning was Katy's question about herself. Was Katy really considering matrimony? Had Jim asked her? Anna couldn't quite imagine him doing that. Oh, she knew how much he liked Katy—perhaps even loved her—but he was too sensible, too mature.

He wouldn't impulsively suggest an impromptu marriage then jump on a train. At least she hoped not. Because, although she didn't want to say it, she did feel that Katy was too young to marry. She'd really hoped her daughter would wait a few years, that she'd enjoy her young adulthood and feminine independence without being bound in wedlock. Still, Anna knew that if Katy truly wanted to marry Jim Stafford, no one and nothing would stand in her way.

CHAPTER 9

Katy wasted no time in answering Jim's letter, sitting down in Kathleen's business office to respond on the same afternoon she received it. Although dismayed to learn Jim had been sent directly to Camp Lewis and wasn't coming home, Katy could see that he was greatly relieved to discover he'd likely receive an officer's commission as a result of his early enlistment. Katy knew she should be glad for him, but in her imagination, it was the officers who led soldiers into battle . . . and in all likelihood, the first ones to be cut down by the enemy. But, like Jim had done, she tried to keep her letter lighthearted and uplifting.

"Why are you still here?" Ellen asked when she found Katy at the desk. "Mom told me you'd already gone home. We were about to lock up."

"That's fine. Just leave the backroom lights on and I'll let myself out."

"What are you working on?" Ellen leaned over to peer across the desk.

"Just writing a letter." Katy smiled stiffly. Ellen

had only been back at the dress shop for a week, but her pushy ways were already wearing on Katy's nerves.

"You're writing our dear friend Jim Stafford?" Ellen's brows arched with too much interest as she stood up straight.

"That's right." Katy waited, fountain pen poised in the air.

"How is good old Jim?" Ellen sat down on the other side of the desk.

"He's doing quite well." Katy tried to conceal her aggravation as she relayed a few news tidbits.

"It sounds rather dreary to me. Lawrence is glad he doesn't have to go." Ellen lowered her voice. "You know that he's opposed to the US going to war. He's quite vocal about it behind closed doors."

Katy felt slightly vexed—both at Ellen and Lawrence. "Well, I suppose he's entitled to his opinions. After all, this is a free country."

"Lawrence sometimes talks about organizing."

"Organizing?"

"You know, to unite other people opposed to war. Perhaps create a new political party."

"Or perhaps Lawrence should simply move to a different country . . . perhaps Germany?"

"Germany? But they're already at war." Ellen frowned.

"Yes, I know that." Katy kept her voice even.

"But if Lawrence opposes US involvement in the war, one may wonder if he holds an alliance with Germany."

"No, of course not! He's not like that at all."

Katy suspected she'd stepped over some line but wasn't sure she cared. So far, Lawrence had managed to offend a number of people in town, including Katy's mother. Lawrence had seemed to believe he should be hired by the newspaper and was affronted when rejected. "No, I suppose he's not." Katy looked down at her letter, trying to think of a way to get rid of Ellen.

"It's just that Lawrence may have political aspirations," Ellen continued. "Did you know that his grandfather was involved in politics in San Francisco? Lawrence thinks it may run in his family."

Katy pursed her lips, not wanting to encourage this conversation.

"Lawrence feels that he may have more opportunity in Oregon than in California."

"Oh?" Katy wondered if this was because Lawrence had already burnt his bridges in San Francisco.

"I would think you'd appreciate that Lawrence wants to be a leader. I remember how you helped Mayor Wally get elected. And I helped you too. Remember?"

Katy looked evenly at her. "Yes, you did help me, Ellen. And I really appreciated it. But to be honest, you don't seem like the same person . . . as you were back then."

"What do you mean?" Ellen's expression went from a scowl to a catty smile. "Katy McDowell, are you jealous of me for marrying Lawrence?"

"Not at all." Katy had to control herself from laughing. "But I am sad about something. It seems you have changed."

"Of course I've changed. I'm a married woman."

"Yes . . . I know." Katy wondered how many times Ellen had made that same statement. Almost as if trying to convince herself as much as anyone else.

"And as a married woman, I care about my husband's future." Ellen pulled on her gloves. Hopefully because she was about to go. "And I happen to believe Lawrence would make a fine political figure. He's educated and has business experience—not to mention he's good looking. I suppose I thought I could count on you, my good friend, to help us. That perhaps you could help introduce Lawrence to the influential citizens of this town. Perhaps have a dinner or some social gathering." She smiled hopefully. "Sort of introduce him to Sunset Cove society."

Katy didn't know what to say. "Well, I'll definitely keep that in mind." She held up Jim's letter, hoping to change topics. "Jim thinks he may be able to be assigned as a war correspondent."

"What's that?"

"He says he'd be serving in the army, but as a news reporter. He'd write about the battles." Katy wondered if that meant he'd be safer. She hoped so.

Ellen leaned forward with wide eyes. "So, are you and Jim going to get married?"

"No, of course not." She laid down Jim's letter. "We're just good friends."

Ellen smiled. "Yes, that's what I thought. Jim probably still thinks of you as Anna's little girl. He'd never dream of marrying someone so much younger."

"I'm older than you, Ellen." Katy sat up straighter.

Ellen laughed. "Yes, but I'm a married woman."

Katy bristled. "Yes, back to that. So, although it's interesting that Lawrence has political aspirations, how is he doing with his job search?"

"Well, you know how the newspaper treated him." Ellen scowled. "And then we'd hoped that Mrs. Douglas at the Mercantile was going to hire him. Especially after my mother asked Randall to put in a good word with his mother."

"Oh, yes." Katy had heard how Lawrence had offended Mrs. Douglas by making a derogatory comment about her old-fashioned store, acting as if he could change it into something grand. But Mrs. Douglas didn't want grand. She only wanted someone capable of managing the counter and till.

"Poor Lawrence went to meet with her, so full of hope. And then she let him down."

"I heard the Walters Dairy Farm is looking for someone. You know, after they lost Caleb." Katy sighed. "So sad."

"A *dairy* farm? You can't be serious. Lawrence milking cows?"

"Well, I understood they needed someone with business ex—"

"Just think, Katy. Can you honestly imagine Lawrence coming home smelling like a cow barn? Don't you remember how Caleb Walters stank at school? No one wanted to sit by him."

"I didn't mind sitting by him." Katy felt indignant. "We took our graduation exams together. He was a very nice—"

"Yes, yes, I'm sorry. And it was very sad about his death."

Katy picked up her pen again, checking to see the reservoir was nearly empty. "Well, I would think Lawrence would be grateful for any sort of work."

"It's not that he doesn't want to work. If we could just get some money together, Lawrence and I would start our own business."

"What kind of business?" Katy tried to appear interested as she refilled her pen.

"Retail clothing, of course."

Katy concealed her surprise as she replaced the lid on the ink well. Did Ellen and Lawrence plan on becoming competition for Kathleen's Dress Shop? "That's interesting."

"Well, that's Lawrence's family business in San Francisco." Ellen sounded defensive. "They do wholesale and retail. We could probably get merchandise from them at a good discount."

"Yes, the Bouchards do have quite a large business down there." Katy laid down her pen, deciding to finish her letter later—at home and in the privacy of her own room. "I went with Grandmother on a buying trip there. Last December, remember?"

Ellen shrugged. "Yes, well, I was there quite a bit myself. Did you know that Lawrence and I lived in an apartment just a few blocks away? Very handy since he worked there."

"Why did Lawrence quit the family business?" Katy studied Ellen. So far no one had heard a very believable excuse for Lawrence's sudden departure.

"Well, they didn't see eye to eye on things. Lawrence has new ideas. His family is rather old-fashioned."

"I see." But Katy didn't really see. The San Francisco business had appeared modern and well-managed to her. She suspected there was still more to this story.

"So, if Lawrence and I could just get some startup money, I think we could be quite successful." She leaned forward on the desk, peering hopefully at Katy. "And I thought perhaps you could try to convince your grandmother and my mother that Lawrence and I are a good investment risk. I think they may listen to you, Katy. And I know they have money. Perhaps you do as well. Maybe our shop could be associated with Kathleen's. Lawrence suggested it may be an annex of sorts."

Katy felt confused. "Do you think it makes sense for the owners of Kathleen's to help fund a business that would be in direct competition with us? After all, Sunset Cove is a small town."

"Oh, we wouldn't sell women's clothes," Ellen told her. "Lawrence wants to sell high-quality men's wear."

Katy pursed her lips. "That's interesting, but do you really think our small town can support a men's clothing store? Most men around here don't seem terribly interested in fashion."

"Lawrence would like to see that change. And think about the customers here at Kathleen's. How many of those women would like to see their husbands dressing more stylishly?"

"I suppose that could be true."

"So, Katy, could you see your way to asking my mother and your grandmother, perhaps even your grandfather or anyone else who'd be interested in investing?" Ellen looked hopeful.

"I, uh, I promise to think about it."

Ellen picked up her handbag. "Oh, I knew you

were still my friend, Katy. I realize we were at odds because of me marrying Lawrence, but I knew you'd forgive me."

Katy stood, taking in a deep breath. "Ellen, I think you know that I had no interest in marrying Lawrence. I'm sure I made that clear last December. So please do not entertain any thoughts that you stole him from me." Katy was tempted to pick up Jim's letter and declare that if she wanted to marry anyone—and she wasn't sure that she did—Jim would definitely be her first choice. Not that there was any chance of that now.

CHAPTER 10

Anna wasn't surprised to learn that Sarah Rose was experiencing some derogatory comments while working in Daniel's office, but she was relieved that Sarah seemed undeterred by them. Just the same, they all remained careful for Sarah's sake, not allowing her to walk to or from work alone. Despite Sarah's protests that she would be perfectly fine, Anna still insisted on walking with her to work in the morning.

And Daniel continued to escort Sarah home in the evening. Anna actually liked this arrangement since it gave her an excuse to spend more time with Daniel. Sometimes they took a beach stroll. Or if the weather was uninviting, she'd invite him in to visit with her and Mac over tea. Occasionally he stayed for dinner.

"Well, it's been almost three weeks since Sarah went to work for you," Anna said as they walked down the beach together. Daniel had seemed rather quiet and reserved and she was trying to engage him in conversation. "Have you noticed whether patients have become more accepting?"

"Some seem to be fine. Others . . . well, it may take time." He grimly shook his head. "Mrs. Elliott Stone was in today."

"Oh, dear." Anna knew that woman was outspoken and generally unkind.

"And she didn't hide her disdain. But I'm proud to say Mrs. Lewis handled her with poise and politeness."

"Oh, that's good to hear." As usual Anna had to remind herself that Mrs. Lewis was Sarah Rose.

"And Mrs. Lewis has done such an excellent job of getting me caught up in the office that I suggested she talk to Katy about spending time at the dress shop. I feel a bit guilty for keeping her to myself, and I actually think she may enjoy the opportunity to be around other women. I've been concerned that she may be feeling a bit isolated."

"I've had similar thoughts. Despite our invitations, she's still determined to take dinner in her room. And, although we said it was unnecessary, she now insists on paying her room and board."

"She mentioned she'd like to get a room at Bella's Boarding House, but I don't think that's a very good idea."

"Not yet anyway. I'll make sure to let her know she's welcome with us."

"Do you think we'll ever live in a world where people aren't judged by exteriors?" His tone sounded dismal.

"I'm not sure. But Katy feels certain it will change . . . in time."

"That Katy. Such an optimist." Daniel let out a slow, sad-sounding sigh.

Anna stopped walking to look at him. "Is something wrong?"

"I got a telegram from my father today."

"Oh?" Anna wished he were about to say the message was to wish Daniel a happy birthday since she knew it was only three days away, but judging by his expression, it was not good news.

"It seems he's developed angina."

"Angina?" Anna had heard the medical term but couldn't remember what it meant.

"Pectoral angina," he clarified. "It's a pain in the chest region that is symptomatic of heart trouble."

"Oh, dear. Does he want you to go home to Boston?"

"He didn't say so, but I suspect that he does."

"Do you think his condition is serious?"

"Hard to say. I sent him a telegram reply as well as a telegram to an associate to inquire as to the severity. But my father did mention he's taking nitroglycerin . . . and that makes me believe it's rather serious."

"Maybe you should go see him."

"That's a possibility." He rubbed his chin, staring out over the ocean. "But I'll wait to see what Dr. Clements says. He's the doctor I telegrammed. His prognosis will help me make a decision."

"Well, I would understand if you felt the need to return to Boston, but I do hope you'll wait until after the groundbreaking ceremony."

"Which has been mysteriously scheduled on the same day as my fortieth birthday?" He gave a suspicious sideways glance that made her smile.

"My, my, what a coincidence."

"I think I can assure you I'll still be here for the ceremony. But it's one reason I'm hoping that Mrs. Lewis can start working for Katy soon. I don't expect her to remain in my office after I'm gone. That is, if I go."

Somehow she felt certain he was going. "How long do you think you'll be gone?"

"I have no idea. It all depends on his condition."

Anna didn't like to be skeptical, but she wondered if the elder Dr. Hollister might be overplaying an illness in order to attain Daniel's sympathy and tug him back East. Although her opinions on Daniel's father weren't nearly as negative as Mac's, she did feel wary. He seemed the sort of person to manipulate situations to his advantage. She would never want to play poker with him—not that she played poker.

"I met with Randall's architect friend this morning." Daniel's tone brightened.

"I heard he was in town. Mac invited him to dinner tomorrow night. Perhaps you'd like to join us."

"I'd love to." Now Daniel told her about

going over the building plans. "I had no idea the building would be that big. I hope the budget committee knows what they're doing."

"Mac and Wally keep saying they need to build for the future."

"That's a good theory, but I hope they keep in mind there's a war going on."

"Why should that make a difference? The hospital will be locally funded."

"Yes, but it's possible there will be shortages or other challenges. I had even suggested to the committee that they put the hospital on hold until after the war."

"But we need a hospital now," she insisted. "Don't forget what happened to young Caleb."

"Believe me, I haven't. But I have a feeling this war is going to take its toll on our country. Maybe not right at first . . . but in time."

"Then we'd better get that hospital built fast."

He chuckled. "You McDowells are certainly a determined family."

"Or stubborn or obstinate or just plain mule-headed. I'm sure we've been called all those things and worse." Hearing Daniel laugh made Anna feel better. She knew he was worried about his father, and she knew he would probably be heading east within the week but at least he was happy now. And hopefully he'd remember his last few days in Sunset Cove as happy ones . . . and want to come back.

• • •

Katy wrote to Jim almost daily. She knew he didn't have that kind of time to respond to her letters, but she continued to reassure him it didn't matter. So far she'd only received three letters from him, but she treasured them. The one she received on Friday afternoon sent her heart racing. Not wanting to read it under Ellen's prying eyes, Katy carried it over to Brown's Café and, after ordering a piece of lemon pie and a cup of coffee, took her time to read it.

Dear Katy,

Thank you for your delightful letters. I try not to feel overly guilty for not answering each one. But, as I've already told you, days here start long before dawn and continue at an exhausting pace until well after dark. We fall into bed exhausted each night. But tonight, I'm staying awake long enough to pen this to you.

I have one regret about enlisting so quickly into the army, Katy, and that is not having enough time with you. I suspect you know how much I care about you, but I'm not sure if you realize how deeply my feelings for you go. Until now, I had no intention of revealing those feelings. But after reading your last letter, which was

130

lovely, I have decided to lay my cards on the table.

Katy, dear, I love you. I have loved you almost from the first time I met you in front of your grandfather's house. I still remember you standing there in a pale blue summer frock, with paint smudges on your fingers and a beautiful seascape painting in your hands. Of course, I told myself you were far too young for me. And I reminded myself I was employed by your grandfather and that your mother was my boss. Both good reasons to keep my distance.

Then I remember the sweet evening you taught me how to dance the turkey trot on the moonlit beach. Yes, Ellen was there too, but I only had eyes for you, Katy. How we sang and laughed that night.

And then I recall so many other random but wonderful memories, moments that will keep me warm while I'm holed up in some European trench on a dark, cold night. Thank you for that!

If I could, dear Katy, I would like to get down on one knee and ask you to marry me. How I wish I could . . . or wish that I had done so on that last day as we stood out there in the rain on the train platform. I almost did that. It took all my self-control not to. Because, at the time, it felt selfish of me. What right did I have to tie you down to me like that, knowing that I would soon be sent overseas? I had to bite my tongue.

I've just learned some of our troops are due to ship out soon. No one says the exact date, but I believe it could be, at the soonest, within the next few days . . . or at the latest in two weeks, in early July. So before that happens, I just wanted to state my case clearly. I love you, Katy McDowell, and when this war is over, I want to marry you. I humbly and respectfully ask for your hand in marriage. There, I've said it.

One more thing before I collapse onto my bed. Your mother is somewhat aware of my feelings for you. She told me that you're an independent woman of independent means who may not wish to marry for years to come. And I will understand that. I only hope that when you are ready for marriage, you will want to marry me. If not, I will try to understand, and I will pray for our friendship to continue unhindered.

All my love,
Jim Stafford, 2nd Lt.

Katy's hands trembled as she put the letter back into the envelope then slipped it into her handbag. Had she really read it right? She looked around the café and then extracted the letter again and slowly and carefully reread it. Jim wanted to marry her. She hadn't imagined it. He really, truly wanted to marry her! But why did he want to wait until the war ended? What if he never made it back?

Katy had planned to return to the dress shop after the post office, but now she decided against it. She didn't want anyone—particularly Ellen—questioning her about the letter. Instead, she slowly walked home and went up to her room. And there she began to pace . . . back and forth . . . trying to gather her thoughts. Oh, she had no doubt that she would marry Jim Stafford. She had practically told him this very thing in her last letter. But now she had to figure a way to do it before he left for the European front.

Tomorrow was Saturday, and Kathleen's Dress Shop would be closed all morning for the hospital's groundbreaking ceremony. Naturally, Katy was expected to attend. But afterward . . . Well, that would be up to her. And her mind was made up. She was going to Jim and, if he wanted, she would gladly agree to become his wife.

A part of her felt like she should tell her mother and probably her grandfather and grandmother too. Except that she felt worried. If she confessed her impulsive plan to them, one of them would surely attempt to stop her. They would say she was "too young" or that she "hadn't thought this through" or that it was an "impetuous decision" that she would live to regret. But she honestly didn't think so. In her heart, she knew it was right. And she knew if Jim did not survive this war—and that was a real possibility—she would never forgive herself for not going through with this. But how to pull it off?

Somehow she needed to quietly sneak to the train station—with her luggage. No small feat. There was only one train on Saturday, and she knew it departed at two-ten in the afternoon. Plenty of time to be done with the ground-breaking ceremony and Dr. Daniel's birthday party. She would have her bags all packed and, after everyone got home, she would somehow sneak them out to the Runabout. Mac would eventually forgive her for leaving his car at the train station, but she'd arrange to have it returned home later that afternoon. After she was well on her way.

Now to send a telegram to inform Jim of her plans to depart on Saturday. But she would tell him not to respond. She didn't want a telegram to arrive at the house and tip off her family. After that, she would withdraw some funds from her bank account then go home to carefully pack her bags . . . and hopefully she'd be able to sleep through the night. As she went through these preparations, she imagined herself a character in one of the motion pictures she'd seen while living in Portland. It all felt very dramatic and beautiful and exciting. Something she would probably remember for the rest of her life. If only no one tried to stop her.

CHAPTER 11

By Saturday morning, Katy was a bundle of nerves. She'd gotten up earlier than anyone else, managing to sneak her bags downstairs and stash them in the carriage house beneath some tarps. She'd also written a letter to her family but wasn't sure where to stash it. Finally, she decided to take a chance by tiptoeing up to Sarah Rose's room.

"I'm sorry to disturb you," she told Sarah after she opened the door.

"No need to be sorry." Sarah frowned slightly as she buttoned her dressing gown. "Is something wrong?"

"No, nothing is wrong." Katy smiled brightly. "Something is very right. And, if you promise to remain quiet, I would like to take you into my confidence."

Sarah pointed to the chair by her window then sat at the foot of her bed, waiting. "Go ahead, Miss Katy. You know you can trust me."

Somehow, Katy knew that she could. And so she poured out her whole story, clear from the beginning of first meeting Jim Stafford. Sarah's eyes grew wider as Katy got to the part about taking the train up to Fort Lewis to marry Jim. "It's not that I'm concerned about my family because I know how much they respect Jim. But I'm worried they'll say I'm too young. And with so much going on today with the groundbreaking and birthday ceremonies, well, I just want to quietly slip away."

"My goodness." Sarah slowly shook her head. "You mean you plan to leave today?"

Katy told her the rest of the plan and pulled out her note. "I hoped you could hand this over to them later today. Perhaps before dinnertime. No one should be worried about me until then. I already told Clara that I wouldn't be at the dress shop this afternoon."

"And I'm not working there today either," Sarah said. "Although I told Clara I could come on Monday."

"Which brings me to another thing. I know that Dr. Hollister is leaving for Boston soon. I haven't heard when exactly. But while I'm in Washington, I was hoping you may be able to put in more time at the dress shop, to make up for my absence. I don't want the work to pile up too much."

Sarah brightened. "As a matter of fact, Dr. Hollister mentioned this very thing to me just yesterday. He was concerned about laying me off for a while, but I told him I'd ask you."

"I'm sure there will be enough work for you to come every day," Katy assured her. "So, tell me, how do you like it so far?"

Sarah's smile looked slightly forced. "Oh, I do love the work. And your grandmother and Miss Clara are very nice . . . and I think the other seamstresses are getting used to me. Especially after they saw that I *do* know how to sew."

"But Ellen?" Katy had heard Ellen's comments when Sarah wasn't there. Hopefully she hadn't said anything mean to her face.

"Miss Ellen, well, she is a bit prickly."

Katy chuckled. "If it makes you feel any better, she's a bit prickly to me too."

"I think she's unhappy."

Katy considered this. "You could be right."

"But back to you, Miss Katy. Are you certain this is the right thing?"

"I am certain, Sarah Rose. I love Jim, and I don't want him going to war without knowing I want to marry him. If he still wants to wait until after the war, I will agree. But I hope he doesn't."

"You really are all grown up, honey." Sarah Rose came over and placed a hand on her shoulder. "I knew that the moment you picked me up at the train station. And if this is what you really want, I will keep your secret until dinnertime."

Katy hugged her. "I knew I could trust you."

Sarah Rose had tears in her eyes. "I just hope you'll be safe on the train . . . alone."

"You came on the train alone," Katy reminded her.

She nodded somberly.

"I'll be fine, Sarah. I plan to spend the night with my friend Rebecca and her family in Portland. I already sent her a wire. Then I'll take the next train to Tacoma—that's the city near Fort Lewis. I'll stay in a hotel there and wait to hear back from Jim. And, like I said in the note to my family, I will send a wire here to let everyone know I'm okay."

Sarah Rose slowly shook her head. "You truly are a modern young woman, Miss Katy. I admire you greatly."

Katy grinned. "Thank you. I feel like I'm about to embark on a great adventure." She looked at the alarm clock by Sarah's bed. "And I better let you get ready for the day. I know you're going to the celebration too. Mother is going with Dr. Hollister. And I'm driving Grandfather, but you can ride in the rumble seat if you like."

"Thank you, I'd appreciate it."

Feeling confident that the pieces were all falling neatly into place, Katy went downstairs to finish getting herself ready for the day. Hopefully no one would notice that her ensemble wasn't as festive as usual, but she knew she wouldn't have much time to change into traveling clothes. And since her family would assume she was going to work, she'd decided to wear something appropriate for that. As she went down to breakfast, she tried not to feel guilty for deceiving them, but in her heart she believed it was for the best. And she felt that, in time, they would understand.

At least, she hoped they would.

Anna had mixed feelings as Daniel drove them up to the hospital site. Although this was a day of celebration, it was also a day of sadness because she knew that Daniel was preparing to leave for Boston. He would've been gone by now if not for today's festivities. And despite his reassurance that he was only going away temporarily, she knew that he was uncertain. If his father were truly in a dire condition, he might feel the need to stay on indefinitely. But at least he'd promised to communicate with her during his absence.

"I'm so glad we have fair weather today," Anna said as Daniel drove up the hill to the site. "Even the fog seems to have burned off."

"Oh, my." She pointed at the people walking up the hill and the cars parked along the road. "It looks like we'll have a nice crowd."

"From what I've been hearing, almost everyone is in favor of a local hospital."

"The voters certainly approved." Anna waved at Randall as he helped his mother and Clara from his car.

"I'm still marveling that the committee approved those hospital plans," Daniel said as he parked. "It will be an impressive structure in our small town."

Anna liked that he'd called it "our" town. It gave her hope.

"Well, here we go." He opened the creaky door of his old truck and helped her out. "Sorry we couldn't arrive in more style."

Anna knew that Daniel sometimes felt apologetic for driving an old delivery truck. Especially when some fellows, like Randall Douglas, sported flashy modern vehicles. "Don't worry, I've never been the least bit troubled by this truck. I think it has personality."

"You should've heard what my father called it."

Fortunately, Anna didn't have time to respond or find out because suddenly the mayor and council members were warmly greeting Daniel, shaking his hand, and inviting him to come join them in front of the building site where some chairs and benches had been set up and near where the blueprints for the two-story hospital were prominently displayed.

Before long, with an impressive crowd gathered around, speeches began to be made. Everyone took turns, followed by enthusiastic applause until it was finally time to break the ground. Chief Harvey provided a golden shovel, and Mayor Wally and Daniel held the handle, plunging it into the soft ground while the crowd cheered. It was a good moment.

"And now everyone is invited to join us for a birthday celebration for Dr. Hollister," the mayor announced loudly. "We'll meet up again down at the City Park. As you've probably heard, it'll be a potluck picnic with birthday cake for everyone. We hope to see you there!"

Daniel acted surprised, but Anna was pretty sure he already knew about the park party in honor of him. "Just think of it as a nice sendoff," she told him as he helped her back into the old delivery truck. "A chance to say goodbye."

"You make it sound as if I'm never coming back." He frowned as he closed her door.

She watched as he bent down, working hard to crank the old engine to life. And she wondered . . . Did she really believe he was coming back? For a split-second she imagined Daniel dressed in a stylish suit, driving a shiny new car, and being the respected chief of staff at the prominent Boston hospital. Really, how could their Podunk town and small hospital hope to compete?

"Is that what you really think?" he asked as he hopped into the driver's seat.

"I don't know that I'd blame you," she said quietly.

"But what about this hospital? And all the community support?" He waited as another car pulled out. "Don't you think I'm eager to return for all this?"

"I don't know."

He turned to look at her. "And what about you, Anna? Don't you think I'd come back for you?"

Before she could answer the car behind them blared a loud horn that made her jump. "Oh, my!" She turned back to see Chief Rollins waving at them with a big smile and his wife Gladys looking embarrassed. "Looks like you better move."

As he maneuvered the bulky truck around, finally turning back toward town, Anna tried to gather her thoughts. "I just want you to know, Daniel, that I will understand if you need to remain in Boston for a . . . *for a while.* I remember how just one year ago, Katy and I came to Sunset Cove because you'd sent me that telegram informing me Mac was in a bad way. Even though we'd been estranged, it was the right thing to do, and I'll never regret it. Family is important."

"I completely agree. But there are many kinds of family." He paused at the bottom of the street and looked at her. "Some we are born with and some we gather along the way, Anna."

She felt her cheeks warm but said nothing.

"And I think of you and Mac and Katy—and even Lucille—as family. You're all as important to me as anyone back in Boston."

"I appreciate knowing that," she said quietly as he pulled onto Main Street.

"Do you mind if I park the truck behind my office, and we walk to the park?"

"Not at all." She was actually glad for this—a little more time of having Daniel to herself.

"I've closed up things in my office," he said as he helped her from the truck again. "And I've let Mrs. Lewis know that she's free to work full-time at the dress shop if she likes."

"Yes, she told me." Anna adjusted the brim of her oversized hat. It was something Katy had insisted on for today's festivities, but Anna felt slightly conspicuous. "Although she was disappointed, she was appreciative of the several weeks she got to work for you."

"She was a Godsend." Daniel held out his arm for her. "And I was impressed with how quickly most of my patients adjusted to her."

She looped her hand through his arm and smiled up at him. "I know Sarah Rose was very grateful for your confidence in her."

Although they continued to make small talk as they walked toward the park, Anna couldn't stop thinking about what he'd said about family. She wished she could nudge him back onto that topic to attain a bit more information. Had he simply meant he'd adopted her family in general . . . or had her family grown more special to him because of his feelings for her? Naturally, she wished for the latter. And hadn't he said almost as much before? Yet it seemed like life and circumstances and family continued to tug them apart.

As they approached the park, Anna wondered what she'd say if Daniel were to invite her to go to Boston with him. As hasty and reckless as it seemed for a normally careful person, she thought she would throw caution to the wind and say yes. After all, her father was in good health and taking on more at the paper. Her daughter was living as a responsible adult with her own business. Even the recent criminal elements had died down in their small town. Perhaps it really was Anna's chance to do something completely unexpected . . . time for her to follow her heart.

But as they entered the park, where merry-makers were already gathered and a band was cheerfully playing in the gazebo, Daniel was suddenly being greeted and congratulated by many well-wishers. Anna knew her chance to be alone with the good doctor had temporarily slipped away. She also knew he would be leaving later in the day. Still, she was glad to see him being so fully appreciated by the townspeople, many of whom had been his patients. Perhaps their enthusiasm would be more persuasive than anything she could do to entice him back to Sunset Cove. She could only hope.

CHAPTER 12

Anna was helping to serve birthday cake when Frank Anderson quietly asked if he could speak to her privately. For the last month, ever since Jim left the paper, Anna had been trying to win Frank's respect. She knew that she'd earned his approval in the past year, and that he now trusted her skills as a newspaperwoman and editor in chief of the *Sunset Times*. But she still wasn't sure that he respected her. Because she was a woman.

As she walked over to the far side of the park, she noticed Frank's wife Ginger and their three boys by the gazebo. The oldest boy looked to be about six and the youngest one a toddler. The Andersons seemed such a happy, wholesome family. And Frank had been with the newspaper for around fifteen years. She hoped that he wasn't about to tell her he was leaving the paper to go to war. Wasn't he too old for that? Or with too many dependents?

"I'm sorry to interrupt you," he said as she

joined him. "But I just overheard something that I think may interest you."

"Interest me?"

"As a potential news story."

Anna felt a wave of relief. Frank wasn't about to leave. "What is it?"

He nodded over to where Lawrence Bouchard was visiting with a couple of young men. "Your friend Lawrence was—"

"First of all, he is not my friend."

"Oh." Frank nodded. "Well, I know your daughter is friends with his wife. And didn't you interview him for a job at the paper?"

"I didn't hire him." She lowered her voice. "To be honest, I do not trust the young man."

"Maybe for good reason. Do you know the fellows he's talking to?"

Trying to be discreet, Anna glanced their way and then turned back to Frank. "Not exactly, but I'm sure I've seen them around town. To be honest, I'm surprised Lawrence would give fellows like that the time of day." The young men both had an unkempt appearance—nothing like Lawrence, who always looked like an advertisement for fancy menswear.

"The short stocky guy is Bud Griggs, and the other one is Fred—I can't recall his last name. They were both fishermen and acquainted with AJ Krauss."

"Were they involved in any of the criminal activities with AJ and his dad?"

"Not that I'm aware of. I think they were legitimate fisherman back when the rum-running was getting out of control. And I still see them take out Bud's boat sometimes. Bud seems to know fishing. Even points me in the right direction now and then. And remember I did that piece on him for catching a trophy salmon last fall?"

"Oh, yes. I do remember." She controlled the urge to look back at the three men. "I know Lawrence Bouchard is still looking for employment. Do you think he's interested in becoming a fisherman?"

"Do you?" Frank removed a pipe from his jacket pocket, gave it a whack, and began to fill it.

She chuckled. "I guess I'd like to see that."

"Well, what I overheard suggests to me that Bouchard is interested in something else. Something that would involve a boat." He narrowed his eyes. "And I don't mean fishing."

"Rum-running?"

"Yep." He paused to light his pipe. "I didn't hear it all, but I did hear Bouchard mention connections in California. He asked Bud if his boat was seaworthy enough to take a trip down there."

"Californian wine," she said quietly. "He probably wants to bring it up here and sell it for profit."

"That's what I was thinking. I hear there's been

activity up and down the coast. Wouldn't be surprised if some of it was going on right beneath our noses."

"With those guys?" Anna turned a bit, putting her back to them to keep herself from taking another peek.

"From what I hear, fishing hasn't been too good this spring. Running black market goods may be tempting. Easy money."

"Makes for a good newspaper story too." Anna imagined the headline . . . and the possibility of getting the story picked up across the country. Many states were preparing to adopt prohibition, and there were rumors it could become federal law in the not-too-distant future. "You know, Frank, I need someone to replace Jim. Both as managing editor and reporter. I need someone who can chase after some of the more challenging stories. I considered talking to you about the position, but you always seem so content with writing about sports and wildlife. . . ."

"Well, it's familiar territory. I'm comfortable with it."

She glanced over to where his young wife and sons were still enjoying the music. "And you're a family man. I wouldn't want to assign you to a position that would put you in peril. Don't forget what happened to Jim. It can be, well, unsafe at times."

"Fishing and hunting can be pretty dangerous

too." He puffed on his pipe with a faraway look in his eyes.

"Would you be interested?" she asked hopefully. "The position would come with a raise."

"What about when Jim comes home from the war?" he asked.

"Jim knows he'll always have a job at the paper," she assured him. She almost added that she was willing to give up her position but thought better of it. "In the meantime, I can't do everything on my own. I need someone to step up. And Ed seems, uh, unwilling."

"You mean Ed still doesn't trust your leadership," he said with a knowing expression.

"He doesn't exactly make a secret of it."

"Well, if push came to shove, you could count on Ed. He may grumble some, but he knows that you're a good newspaperwoman."

She smiled. "That means a lot to me."

"That said . . . you can count on me too. I'll take you up on your offer. And here's what I'm thinking about this particular story." He took a nonchalant puff of his pipe. "We can do a little surveillance this afternoon. Based on what Bouchard said, I think he's already put together a plan of sorts."

"Well, I've heard he's desperate for money. I wouldn't be surprised if it's urgent." She didn't want to mention that Ellen had borrowed money from Clara to remain in the hotel.

"I don't really expect the three of them to leave this shindig together. I thought I could get my fishing gear and act like I'm going down to the dock to fish. That's pretty normal for me on a Saturday anyway. In the meantime, if you were so inclined, you may be able to keep an eye on Bouchard."

"I could invite someone to have tea with me at the hotel." She glanced over to where Lucille and Clara were visiting—probably shop talk but surely she could entice one of them to meet her for an overdue social visit.

"Then if Bouchard comes down or seems to be preparing for some sort of fishing trip, you could get word to Chief Rollins, and he could alert the Coast Guard to be on the watch for their boat. Not on the way down, of course, but on the way back up here."

"How long do you think it'll take a small boat to get down to California?" Anna checked her pocket watch and saw it was close to one.

"The California border is over a hundred miles away. A small fishing boat like Bud's probably averages about ten miles an hour. Maybe more on a calm sea . . . like today."

"So that's about ten hours. Twenty for round-trip. They could be back here with illegal alcohol by tomorrow evening."

"Just what I was thinking. But realistically, I'd guess longer. A trip like that wears a person out.

They'd probably need to rest . . . and to make their connection."

"Even so, they could easily be back here by early next week."

"Yes, and that's where the Coast Guard will come in handy."

Anna knew this could be another big newsbreak for their small paper. The stories they did on the rum-running last year had been picked up by the *Oregonian* as well as other larger papers across the country. Little Sunset Cove was of high interest with the talk of more widespread prohibition. "Maybe we shouldn't tell Chief Rollins too quickly," she said. "After all, we don't know anything for sure. And there's nothing the chief can do about it yet anyway."

"That's true." Frank's eyes lit up. "And it may be nice to scoop this story."

She smiled. "Well, I'm glad you were wearing your reporter's hat today. It'll be a pleasure to have you in this new position."

"And it looks like our work is about to begin." Frank was looking beyond her. "Don't look now, but Bouchard is shaking the boys' hands, and it looks like they're about to part ways."

"I'll keep an eye on Lawrence," she assured him. "I think I'll start with his wife."

"And I'll make a beeline for home and my fishing gear. Would you mind letting Ginger know? Not with all the details, of course. Just tell her I'm following up on a fishing story. She'll understand."

So Anna went directly to Ginger and quickly explained he was researching a story. "He went home to change."

"Oh, he's probably just using that as an excuse to get some peace and quiet," Ginger said with a knowing smile. "Poor Frank. When I met him he was a confirmed bachelor. Happily working for the paper and fishing and hunting in his spare time. Then I snagged him and brought all this into his life." She laughed as she ruffled her oldest son's hair. "I think he goes hunting and fishing now just to get away from the noise. But I don't mind. Especially if he brings home dinner."

Anna smiled. "Frank's fortunate to have such an understanding wife. Now, if you'll excuse me." She hurried over to where it looked like Daniel was getting ready to exit his birthday celebration.

"I was just coming to tell you goodbye," he said when he saw her. "I hate to run out on my own party like this, but I have to catch the two-ten train."

"Oh?" She blinked. "I knew you were leaving soon, but today?"

"I booked it yesterday." His eyes were sad. "I meant to tell you but never got the chance."

"Do you need a ride? I could borrow Mac's Runabout and—"

"No, Randall Douglas offered to take me to the station when we met for coffee yesterday. My bags are already in his car." He waved to someone behind her. She turned to see Randall striding toward them and then noticed that Lawrence was still talking to Fred, but Bud had disappeared. Not far away, Ellen was talking to a young woman.

"So I guess we'll have to say goodbye here," Daniel said.

Anna felt a wave of sadness. "I will miss you," she said quietly.

"I'll write you as soon as I get to Boston. I'll keep you informed as to my father's condition . . . and my plans."

"So is the birthday boy ready to go to the station?" Randall asked in jovial tone as he joined them, as if oblivious as to how painful this parting really was. At least to Anna.

"I'm ready." Daniel looked into Anna's eyes, grasping her right hand with both of his. "I'll miss you too."

She forced a smile, savoring the warmth of his hands around hers. "I wish you a safe journey, Daniel. And I hope you find your father well on the road to recovery."

"Give my best to Mac and the rest of your family." He continued to hold her hand. "Assure them I'll be back."

She nodded but wondered if that were really

true. Would he be back? Or would Boston hold onto him?

Randall dangled his pocket watch in front of Daniel. "If you want to catch that train, Doctor Dan, we better get moving."

Daniel squeezed her hand again. "I'll be in touch."

"And I'll write back." She felt a lump in her throat as he released her hand. Trying to be brave, she smiled and waved. Then Randall whisked him over to where his fancy new car was waiting with the motor already running. She watched as the men got in and the car headed away.

Seeing Ellen was still nearby, Anna suddenly remembered her promise to keep tabs on Lawrence Bouchard. She hurried over to Ellen, trying to think of an excuse to disrupt her conversation with the other two young women. As she got there, it hit her. "I'm sorry to interrupt," she told Ellen. "But have you seen Katy?" Anna peered around the park, surprised that she actually did not see her daughter anywhere.

"I think she went to open the dress shop," Ellen told her.

"Oh, yes, of course. I forgot she was working today." Anna smiled at Ellen. "I haven't had much chance to welcome you back to town. Are you and Lawrence settling in nicely?"

"As nicely as we can for now." Ellen's eyes

narrowed slightly. "It would help if Lawrence could find employment."

"Yes, I know he's looking. I'm sure something should open up for him . . . in time."

Ellen brightened. "We actually have been discussing a business idea, but we're looking for financial investors."

"Oh?" Anna had no interest in investing, but to prolong the conversation—and perhaps extract some news—she played along. "What sort of business?"

"Well, we don't want to say . . . not yet anyway. But I've already approached my mother and your mother, and they both seemed intrigued. I thought perhaps you and your father may like to hear more about it as well."

Anna tried not to act surprised. Did Ellen really think they would all want to invest in what appeared to be a rum-running business? Or perhaps Frank's assumptions were wrong. "Well, I can't speak for Mac, but I may be interested to hear more. Perhaps we can plan to meet up next week." Anna forced another smile for Lawrence, who was coming directly to them.

"I was just telling Anna about our business venture," Ellen told him.

His smile faded. "What do you mean?"

"Don't worry, dear. I didn't give away any secrets. I simply mentioned that we're looking for investors."

"Oh, yes." He smiled stiffly at Anna. "Well, that's true. We do have room for a couple of solid investors." He turned back to his wife. "If you'll excuse me, I have an appointment with someone."

"Potential investors?" she said hopefully.

"Yes, something like that." He tipped his bowler hat then hurried toward Main Street.

"Well, do feel free to call on me next week," Anna told Ellen. "Please, excuse me." Now Anna hurried over to her mother, quickly explaining that she wanted to catch up with her.

"But not here," she said quietly. "I'd like to chat privately, if you don't mind. Would you like to join me at the hotel for a nice hot cup of tea?"

Lucille beamed at her. "I would love that. In fact, I was just trying to think of an excuse to leave. That chilly sea breeze is starting to aggravate my lumbago."

Anna glanced across the park. "It looks like a lot of folks are leaving now."

"Katy already took Mac home. He was a bit worn out." Lucille waved to Clara. "But I do need to speak to Clara before I go. Do you have a—"

"How about if we meet at the hotel?" Anna smiled. "And take your time."

"Perfect."

Anna had lost sight of Lawrence Bouchard by now, but based on the direction he'd headed, she suspected he was at the hotel. She cut across the park, avoiding the path of anyone inclined to chat, and hurried to the hotel which, thanks to the earlier celebrations, appeared somewhat deserted. The restaurant was nearly empty too, so taking a table near the lobby, she was able to keep an eye on both the stairs and the front entrance. Now to think of something benign to discuss with her mother, something to help justify this impromptu tea party that was really just a sleuthing session.

CHAPTER 13

Mac had provided Katy the perfect excuse to depart from Dr. Hollister's birthday party in the park. Which was fortunate because, prior to him announcing he was worn out, every time she started to leave, someone would stop her. Even when she claimed she needed to open Kathleen's, Clara and Grandmother pointed out that everyone was still at the park.

So Grandfather's request to go home came just in time. She hadn't, however, counted on him needing help to unbutton his jacket and get settled into his sitting room. And he'd wanted a cup of tea. Naturally, Bernice and Mickey were still at the festivities and not around to help.

While waiting for the teakettle to whistle, Katy raided the icebox and cupboard to pack a box with food for the trip. Then she stowed her baggage in the rumble-seat of the Runabout, covering it with a blanket, just in case. She'd already paid a dollar to the delivery boy from the mercantile, asking him to walk to the train station and pick up Mac's Runabout. Grateful for the generous wage, Tommy had promised to deliver the car to the house at six o'clock sharp. By that time, she planned to be on her way to Portland. As long as she didn't miss the two-ten train.

Finally, with Grandfather comfortable with tea and sugar cookies, Katy hurried out the carriage house and pulled her driving coat over her traveling suit and was on her way. She'd have to drive fast to make the train, but speeding had never worried her before. Fortunately, thanks to the festivities in town, no one else was on the road. Although when she was almost there, she was surprised to see Randall Douglas's car coming toward her. Tempted to duck her head, she realized that would only draw more attention. Instead, she smiled and waved as if nothing were out of the ordinary. And Randall just honked his horn.

With her heart still beating fast, she parked in front of the train station and hurried inside to find a man with a cart. While he fetched her luggage, she paid for her fare. As she was handed her change, she heard the train whistle blow.

"You sure cut it close, ma'am. There's the train now." The station master handed her the ticket to Portland with a curious look. She simply thanked him and hurried to the platform just as the baggage man wheeled out her luggage. Checking to see it was all there, she took the smaller bag and handed the man two bits. Overly generous perhaps, but she was grateful for the help. With her smaller bag in hand, she climbed aboard the train, and it began to roll even before she found her seat in the rear of the passenger car.

As the train took off, Katy let out a slow, relieved breath. She'd made it. She studied her ticket. Her first stop would be in Salem at four-fifty. There she would take the six-fifteen to Portland, which was scheduled to arrive at eight-forty. There, if all went well, her old friend Rebecca and her family would see she was picked up. At least she hoped so.

"Katy McDowell!"

Katy looked up to see Dr. Hollister looking down at her with a surprised expression. "Oh!" She blinked, unable to think of anything to say.

"I didn't know you were going . . ." He frowned. "Somewhere."

"I, uh, I didn't know you were going either." She felt her heart beginning to pound again. "Did Mother send you?"

"Your mother?" He looked confused as he took a seat across from her. "Why would she do that?"

Katy realized her blunder. "No, of course not." She smiled to cover her mistake. "Of course, you're on your way to Boston, aren't you? Mother mentioned your father was ill, and that you planned to go see him."

"That's right." He nodded but still looked

suspicious. "But she didn't mention that you were going, uh, anywhere. If I'd known, we could've given you a ride to the station. Randall Douglas brought me."

"Yes, I waved to him on the road."

"So, where are you headed?"

"Well, for now I'm headed to the Eugene station."

"Yes, well, that's the obvious answer. Is that your final destination?"

"No, from there I am bound for Portland." She tried to keep her smile natural. "I'm being met by my old school chum, Rebecca Strong. I haven't seen her in over a year. I will stay at her house, and it will be so delightful to catch up with all the goings on there and hear about my old friends." She felt glad that this was actually the truth. She was looking forward to seeing Rebecca again. Hopefully, she'd received the wire and planned on being there.

"I'm surprised your mother didn't mention this." Dr. Hollister studied her closely. "Is Portland your final destination?"

Katy hated to lie . . . so she said nothing and just stared at the ticket still in her hand, concealing the section that revealed her last stop—Spokane, Washington.

"Let me guess," he said quietly. "You're on your way to see Jim Stafford."

She looked up. "How did you know?"

"It's not a giant leap," he said gently. "I could tell for some time that he had feelings for you. But I wasn't sure you returned those feelings. May I assume that you do?"

She simply nodded.

"To be honest, I had almost expected him to propose marriage to you before he left for the army."

"I wish he had."

His brows arched. "So is that why you're going? Do you plan to marry him?"

Well, since the cat had slipped out of the bag, she poured out the whole story. Even to the part of not telling anyone. "Except Sarah Rose," she admitted. "I took her into my confidence so she could give a note to my family. They should have it by the time I'm on the train to Portland."

"I see." He nodded with a slightly grim expression.

"Don't get me wrong," she said defensively. "I wasn't worried they would disapprove of Jim."

"No, I shouldn't think so."

"But I was worried they would try to talk me out of it. They would say I'm too young."

"*Are* you too young?"

"Not at all." She stuck out her chin. "I'm a high school graduate. I am part owner of a thriving business." She paused with uncertainty. "Do you think I'm too young?"

He chuckled. "No, as a matter of fact, I don't.

Lots of young women marry at your age. Some even younger."

She sighed. "Oh, good."

"How do you think your mother will react to the news?"

"She'll be sad that I didn't tell her before I left. But I don't think she'll be terribly surprised. She'd already admitted that Jim had spoken to her about me."

"And he knows you're coming?"

"I sent a wire. And I told him I'd send another upon my arrival."

"Well, you seem to have it all figured out." He slowly shook his head. "And I must confess I admire your courage . . . and your gumption. Maybe that's where youth comes in handy."

She peered curiously at him. "Meaning that if you were younger, you may do the same thing?"

"Perhaps."

"With my mother?"

He smiled.

"You do want to marry her, don't you, Dr. Hollister?"

"Well, since you have confided to me, I suppose I can confide to you. I do love your mother, Katy. It was the hardest thing to leave her today."

"Why didn't you ask her to go with you?"

He frowned. "She has the newspaper . . . her family . . . her life in Sunset Cove. I can't ask her to leave all that behind."

"Oh? Does that mean you don't intend to come back to Sunset Cove? Are you leaving us for good?"

"I hope not. But it's hard to say. I won't know until I see my father."

"But if not for your father's poor health, are you saying you would want to marry my mother?"

"Can I trust you not to say anything?"

She arched her brows. "Haven't I just entrusted you with my secret?"

"Yes. And I appreciate that. Can I ask you a personal question?"

"What?"

"How would you feel about your mother remarrying? Getting a stepfather?"

"If it were you, I'd be quite pleased. But only because I'm fairly certain my mother loves you. And now that I know you love her, I would be even happier."

His smile seemed more relaxed. "Well, I would love to propose to your mother. And I would love to return to Sunset Cove. But like your mother told me this morning, family is important. And I'm the only family my father has. I can't abandon him when he needs me."

"Why don't you bring him back to Sunset Cove with you? That seems as good a place as any to recover from an illness. And it won't be long until we have our nice new hospital."

"That's true. But my father can be a bit stubborn."

"Just remind him that my grandmother still lives there." She grinned. "And that she's still single."

His eyes lit up. "I like how you think, young lady."

"Perhaps you should warn him, though, that if my grandfather suspects your father is returning, he'll probably try to get Grandmother to the altar before it's too late."

"I wouldn't be surprised."

"But knowing my grandmother, she's in no hurry to rush into matrimony. She's quite content being on her own."

"Good for her."

Katy opened her small bag and removed a cardboard box. "I brought some food along." She opened it up, holding it out for him to see her well-packed provisions. "I was so nervous today that I had no appetite." She giggled. "But it looks like I brought enough to feed a small army. Please, help yourself."

"I was rather anxious this morning too. Other than a piece of birthday cake that was too sweet to finish, I haven't eaten either." He took one of the sandwiches. "Thank you."

For the rest of the trip to Salem, they visited pleasantly, and Katy found that she was actually relieved to have taken Dr. Hollister into her confidence. It was reassuring to have him aware of her plans without judgment or disapproval. But when they both disembarked the train in Salem, Katy began to feel uneasy. Dr. Hollister helped her to press her way through the boisterous crowd on the platform, going to the baggage car to ensure that her luggage was removed and ready to be loaded onto the next train.

"These young men must be on their way to army camps," Dr. Hollister told her as they stood by the luggage cart. "I've never seen this station so busy."

She glanced around, hoping to see another lone female traveler, perhaps someone she could sit with on the way to Portland, but most of the women seemed to be there to see off their men with tearful goodbyes and tender moments.

Dr. Hollister suddenly became quite fatherly, giving her travel tips and warnings as if he were worried for her welfare. Finally, he inquired about her plans upon arriving in Portland. "It will be rather late and dark by then."

Katy quickly explained about Rebecca, trying to appear more confident than she felt. "It'll be so great to see her again."

"And you're certain she'll be there?" he asked above the noise of the incoming train. "She confirmed this to you?"

She pursed her lips. "Not exactly. I asked her not to wire me. I didn't want to chance anyone at home seeing it."

His brow creased as he rubbed his chin. "Well, if by some chance your friend isn't at the train station in Portland, do not loiter outside on the street. Return to the terminal and use the telephone to call your friend's home. And if you can't reach her and she doesn't show up, ask a station employee to make a reservation at a reputable hotel and to call a cab for you." He pulled out his billfold then pressed a ten-dollar-bill into her hand. "Just in case—"

"I have money," she assured him, trying to give it back.

"I will feel better if you have this." He pointed to her soft leather purse. "But don't put it in there. You tuck this into your pocket, Katy, or your glove or your shoe while you're traveling. Just in case."

"But I—"

"Please. Do it for me. Call it a wedding gift, if you like."

"All right." She took the bill and slid it into her glove just as the porter called "all aboard."

"That's my train." Dr. Hollister gave her a quick hug. "I wish you the very best."

"Thank you for everything." She watched him pick up his bags and board.

"Tell Jim congratulations for me," he called as the train began to move.

She nodded, waving vigorously. Maybe she'd get to tell the good doctor congratulations on his own marriage someday. She hoped so. He would make a good stepfather. As she watched the train grow smaller, she felt surprisingly alone. More so than when she'd boarded the train by herself earlier.

Dr. Hollister's advice was well-meaning, but suddenly she felt uneasy. Like he'd just told her, Portland could be a rough town. Especially for a lone woman at night. Why hadn't she considered that before? And why hadn't she confirmed everything with Rebecca? She glanced at her pocket watch, wondering how long it would take to go inside the terminal and ask to place a long-distance call to Portland. But the Portland train was already pulling into the station.

As Katy picked up her small bag, she wondered if she'd finally bitten off more than she could chew. Hadn't friends and family accused her of this very thing many a time before? But hadn't things always turned out all right in the long run? Besides that, there was no turning back now. There wasn't even a return train to Sunset Cove until Monday afternoon. And, she reminded herself as she pushed through the crowded plat-form, she was going to Jim. Once she saw his happy face, this would be all worthwhile. And their new life would begin.

CHAPTER 14

After a busy and somewhat emotional morning—thanks to Daniel's unexpected announcement to go back East—followed by an afternoon of trailing Lawrence Bouchard, Anna needed a break. And she knew her mother deserved an explanation for the way Anna had hastily excused herself from their impromptu tea party. For that reason, she stopped by Lucille's house before going home.

"Welcome, welcome to my runaway daughter." Lucille threw her door wide open. "Have you come to finish our tea?"

"I would appreciate a hot cup of tea." Anna removed her hat. "I apologize for dashing off like that."

"No worries. I suspect you were following a story." Lucille led her to the front parlor then pulled a cord for the maid's bell. "And I suspect it has something to do with Lawrence Bouchard." She sat on the couch, patting the seat beside her. "Come tell me what's going on. I'm all ears."

Anna hadn't counted on disclosing any of this

to her mother. "Perhaps I should hire you as a reporter." She sat down, slowly removing her gloves. "You seem to have a natural sleuthing skill, a real nose for news."

Lucille laughed. "Well, the more I've gotten to know Lawrence, the less I trust the young man."

"I don't trust him either."

"So, was he up to something newsworthy?" Lucille's pale brows arched.

Anna shook her head no. "Not yet anyway."

"Where is that silly girl?" Lucille reached for the cord again then stopped. "I think I'll go see where Sally is hiding."

As Lucille went off in search of her maid, Anna replayed her last two hours of trailing Lawrence Bouchard. His first stop had been the Mercantile. While she'd browsed the magazine rack, he'd made some quick selections. Claiming he planned to do some fishing, he'd gathered rubber boots and a heavy oilskin coat and hat. But not a single piece of fishing gear. Next he'd gone to the hardware store, but still he didn't buy anything related to fishing. Instead, he'd gotten an oil lantern, a canvas tarp, and a coil of rope. All seemed rather suspicious. He'd then carried his loot toward the docks.

Naturally, that was where Anna discontinued following. Stopping by the post office, she visited with Gladys Rollins while keeping one eye on the waterfront. But since Frank was down there, she knew he'd take over the surveillance. It wasn't long, however, before Lawrence returned . . . empty-handed. So Anna had excused herself from Gladys and, from a distance, trailed Lawrence back to the hotel. She'd stayed outside for a bit, chatting with Virginia Proctor. Although she didn't tell the trusted newspaper receptionist about Lawrence Bouchard, she did inform her of Frank's agreement to step in for Jim Stafford. Like Anna, Virginia was pleased by this news, affirming that Frank would be an ideal replacement. Finally, assured that Lawrence wasn't coming out of the hotel anytime soon, Anna had sent a note, by way of a hotel bellboy, down to Frank, asking him to call her at the house if anything new developed.

But now it was nearly four o'clock, and Anna was relieved to sit in a comfortable room where Lucille, followed by Sally bringing in a loaded tea tray, rejoined her. "Sorry for the wait." Lucille sat down. "Now, where were we?"

Instead of discussing young Bouchard's possibly diabolical plans, Anna told her mother about Daniel's unexpected quick departure to Boston.

"Our dear doctor—*gone?*" Lucille frowned as she filled their teacups. "I barely had a chance to wish him happy birthday. And I never got to tell him goodbye. Well, at least he stayed long enough to enjoy the celebration. Goodness, what a crowd we had. Wasn't it wonderful to see the big turnout?"

";I think it encouraged Daniel too." Anna reached for a ginger cookie.

"But not enough to keep him here. That's too bad." She patted Anna's hand sympathetically. "I'm sorry, honey . . . for your sake as much as for the town's."

Anna explained about Daniel's father's angina. "You see, Daniel only just learned of it this week. He would've left sooner but didn't want to miss the groundbreaking ceremony. Still, I know he was quite concerned for his father's health."

"Oh my, I do hope the poor old fellow is all right. I so enjoyed my time with him last winter. Such a well-mannered gentleman."

As Anna sipped her tea, she refrained from pointing out that although the elder doctor had been polite to Lucille, he'd been rather rude to almost everyone else. "Well, I hate to have tea and run." Anna set her empty cup down. "But I told my reporter that he could call me at home."

"Aha." Lucille held a finger in the air. "So, you are following a story on young Lawrence Bouchard."

"I know I can trust you to keep this quiet." Anna picked up her gloves. "I don't want Clara or Ellen to suspect anything."

"I wouldn't think of burdening Clara with that. She's already concerned that her new son-in-law is a lazy bum, and she swore to me she wasn't going to loan him another cent." Lucille followed Anna to the front door. "I couldn't believe it when he came to me for a loan." She lowered her voice, glancing over her shoulder as if worried that her maid was nearby. "Lawrence doesn't know that I've been in contact with his family, or that I know he left San Francisco under suspicion . . . of embezzlement."

"What?" Anna paused by the door.

"Please, don't repeat that." Lucille looked worried. "It's little more than a rumor."

"I assure you I won't."

"Because the Bouchards are good people—well, except for that boy." Lucille grimly shook her head. "And poor Ellen—oh, I know she's been riding her high horse—but I fear she's in store for a big fall."

"Can I trust you?"

"Of course you can. I'm your mother."

"I want to speak to you privately." Anna grabbed Lucille's hand, pulling her out to the covered porch then closing the door. "We suspect Lawrence may be about to embark on a rum-running scheme."

Lucille just shrugged. "That doesn't surprise me in the least."

"Well, since you see Ellen almost every day at the dress shop, perhaps you could keep your ears and eyes wide open. If you hear anything—

like Lawrence taking a fishing trip or going anywhere—see if you can find out when he left and when he'll return and let me know. That would be immensely helpful."

Lucille's eyes lit up. "Oh, this sounds exciting. I'm happy to help."

"Thanks. And now I better get home in case Frank has called."

"I'll stay in touch." Lucille winked as she waved.

As Anna went the two houses down to Mac's place, she hoped that it wasn't a mistake to involve her mother like this. But Lucille was in an excellent position to sleuth. And who would suspect someone like her?

She went directly to Mac's sitting room. She'd been a little concerned about him wearing out earlier in the day, but all the activities had distracted her. She found him sitting in his favorite chair. "How are you doing?"

"I'm all right," he said in a slightly gruff voice.

"Are you sure?" She sat down across from him. "You don't sound all right to me."

"That's because I'm *not* happy." He jutted out his jaw. "First my good buddy Jim Stafford leaves for the war. And then Doctor Daniel up and goes as well."

"So you heard?"

"He told me himself. At his birthday party." He

huffed out a sigh. "That's why I asked Katy to bring me home early."

"I see." Anna knew that Mac would miss Daniel almost as much as she would. "Speaking of Katy, I noticed your car wasn't in the carriage house." She glanced at his mantle clock. "But it's five-thirty. I would think she'd be home by now."

Mac just shrugged.

"I forgot to ask earlier—Bernie mentioned we'd have dinner at seven, but is anyone joining us?"

"Who would that be? Daniel's gone. Jim's gone." He shook his head with a gloomy expression. "It's going to be awful quiet around here."

"Oh, Mac." She forced a smile. "We still have Lucille. And there are your older friends—Wally and Harvey and their wives. I'm sure you'll still enjoy an adequate social life."

"I wasn't just thinking about myself, Anna. I like having younger folks around for your sake too. And for Katy's."

Anna stood. She understood his implication. He was worried for her romantic interests . . . and for Katy's. Well, there was nothing they could do about that. "I suppose it will be quieter." She picked up her hat and gloves. "If you'll excuse me, I'd like to get cleaned up for dinner." As she went up the stairs, she couldn't wait to remove her shoes. They were pretty enough—something Katy had insisted went well with today's festive ensemble—but they were not comfortable. She was eager to bathe, get into something more comfortable, and put up her feet for a while. If she could escape dinner downstairs, like Sarah Rose did, she would gladly do so. But she knew that Mac and Katy would probably miss her. Especially when Mac already seemed discouraged.

Anna took her time with her bath and was finally relaxing in her easy chair, gazing out the window to where the sun was dipping low in the sky. She'd been trying to read but was distracted with a plethora of worrisome thoughts. Although she was determined not to feel sorry for herself over Daniel's hasty exit, she was still saddened by his absence. Like Mac, she felt like life here was changing—first with Jim's departure and now with Daniel's.

Not only that, but Anna knew that right this moment American troops were being transported overseas, preparing to go into active battle. It had come in over the wire just yesterday. She hadn't wanted to mention it to Clara, but Anna felt fairly certain AJ's unit was one of the early ones that had already shipped out. She knew it wouldn't be long until Jim Stafford went to Europe as well. Maybe he was even now on a boat. This war had already changed so much of the world . . . America would be changed as well.

American lives would be lost overseas, and

there would be shortages and deprivations on the mainland. It was even possible that there could be enemy attacks or invasions as well. England had been routinely bombed by German warplanes and zeppelins. Hundreds of civilians had been wounded and more than one hundred and fifty had died just two weeks ago. Germany was eager to show off its war machine with no concern for who was hurt along the way. Women and children—it made no difference to the heartless High Command.

No one knew for sure what this war would cost the United States in the long run, but it was sure to be thousands of lives and millions of dollars. The hope was that with more allied forces, the war would end more quickly. But no one really knew. Predictions seemed to blow up in the face of predictors and, often, when leaders thought it was about to get better, it would simply get worse.

Anna suddenly noticed something on the floor by her door. It appeared to be a white envelope. Curious to its origin and content, she hurried over to pick it up. The lovely artistic handwriting looked like Katy's, and the letter was addressed to her. Thinking it was perhaps an invitation to some sort of impromptu social activity this evening, which would be most welcome, Anna eagerly opened it. But upon reading the first line, her heart plummeted like a stone.

Dear Mother,

I'm so very sorry I can't say this to you face to face, but I feel this is for the best. I have left by train to go to Jim Stafford. It is too late for you or anyone to attempt to stop me. Jim has asked me to marry him, and I have accepted. I know that you'll be disappointed that we did it like this, but I am so worried that he will leave for the war before we have a chance to say our vows. So I have taken matters into my own hands.

Please, do not worry about me. I have carefully gone over all my plans and the details. I've made the proper arrangements and have taken my own money. As you have often told me, Mother, I am old for my age and an independent woman.

I know that you believe in Jim. You and Grandfather both know he is an honorable and trustworthy man. And I love him. I believe when you think about all this, perhaps not right now, but after a bit of time, you will agree with me that I have done the right thing. I want Jim to go to war knowing that he has a loving wife to come home to . . . and if he doesn't make it back home, which is something I can scarcely bear to think about, I will know that I have honored him by becoming his wife.

I will ask Sarah Rose to deliver this note to you before dinnertime, but I will not burden her with any other information. I will send you a wire when I make it to my destination in Tacoma, Washington, which is near Jim's army camp. Please, do not worry about me, Mother. And please explain everything to Grandfather and Grandmother. I hope and pray they will understand.

All my love,
Katy

Anna sank into the easy chair with a defeated, long sigh. She felt as if someone had just socked her in the stomach and knocked the wind out of her. How could Katy do this to them? Running off to be married like this and telling no one? No one besides Sarah Rose. Of course, Katy would know she could trust Sarah with her secret. Although, Anna felt sorry for Sarah. She probably hadn't enjoyed keeping quiet. Anna had a half-mind to go up and question Sarah, but she didn't want to make her feel guilty. It wasn't her fault. Besides, Anna knew as well as anyone that when her strong-willed daughter decided to do something, there was little to be done to stop her.

Still, she was irked and dismayed. Even if it

was Jim Stafford, didn't Katy understand the pain she would inflict on her family and friends? Didn't she understand how tongues would cluck, innuendo would flow, and people would be hurt? How would Mac take this news? In his mind, his beautiful beloved granddaughter could do no wrong. And now this?

Anna had been honest with Katy about how brokenhearted Mac had been when Anna had done this same thing—at nearly the same age—and how badly that had turned out for all of them. And then just last winter, Ellen's family had been devastated when she'd run off with Lawrence. And that wasn't going too well now. Of course, Anna knew that Jim Stafford was a good, decent man and someone that both she and Mac fully approved. Even so, he was nine years older than Katy and about to be shipped overseas. What kind of marriage would that be? Did Katy think she could go with him?

Anna leaned back in her chair and her tears began to flow freely. They fell for Katy . . . and for Jim. They fell for AJ, as well as all the other soldiers heading into the worst war the world had ever known. And her tears were also for Daniel . . . and for his ailing father. But mostly they were for Katy. How could her beloved child have done this to her—without saying a single word?

CHAPTER 15

A nna had no appetite as she went downstairs. She knew she needed to break the news to Mac . . . but she also knew it would break his heart. It would remind him of what Anna had done to him not quite twenty years ago. And the way she was feeling right now, she wasn't even sure she could take it without breaking down. She tiptoed through the quiet front room and, without putting on hat or gloves, she slipped out the front door and ran down the street to Lucille's house, knocking loudly on her door. She hoped her mother wasn't entertaining anyone tonight.

Sally answered with a surprised look. "Oh, I didn't know that Mrs.—"

"I'm not expected," Anna told her. "Does my mother have guests?"

"No, not tonight."

"Oh, good." Anna pushed past her. "Where is she?"

"She just sat down to take dinner."

Anna hurried straight to the dining room. "I'm sorry to interrupt—again." And without pausing she blurted out the story of Katy suddenly eloping with Jim Stafford. "The problem is I still have to tell Mac." And now she felt tears coming again. "And I—I just don't know if I can."

"Oh, honey." Lucille hopped up from her chair and hugged Anna. "I'm so honored that you came to me for help."

"Will you come have dinner with us?" Anna asked.

"Of course I will." Lucille waved to Sally. "Please, take that away. I'm going with my daughter now." And just like that, she grabbed her hat and gloves, and they hurried back over to Mac's house, where, as usual, the table was set for three.

"Lucille," Mac said happily as he came into the dining room. "To what do we owe this pleasure?"

"I invited her," Anna told him.

"Go ask Bernie to set another place—"

"We don't need it," she said quickly. "Katy's not here tonight."

"Oh, well, perfect." He limped over and, using his one good arm, helped Lucille to her chair. "I'm so glad you could join us."

"So much better than eating alone." Lucille unfolded her napkin. "Especially on a Saturday night. Thank you for having me."

Mac smiled, sat, and bowed his head to ask the blessing. Then the three of them, mostly Mac and Lucille, chatted pleasantly while Bernice served their dinner. Thankfully, Lucille was excellent at small talk, and Mac seemed genuinely cheered by her presence. Although Anna did little more than pick at her food, she was determined not to broach the subject of Katy's elopement until Mac was finished. But it was obvious that Lucille was trying to brace him for what was coming. Several times she mentioned Katy's name, saying what a fine businesswoman she'd turned into, how mature she was, how she knew Katy had been greatly saddened when Jim Stafford enlisted. It was all the perfect setup.

Finally, after dessert had been served and Anna felt she could no longer contain her feelings, she told Mac that she'd received some unexpected news. "Just this evening," she said, trying to sound light. "I was quite surprised."

"Someone on the telephone?" he asked. "I didn't hear it ring."

"No. Not by telephone."

"A telegram then?"

"No, it was a note that was slipped under my door." She glanced at Lucille, but the older woman simply nodded. "Katy has gone up to Washington, Mac."

He blinked. "Katy went to Washington? *How?*"

"By train. Jim Stafford will meet her, and they will be married."

His pale blue eyes grew wide. "*Married?* Our young Katy is getting married?"

"Katy loves Jim," Lucille said. "I've known it for some time. I saw how her eyes lit up when he came to take her for coffee or to walk her home from work. I honestly thought they would get married before he left for the war."

"You did?" Mac still looked stunned.

"I wondered myself," Anna confessed. "Jim told me his feelings for Katy. And I suppose I actually gave him my blessing. He's a good man."

"I know he's a good man," Mac said loudly. "But Katy is just a girl."

Now both Lucille and Anna attempted to reassure him that Katy was a young but independent woman. "I, for one, am proud of her," Lucille declared.

"Proud of her?" Mac scowled. "For secretly running away to get married?"

"Isn't that what you did with me?" Lucille challenged him. "Don't forget your mother was none too pleased when you brought me home with you from San Francisco. Come to think of it, I wasn't even as old as Katy."

"Yes, well, that was then."

Anna had no intention of bringing up her past to smooth Mac's ruffled feathers. "Katy is following her heart," she said quietly. "She loves Jim, and I think she's worried he may not survive this war."

Mac's anger seemed to melt into sadness.

"Katy wanted Jim to leave for the war with the assurance that he has a devoted and loving wife back home," Anna said.

"I guess I can understand that." Mac sighed. "If I were a young man going into battle, it would be reassuring to know my wife was waiting for me."

Lucille reached across the table to grasp his good hand. "If you were going to battle, I would happily wait for you, Mac."

He smiled at her.

"So . . . I guess we should be happy for Katy and Jim," Anna said without much genuine enthusiasm.

"Yes." Lucille lifted her water goblet in a toast. "Here's to Jim and Katy. May God bless them."

Mac and Anna followed her, but Anna's heart wasn't in it. Still, she was glad that Mac seemed to be adjusting to the idea. But when Bernice offered to serve them coffee in the living room, Anna excused herself. "I've had a long day," she said in a weary voice.

Fortunately, they didn't seem to mind, and hearing the sound of their voices as she went up the stairs reassured her that both of them seemed to have accepted that their granddaughter had run off—and was right now on her way north—to get married. Poor Katy, feeling so grown up but without family or friends there to cheer for her on this big day . . . without her own mother there to support her. Anna was relieved her parents were unconcerned, but she had a feeling she would be crying herself to sleep tonight.

By the time the train pulled into Portland Union Station on Saturday night, Katy felt decidedly uneasy. And despite the coach car's overloaded conditions, where some of the young men actually had to stand or share seats, she wasn't eager to disembark the crowded, noisy train. By now she realized that most of her fellow passengers—draftees on their way to Camp Lewis—would continue north to Tacoma, and she actually wished she could go with them. Of course, that would mean arriving in the wee hours of the morning, which was not ideal for a lone young woman. But even so, since her ticket to Tacoma wasn't good until Monday morning, she had no choice but to get off.

She waited by the baggage car to make sure her bags were unloaded and placed onto a luggage cart. Even though the railroad employee followed her, pushing the cart toward the terminal, she felt strangely alone. And, once again, questioned her judgment about making this trip. Was there any place as lonely as a railroad station at night with almost no one else around?

As a child, Katy had seen Union Station being built and had even accompanied her mother to its grand opening a few years ago. It was a beautiful structure with a tall tower visible from many parts of Portland. But she'd never been here at night . . . or alone. And something about the whole thing felt scary. What if Rebecca hadn't received Katy's telegram? Or what if she and her family were unable to pick up Katy? Worse yet, what if Rebecca's family had moved away? Katy hadn't exchanged letters with Rebecca since Christmastime. Who knew what might've happened since then?

As she entered the well-lit terminal, Katy felt a little better. Although it was relatively quiet with few other people milling about, the large space was light and bright and clean. She glanced around, hoping to spot Rebecca and her family, but didn't see any familiar faces.

"My friend is supposed to meet me," Katy told the old man helping with her bags. "Can you take those to the front entrance? I'm sure she'll be there." She wished she was surer as he unloaded her bags, which were too big for her to carry alone. Why hadn't she packed lighter? Did she really need all that? What if she'd done it all wrong?

Forcing a smile, she gave the cart man a tip then eagerly looked up and down the darkened street, hoping to see Rebecca's family car coming her way. "They should be here," she said more to herself than to him.

"You need me to call a cab, miss?" He looked concerned.

"I, uh, I'm not sure." She thought of what Dr. Hollister had told her, and the cash he'd given her in case she needed a cab and hotel room. Then she remembered he'd said to call Rebecca's house. "Can you watch my bags while I make a telephone call?" she asked.

He assured her he could do that, but before she left, she heard someone calling her name from behind her. "Katy! Katy McDowell!" Turning, Katy saw Rebecca rushing toward her. "I'm so sorry we're late," she said breathlessly. "My brother Aaron drove my dad's truck and we got lost." She laughed as she hugged Katy. "But we're here now." She pointed to a truck parked down the street, and in the next moment the two of them were lugging her bags to it, and her older brother Aaron loaded them into the back.

"I don't know if I've ever been happier to see anyone in my entire life," Katy told them after they were all seated inside. "I was starting to get scared I'd been forgotten."

"How could I forget you?" Rebecca shook her head, smiling. "You've been my best friend since second grade. And, oh, how I've missed you."

Katy smiled warmly. "Thank you for finally finding your way."

"I've never been to the train station at night," Aaron said as he carefully drove away. "My dad says it's not safe."

"Yes, our parents were quite concerned for

your welfare," Rebecca told her. "You're so brave to come to Portland by yourself. But I'm so glad you did. We're going to have so much fun catching up. Wait until I tell you about what Lottie Peterson did last week."

As they chattered happily together, Katy realized that she hadn't told Rebecca the real reason she was in Portland, or that she'd only be here until Monday. But she could explain all that later, when the two of them were alone in Rebecca's room. Katy didn't want to take any chance of Rebecca's family reacting to her plans or trying to prevent her from continuing to Washington. She was pretty sure she could trust Rebecca with her secret, but at the same time she wasn't sure how her school chum would respond to the news that Katy was getting married—especially if she knew that Jim Stafford was nine years her senior. Perhaps Katy wouldn't tell Rebecca everything.

CHAPTER 16

Despite her parents seeming to accept Katy's surprise elopement, Anna was worried— perhaps even more so when she realized Mac and Lucille were taking it all in stride. Did they not see the dangers that could crop up for a young girl traveling by herself to another state? But for some reason they seemed to assume that Katy was all grown and capable of handling life's challenges on her own.

Even though Anna prayed for her absent daughter at church on Sunday morning, she was too distracted to absorb much of the sermon. And when church let out, she excused herself from Lucille's invitation to take Sunday dinner at her house, claiming she had a headache. In all truthfulness, she did. After a sleepless night of fretting over her missing child, she ached all over. And, at this point, she had no desire to do anything with anyone. Just the same, Anna was glad when Sarah Rose accepted the dinner invitation. Although it was only because Lucille refused to take no for an answer from her.

Relieved to be alone in the quiet house, Anna went straight home and immediately started to pace back and forth. Just like last night, she tortured herself with the same answerless questions. Where was Katy right now? Had she made it safely to Washington? Had Jim met her at the station? Or was she stuck somewhere in between? And if so, what would she do? Was there anything Anna could or should do to check up on her daughter? And if so, what?

As expected, Sarah Rose had been tightlipped about the whole thing last night. And Anna didn't want to push her since Sarah claimed she'd given Katy her solemn word. All Sarah could say was "Don't worry. Miss Katy will be just fine. She's a smart, independent young woman. The best thing you can do for her is pray."

And so Anna had been praying. As she paced, she begged God to keep her little girl safe and to get her to wherever she needed to be. "Even if it's not home with me." The sound of the doorbell interrupted Anna's prayer, and thinking it might be Katy—although she didn't know why she'd ring the doorbell—Anna dashed down the stairs in time to see Mickey coming toward her with an envelope. "Telegram for you," he said with a somber expression.

Anna's heart skipped a beat as she reached for the telegram. Hurrying to open it, she rushed into Mac's sitting room to see what was inside.

Everyone knew that telegrams usually brought bad news. Bracing herself, she read.

Saw Katy on train STOP Seemed fine STOP Don't worry STOP Best Daniel.

Anna couldn't help but smile at the brief message. Of course Daniel and Katy had shared the same train. Why hadn't she thought of that earlier? Well, perhaps that was a good omen. At least it was somewhat encouraging. And she would try to take his and Sarah Rose's advice— and stop worrying.

After a day and a half of catching up, Katy was keenly aware of two things. First, she had out-grown Rebecca, and second, she couldn't wait to see Jim! But she did appreciate Rebecca and her family welcoming her into their home. And she'd tried to show her gratitude by acting like the carefree young girl that Rebecca remembered from school days. She laughed at Rebecca's stories, helped Rebecca's mother in the kitchen, entertained Rebecca's little sister by drawing some dress designs in her scrapbook, and even pretended to enjoy Aaron's attentions—which were unwavering. But on Monday morning, when Rebecca's father dropped Katy off at Union Station on his way to work, Katy was relieved. By now she accepted that she and Rebecca lived in two different worlds. Maybe they always had.

Katy had time to consider such things as she waited for her train, which wasn't due until ten-fifteen. Rebecca had grown up with a father who worked hard to provide for his family, a mother who baked daily and kept a tidy house, a sweet little sister, and a protective older brother. Katy had experienced none of those things. In many ways, she'd always been like the child with her nose to the candy store window when spending time at Rebecca's house. But it no longer seemed to matter now. Katy was glad she'd grown up with independence and freedom. She loved that she was part-owner of a prosperous business, that she could design clothes that women wore, and that she was about to marry Lieutenant James Stafford. All parts of her life that she'd kept under wraps while being a guest in Rebecca's home.

After checking her luggage, Katy casually strolled through the train terminal, stopping at a newsstand to purchase a new edition of *Vogue*. She didn't mind being in the terminal by herself today. Not in the least. By the end of the day, she would be in Tacoma, about twenty miles from Camp Lewis . . . and Jim. Although she hoped that Jim would be at the station to meet her, she knew she couldn't count on it. Most likely he wouldn't have gotten any leave yet. Her plan was to get a room in a hotel, send him a telegram, and wait. She'd brought sufficient funds for her return trip and to cover enough room and board for up to two weeks—perhaps longer if she was frugal. She hoped it wouldn't take that long for her to connect with Jim.

As she sat down to leaf through her magazine, she vaguely wondered what she'd do if Jim were unable to get leave time, or if he insisted on waiting until the war ended to marry her, or worse yet, if he'd already departed with his unit for Europe. She hoped and prayed he had not. But, she told herself, even if that happened, she would not regret making this trip. After all, it was an experience—an adventure.

She sat and watched people coming and going through the train terminal. So many young men—some in uniform, some not—and so many goodbyes. After a while, she couldn't bear to look at them because she kept wondering how many of these farewells would be the final. And she knew—especially from hearing her mother and grandfather and Jim talking about newspaper stories—that many, many soldiers would never come home. Just the thought of that made her teary eyed.

So, putting it out of her head, she studied the latest fashions depicted in *Vogue*. Katy had heard that the war was changing styles, not only due to a lack of materials being shipped from various foreign locations but because of predicted shortages in the States. But beyond that, Katy could see that designers were moving from the elegant ruffles and furs and laces and silks to more sensible designs. More practical and serious. As dismayed as she felt to see this change, she also liked the challenge it would bring. And right there in Union Station, Katy decided that Kathleen's Dress Shop would stay current with the times. Oh, certainly there would still be events that called for feminine frills, but Katy felt ready to embrace a fashion shift to what one designer was calling "wartime wear."

Feeling a gentle tap on her shoulder, Katy looked up from her magazine. And there before her stood a handsome uniformed soldier.

"Jim!" She dropped the magazine to the floor and leaped to her feet, nearly falling into his opened arms.

"Katy—my Katy!" He leaned down to kiss her. "I can't believe it. You're really here."

"But how did you find me? What are you doing here?" she finally managed to ask. "You're supposed to be in—"

"I'm on leave." He gazed lovingly into her eyes. "My CO—that's commanding officer—gave me seven days leave to come down here and meet you. I knew you'd be waiting for the ten-fifteen. I just got off the southbound train."

Katy was confused. "But I'm supposed to board the northbound train." She glanced up at the

196

big station clock. "In about ten minutes too."

"Well, I have a different plan." He tenderly touched her cheek. "I'm taking you back to Sunset Cove, Katy."

"What?" She frowned in dismay. "Why?"

"So we can have a real wedding with friends and family. Maybe in the church if we can work out the details in time."

"Really?" She blinked. "You'd do that for me?"

"Of course. For you and me both. I already got our tickets, and the southbound train will depart in about fifteen minutes."

"But my bags." She looked toward the baggage check area. "They're probably being loaded onto the northbound train now."

"Not for long." He picked up his suitcase and grabbed her hand, hurrying outside to the platform. "Give me your claim ticket and I'll take care of it." He set down his suitcase. "You wait here."

Katy's mind was whirling while she waited. It seemed impossible. Would they really have a wedding in Sunset Cove? It wasn't that she didn't want to share a ceremony with family and friends, but what if they weren't supportive of the idea? What if her mother was hurt about Katy leaving without telling her? That seemed quite likely. Even dear Grandfather might be nursing hurt feelings. But Jim seemed determined to do this, and for his sake, she would go along with it, even if it meant eating crow or profusely apologizing to everyone.

Katy pulled her little notepad from her purse and began to write a telegram to her mother. Starting with an apology, she explained the change in plans and Jim's hope to have a church wedding, hopefully as soon as possible.

Jim returned, slightly breathless. "Your bags are being loaded on the southbound train right now."

"Do we have time to send a telegram to my mother?" she asked eagerly.

"Let's send it from Salem," he suggested as he took her small bag, leading her toward the train. "That way we can take our time to work out all the details while we're riding the train."

"Yes, that's a smart plan." She took his arm as he helped her up the steps. Before long they were seated in the coach car, and Jim was looking over her notes for the telegram.

"Let's send it directly to your mother at the newspaper office," he suggested. "That way she'll get it right away. And what do you think about having the wedding on Wednesday? That'll give us one day to get ready and spend some time with family and friends."

"That's fine with me," she agreed as the train began to move. "Even if we can't get the church on Wednesday, we could still be married at City Hall."

"And unless you have any objections, I'd suggest we get married in the morning."

"A morning wedding sounds nice. Especially if we can have it in the church." For some reason that sounded more elegant to her. She loved how the morning sunlight looked coming through the stained-glass windows. And perhaps they could light candles too.

Somehow, thanks to Jim's editing skills, they managed to get all the information down without using too many words. "I can barely believe it," Katy said after Jim tucked the paper into his pocket. "You're really here, Jim. We're really together. And we're going to be married. It feels almost like a dream."

"I can hardly believe it myself." He reached for her hand. "I was over the moon to get your telegram. I started requesting leave time immediately. Of course, it was touch-and-go at first. My CO wasn't sure when our unit would ship out. But when he finally got word from his superiors in DC, he gave me permission to take a full week of leave." His smile faded slightly. "But I can't be late in returning. I assured him I'd be there next Sunday evening by seven. Because we're scheduled to depart the next day."

"Oh." Katy didn't know what to say. She knew it was inevitable that Jim would go to battle, but she didn't like hearing about it . . . or thinking about it.

"That's why I want a morning wedding," he explained. "So we can get the afternoon train out of Sunset Cove and make it back to Portland by that evening. We'll stay overnight there and continue to Seattle on Thursday. That gives us from Thursday evening until Sunday afternoon to enjoy Seattle. And then I report back to Camp Lewis."

Katy felt her head spinning slightly as she attempted to absorb all this information. She and Jim . . . a morning wedding . . . a train trip to Portland . . . honeymooning in Washington. "What's Seattle like?" she asked.

"I'll admit I picked Seattle to ensure I don't miss departing with my unit. But I also believe it's the perfect place for our honeymoon." His eyes lit up. "You've got to see it, Katy. Seattle is one of the most beautiful places on earth. It has snowcapped mountains and the sea and all sorts of things to see and explore. Like no place you've ever been before. Do you think you'd like that?"

"I would love that!" She nodded eagerly. "I was so excited about seeing Washington, and now I'll get the chance."

He studied her for a long, quiet moment. "I forgot to tell you how beautiful you look today. Of course, you always look pretty. But today you look even more beautiful."

"Thank you. It's probably because I'm so

happy." She smiled. "And I must say that you, Lieutenant Stafford, are strikingly handsome in uniform."

He sat up straighter. "Well, thank you."

Katy glanced around the half-filled coach car. "This train isn't nearly as packed as the last one I was on." She described the boisterous young men, some standing in the aisle. "Most of them were on their way to your army camp."

"Men come pouring in every day now. Which reminds me—we better ticket our trip back north while we're in Salem to ensure we have passage."

"Yes, that's a good plan." She patted his hand. "I can see why you're an officer, Jim. You're good at figuring these things out. You'll be a great leader."

"I know we don't have much time, Katy, but I'd like to make the most of it."

"It all sounds perfect," she assured him. "I knew when I left Sunset Cove that I would have to accept whatever came my way. Even if we only had a day or two together, I thought it would be worth it. And now we have a week. It'll be fabulous. I know it will." She didn't want to admit that she'd worried that she might not have even seen him . . . that he might've shipped out already. Compared to that, everything seemed perfectly lovely.

"To think I get to marry my sweetheart in my

hometown. What a wonderful way to start our new life together."

"Yes, it's far better than I'd hoped for." Now if only her family and friends could be as enthused over this wedding as her bridegroom. If only her mother could be happy for her. Katy hoped and prayed she would be.

Anna's heels seemed to drag at the newspaper office on Monday morning. She'd hoped that work would distract her, but so far it wasn't helping much. She hadn't mentioned Katy's elopement to anyone at the paper yet. Not even to Virginia at the front desk—and Anna usually told her wise older friend almost everything.

It didn't help to know that if someone else's daughter were getting married, the news item would certainly make the wedding section on their society page. Especially since Katy was not only part-owner of Kathleen's Dress Shop but the fashion columnist for the newspaper as well. Truly, the public had a right to know.

But Anna's lips were sealed. At least for the time being. Maybe it was selfishness or just foolish pride, but Anna had no intention of printing her daughter's elopement story in their paper anytime soon. Mac had wholeheartedly agreed with her at breakfast this morning. And Lucille and Sarah Rose had promised not to say anything either. They all knew the word would spread quickly enough without anyone's help. And, to be fair, no one knew for certain that Katy and Jim had wed. Until Anna received reliable information that Katy and Jim were actually married, it was nobody's business.

"Telegram for you," Virginia announced, poking her head through Anna's partially opened office door.

Anna hid her eagerness in the hopes it was from Katy. Instead, she smiled as if nothing were wrong. "Did you have a good weekend, Virginia?" She neatly slit the edge of the telegram with her letter opener.

"What a lovely gathering for the ground-breaking. And Doc Hollister's birthday shindig—it was all so nice."

"Yes." Anna nodded absently as she unfolded the page and read. Then, hoping she hadn't misunderstood, she read it again. "Oh, my!"

"What is it? Bad news?"

"No, no." Anna slowly shook her head. "It's very good news." She looked up at the older woman with happy tears. "It's—it's from my daughter."

"Katy?" Virginia blinked. "Why in the world would she waste good money on a wire when she's just down the—"

"Katy has, well, you see, she was visiting a school chum in Portland this weekend. But now she's on her way home. With Jim."

"With Jim? *Our* Jim?" Virginia's eyes grew wide.

"That's right. And they want to be married right here in Sunset Cove. Jim has one week of leave time, Virginia. They want to be married on Wednesday."

"Wednesday?" Virginia scratched her head. "Why, that's only two days away."

Anna studied the telegram. "They want a morning wedding, preferably at the church. That way they can take the afternoon train and get back to Seattle."

"A wedding on Wednesday." Virginia brightened. "Would you like me to help with anything? I can call the church for you. And my neighbor Lenora is an expert at making wedding cakes. Want me to call her?"

"Yes, I'd appreciate any suggestions. I've never planned a wedding before. And on such short notice too."

"I helped with my niece's wedding a few years ago." Virginia pulled out her notepad. "Being that it's a morning wedding, perhaps they'd like a luncheon afterwards."

"Yes, that's a good idea. I'm sure Mac wouldn't mind hosting it at home."

"And what about flowers? I have some lovely pink roses just coming on . . . and delphinium and sweet pea and peonies. My sister-in-law has a real knack for floral arrangements. She did them for her daughter. Want me to see if she can help?" Virginia jotted something on her notepad.

"Oh, that sounds perfect." Anna reached for the telephone. "I need to call my parents and let them know about this. You see if you can reach all those people." As Virginia scurried away, Anna called Mac at home, telling him the happy news.

"Well, that's a relief," he said. "When will they arrive?"

"On the afternoon train."

"I'll tell Bernice to plan a good dinner."

Anna told him Virginia's suggestion about a luncheon, and he eagerly agreed. "I'll let Bernice know," he said. "And maybe we can find someone to help her with it."

Next, Anna called Kathleen's Dress Shop, relaying all the latest to Lucille.

"Oh, that's just wonderful," Lucille gushed. "And we have the perfect dress for Katy. It's one that she designed for our summer line. Ivory satin and lace with rosebuds embroidered along the hemline. Sarah Rose is sewing the floor sample right now. With a few more hands, we could have it ready by Wednesday."

"Speaking of more hands, I know Bernice could use some help with the luncheon after the wedding."

"I'll send Sally over and ask our seamstresses if they'd like some extra work. Oh, Anna, this is so exciting. Getting to see our dear Katy wed. I'm so happy."

Not long after Anna hung up, Virginia returned with updates. Reverend Williamson confirmed the church was free, and he was glad to perform the ceremony. Virginia's neighbor was delighted to make a cake. And her sister-in-law couldn't wait to start arranging the flowers.

"What about inviting folks? Do you have a guest list?" She held up a box of blank stationary cards. "I can write them out for you if you like. I'm not very busy today."

"I'll put a list together."

"Then I'll have one of our delivery boys carry them by hand. Hopefully before five o'clock."

"Thank you, Virginia. You're truly a godsend."

"And will you put an announcement in the society page?" Virginia asked hopefully. "I could mention it to Reginald. I'm sure there's still time. And we have their photographs on file."

"Good idea. Tell Reginald to come see me for the details."

"Will do." Virginia nodded eagerly.

Anna thanked her again. "But we still have a newspaper to get out." She held up the article about the upcoming Founders Day festivities she was writing. She no longer felt very enthused about it, but still, it needed to be done.

But before Anna returned to writing, she made a list of wedding guests. Naturally, she thought of Daniel. How she wished he could be here for this special day. But at least she could send him a telegram. She wasn't even sure if he was in Boston yet, but he'd given her the address of the hospital, and she felt certain he'd enjoy this bit of good news. And perhaps it would be a reminder to him that she still wanted him to be a part of their lives.

CHAPTER 17

A nna had just handed the guest list to Virginia when Frank pulled her aside. "I need to talk to you in private," he said quietly.

"In my office." Anna suspected this was related to Lawrence Bouchard and his fishermen friends. Last she'd heard, Bud Griggs's boat motor engine was being worked on, but perhaps it was fixed by now.

"I strolled down to the dock during my lunch hour," Frank began. "Looks like Griggs's boat engine is working again. At least, he seemed to be testing it out."

"Any sign of Lawrence Bouchard?"

"I didn't see him, but Bud and Fred looked like they were getting ready for a fishing trip."

"Did you notice any fishing gear?" she asked.

"Nope." His brows arched. "Looked more like they wanted folks to *think* they were going fishing."

"Well, feel free to keep an eye on them." She glanced at the clock, surprised to realize she'd completely missed her lunch hour. "Take your fishing pole if you like."

"I've got it in my office." He nodded. "I'll let you know what I find out."

"If I'm not here, call me at home," she told him. She didn't want to mention her distraction of Jim and Katy's arrival or that she in fact felt more interested in the wedding than in getting the rum-running story. "And if I'm not there, feel free to fill in Mac. He'll know how to handle it and whether or not to call the chief."

"Will do." Frank made a mock salute and then took off. She suspected he was looking forward to an afternoon of sleuthing around the docks. Maybe he'd even catch a fish or two while he was at it. And hopefully Lawrence and his buddies weren't really about to embark on a big rum-running expedition. What bad timing!

As much as she cared about chasing a good news story, Anna didn't want anything to detract from the wedding plans over the next couple of days. Perhaps having Ellen and Lawrence on the invitation list would help with that. She'd almost left them off because she knew Katy wasn't feeling close to the couple of late. But it had felt wrong since Ellen worked at the dress shop and was Clara's daughter.

Suddenly she got an idea. She would hand deliver the invitations to the dress shop in person. She called Virginia, asking her to write out the ones for the dress shop employees first and explaining she was headed over there. A few minutes later, she was on her way, making a plan and preparing a speech.

Ellen was working the front part of the dress shop and, to Anna's relief, there were no customers. "You're just who I wanted to see," Anna said cheerfully.

Ellen looked somewhat surprised. "I just heard the news about Katy and Jim," she said a bit glumly.

"Yes, isn't it exciting?" Anna handed her the envelope addressed to *Mr. and Mrs. Bouchard.* "I know Katy will want you and Lawrence to be part of all the festivities. I realize it's short notice, but we plan to fill the next couple of days with a number of functions, and I do hope you and Lawrence will be free to attend." Anna briefly described what would be going on. "Tonight will be just family, and Wednesday morning is the wedding and the luncheon for close friends and family, but I thought we should do something festive tomorrow night. A party with music and dancing for everyone to attend. I know Katy and Jim would love that. I hope you and Lawrence will celebrate with them."

"Of course we'll come," Ellen said happily. "We haven't been doing much of anything socially. Not since moving back here. I've been hoping for something to get dressed up for."

"Oh, you'll certainly want to dress up for tomorrow's party." Anna smiled. "And it will be so nice to have other young married couples in attendance too."

"Lawrence and I will definitely be there." Ellen nodded firmly.

"We'll send more details about the dance time and location later," she promised. Of course, Anna knew this meant she'd have to plan for an evening of merriment tomorrow night, but she also knew that Katy and Jim would probably enjoy it. No one needed to know that this also would provide a way for Anna to keep an eye on Lawrence.

"There she is—my favorite daughter," Lucille said as she carried a box into the shop. Anna greeted her and handed over the invitations for the other shop employees.

"Do you have time for a cup of tea?" Lucille asked as she set the box on the counter.

"In fact, I still haven't had lunch so—"

"What are we waiting for?" Lucille turned the invitations over to Ellen. "Let your mother know I'll be out for a bit, dear. And feel free to unpack that box. It's from New York."

Ellen's eyes lit up. "Ooh, that sounds like fun."

"Just be sure to check the inventory slip that it's all there." Lucille smiled at Anna. "Off we go."

Before long they were seated at the hotel

restaurant, and Anna was telling Lucille about her half-hatched plan to have a dance for Katy and Jim on Tuesday night. "It'll be a chance for everyone—not just close friends and family—to celebrate before the wedding."

"Oh, that's a wonderful idea." Lucille nodded eagerly.

"Perhaps, but there's already so much to be done. I hope I didn't take on too much."

"You let me handle the arrangements for the dance." Lucille glanced around the hotel restaurant. "What about having it right here? If the tables were pushed out of the way, this room would be plenty big for a dance floor. And we could serve refreshments over there and. . . ." Lucille continued with enthusiasm. By the time they left the restaurant, she had it all worked out with the hotel manager, as if they were old friends.

"And I'll be sure to get the word out for the dance," Lucille told Anna as they walked back through town. "Don't you worry about a thing for tomorrow night."

"I can hardly believe it," Anna said as they paused by the dress shop. "How everything is falling into place. It feels almost miraculous."

"Well, the good Lord works in strange ways." Lucille winked. "And it seems he wants our sweet Katy and dear Jim to have a beautiful beginning."

Anna nodded somewhat solemnly. "Before Jim goes to war."

Lucille's smile faded. "Well, we don't have to think about that today." She pointed to the shop. "Why don't you come in and see the dress we're working on for Katy?"

Anna followed her into the back room where Sarah Rose and the two other seamstresses were sewing various sections of the same garment. "It's so beautiful." Anna lightly touched the top layer of the delicately embroidered lace over-skirt.

"The hemline is just above her ankles," Lucille explained. "I set aside a new pair of the most delicate white silk stockings and a lovely pair of white satin slippers."

"Katy will look like a princess."

"I can't wait to see her in it." Lucille picked up another piece of lace. "I don't know if she'll want a veil. It's not mandatory, of course, but we've prepared this just in case."

"Katy is a lucky girl," one of the seamstresses said.

"And Jim is a lucky man," Lucille added.

"And together they will be most blessed," Sarah Rose said quietly.

Anna nodded in agreement. She hoped Sarah was right. But the thought of Jim about to leave for the battlefield loomed like a dark shadow across the pristine white wedding garments.

・ ・ ・

Katy had no idea what would await them in Sunset Cove. Bracing herself for her family's reaction, which could be anything from hurt and disappointment to happy relief, she took a deep breath as Jim helped her off the train. The afternoon fog, not unusual in the summertime, cloaked the platform, but as Jim and Katy neared a lone figure, she heard her mother call out, "Welcome home to both of you." And suddenly they were embracing.

"Thank you for bringing our girl home," Anna told Jim.

"It seemed the right thing to do." Jim set down the smaller bags. "Excuse me. I'll make sure Katy's bags are unloaded."

"So you're not angry at me?" Katy asked her mother after Jim left.

"I'll admit I was shocked and a bit hurt." She pushed a stray curl away from Katy's face. "But I understood. And I respect you for doing what you feel is right. Jim is a good man, Katy. And I know he loves you."

"And I love him," Katy quietly confessed as Jim rolled the loaded luggage cart toward them.

"My bride-to-be doesn't know how to pack lightly," he joked.

Her mother chuckled. "I hope we can fit it all into Mac's Runabout."

"That won't be necessary," Jim told her. "I'm

going to ask to keep most of these here at the station. We'll pick them up on our way out on Wednesday."

"Perfect." Anna nodded. "I should've known you two would have it all figured out." She turned to Katy. "And everything is falling perfectly into place." As they went to the car, she explained how everyone was helping to put together the impromptu wedding, now less than two days away. Then, crammed into the front of the Runabout, Jim drove and Anna continued to tell Katy about the upcoming festivities.

"It seems impossible," Katy said as they got out at Mac's house and waited for Jim to unload the smaller bags, "that you could manage to get so much done in such a short amount of time."

"Many hands make light work." Anna grinned. "And it doesn't hurt that Katy McDowell is a rather well-liked citizen of Sunset Cove."

"I'm so happy, Mother." Katy hugged her again. "I always dreamed of having a real wedding with family and friends."

"But you were willing to give that all up for me." Jim leaned over to kiss Katy's cheek. "I feel like the kid who grabbed the brass ring."

Katy laughed and then, spying her grandfather standing by the open front door, she ran up to greet him. "I hope you'll forgive me for trying to elope with Jim."

"All is forgiven, dear girl." But after hugging

her, Mac gave Jim a rather grim look. "As for you, young man, I'm not so sure. What do you mean by running off with my best girl?"

Jim looked truly contrite. "I'm sorry, Mac. As much as I wanted to marry Katy, I never expected her to pack her bags and come up to—"

"Never mind, never mind." Mac playfully tapped Jim's leg with his cane. "I'm just glad you brought her back for the wedding." He paused to study Jim's uniform. "So, you're really in the army now, Jim Stafford. Think you can do anything to bring that nasty war to an end?"

"I sure hope so, Mac."

"Well, come in, come in." Mac stepped back, waving them inside. "Bernice has a special welcome home dinner planned for this evening." He turned to Katy. "And Lucille and Sarah are waiting for you upstairs. There's something they want to show you."

Katy grabbed her small bag from Jim then hurried up to her room. There, spread across her bed, was the most beautiful lacy white dress. "Oh, you finished it," she gushed as she gathered the soft layers of fabric, examining the lace and embroidery and workmanship. "It's far better than I imagined." She turned to her grandmother and Sarah Rose. "Thank you both!"

"I thought we should do a fitting." Lucille began helping Katy out of her travel clothes.

"And I'll take care of any necessary altera-tions," Sarah assured her.

"This is so exciting." Katy tossed her hat aside and tugged off her gloves. "When I designed that dress last spring, I had hoped someone would use it for a wedding, but I honestly didn't imagine it would be me."

"Well, it seemed meant to be." Lucille and Sarah helped to slide it over Katy's head. "You're going to be a beautiful bride, Katy. We're just glad you came home to share this day with us."

Anna, Mac, and Jim went into Mac's sitting room and, just like in the "old days," began to dis-cuss the newspaper and the most recent current events—primarily the situation in Europe. "It's no secret that troops are already positioned in England," Jim said.

"Even AJ is over there," Anna confirmed. "Clara just got a letter from him. He actually sounded antsy to go into battle."

"It's surprising how eager everyone is." Jim explained how his unit was leaving in less than a week. "But they are already chomping at the bit."

"What is the US Army doing to protect our soldiers from toxic gas?" Mac asked.

"Soldiers are being trained to use special masks," Jim said somberly. "I've heard that special masks are being developed for horses and dogs too."

"Oh, I never thought about that." Anna cringed. "To consider how the poor animals could suffer."

"You mean like soldiers do?" Jim's expression was grim. "As much as I admire the enthusiasm of the younger enlistees and draftees, I have to wonder. If they were better informed of the situation over there. . . ." He shook his head.

"You mean like a newspaperman?" Anna said wryly.

"Yes. It gives one a different perspective."

"Just one more reason you make a good officer," Mac told him. "Experience seasons a man."

"What about acting as a war correspondent?" Anna asked. "Katy had mentioned that was a possibility."

"I'm on the list." Jim shrugged. "Along with a lot of others."

"What about airplanes?" Mac asked. "Any new developments there? When's the US going to get into the air and give those Krauts what-for?"

"We have a lot of catching up to do. England and France are way ahead of us."

"And Germany," Mac growled.

"You've probably already heard that the air service has been formed. As a part of the AEF."

"The American Expeditionary Force?" Anna asked.

Jim nodded. "Some of our young men are over there right now being trained by the best French and English pilots."

"And what will they fly?" Mac asked.

"I recently heard that some motorcar factories are already producing airplanes, but like everything else, it'll take time."

"I just hope it's not a case of too little too late," Mac said dourly. "I can't help but think the world would be in better shape if we'd joined the allied efforts a lot sooner."

Jim grimaced and then turned to Anna. "This is one of those things Mac and I could never agree on."

"Just like the rest of the country." Anna sighed. "Although I think the majority agree that we've done the right thing by joining up."

As they continued to talk war, politics, and newspaper trivia, Anna tried to imagine what Jim must feel like right now. Sitting there looking strong and handsome in his army uniform, but what a contrasting mix of emotions he had to be experiencing. About to celebrate what he was already calling the happiest day of his life . . . and in just a week to be transported across the country and then to board a ship.

And then, finally . . . the war.

CHAPTER 18

Although Anna would've preferred to remain home on Tuesday, she knew there was a newspaper to get out. Plus she wanted to check with Frank regarding the whereabouts of Lawrence Bouchard and his two possibly-criminal cohorts. She and Frank were just discussing this in her office when Jim, still wearing his uniform, appeared at her door.

"Thought I should come in to work." He grinned with a twinkle in his eye. "This a private meeting?"

"Come in," she told him. "I don't know if I mentioned that Frank has stepped up to the managing editor position."

"Congratulations." Jim shook Frank's hand, smiling, apparently with no concern for having been replaced.

"It's possible that we're about to snag a juicy story about rum-running again." She motioned for Jim to close the door and sit down then filled him in on the surveillance they'd been doing on Bouchard and his "fishing" buddies. "Although

I've tried to tempt Lawrence into sticking around for the wedding festivities."

"I don't see the connection." Jim frowned.

She explained her hope to keep the small gang in town a bit longer. "I really want this story, Jim. I want Lawrence Bouchard caught in the act. I'm hoping a lot of liquor will be seized, and we'll be there to cover it—and even get photos. And then I hope our story will be picked up across the country."

"Sounds kind of mercenary to me."

"Really?" Anna blinked. "I thought I was simply being a newspaperwoman . . . a responsible citizen."

He shrugged. "Yeah, I guess that's true."

She studied him closely. "What would you suggest, Jim?"

"Well, it's no secret that I'm not overly fond of Lawrence Bouchard. I never much liked the city slicker, right from the start. But he is Ellen's husband."

She nodded. "That's true." She didn't want to point out that Ellen had changed—and not for the better—since marrying Lawrence.

"Maybe he needs a second chance."

"A second chance?" She drummed her fingers on her desk.

"I guess I'm thinking of AJ. Remember how we all felt he deserved a second chance?"

She barely nodded. "To be honest, I'm not

sure I've even given Lawrence Bouchard a first chance."

Jim smiled. "Maybe someone should."

She considered this. "I know he's desperate for money. He even came in here looking for a job. But I don't think he has newspaper experience, and I'm not impressed with his politics." She explained how Lawrence was vehemently opposed to the war.

"So was I," Jim reminded her.

"Maybe so." She pointed to his uniform. "But when push came to shove, you signed up. And I know you'll do your best for them."

"That's my responsibility as a US citizen. But that doesn't change my opinion on war or neutrality in general."

Anna glanced at Frank. "What do you think?"

He pursed his lips. "I think if Lawrence and his buddies pull off what we think they're planning, well, they could end up in prison for a good while."

"Why aren't they in the army?" Jim demanded. "That may help shape them up."

"Good question," Frank said.

Anna explained that Lawrence was exempt because of his feet. "But I don't know about the other fellows."

"Maybe someone should ask them," Jim suggested.

"Too bad you're not still an investigative reporter," Anna teased.

"Says who?" Jim stood. "How about I give you a hand? Katy's consumed with wedding plans today. I'm at loose ends until tonight's dance."

"Would you really want to?" Anna knew her uncertainty saturated her tone.

"Sure. I'll just go poke around . . . ask a few questions. It'll be fun. Like old times."

"All right." Anna nodded, but she still felt torn. On one hand, Jim's intervention could be helpful for the community as a whole . . . but on the other hand, it might end up killing what could've been a big story. Still, if there were a way that Lawrence and the other guys could be detoured from committing a serious criminal offense, perhaps it was worth the effort.

"What if I ask Lawrence about his interest in working for the newspaper?" Jim glanced at Frank. "Any chance you could find him some low-level job around here?"

"We are a little shorthanded," Frank admitted. "In fact, I have a pile of work waiting on my desk right now." He looked at Anna. "What do you think?"

"I think selective service has already started to take its toll," she said slowly. "Everyone will be shorthanded." Still, she remembered what Lucille had said about embezzlement. Except that she didn't know if it was true . . . and she did believe that a man should be presumed innocent until proven guilty. And yet . . .

"Even if he only helped in the pressroom or made deliveries," Jim suggested. "Bouchard's probably in good enough shape for that. Don't you think?"

"I suppose if he were willing to start at the bottom and learn the ropes . . . and if he doesn't shove his political convictions in our faces . . . Well, I guess I could give him a try." She remembered interviewing Lawrence last month. He'd come across as arrogant and disrespectful. To be fair, she couldn't remember what his qualifications were or if he even had any.

"I'll let him know." Jim reached for the doorknob. "Either he'll be interested, or he's already too committed to his life of crime. It'll be up to him, Anna. But at least it's a second chance."

"It was kind of you to suggest it, Jim." She smiled. "Thanks."

After the men left, Anna took a good, long, albeit reluctant look at herself. It wasn't surprising that she, like Jim, had experienced an instant aversion to the well-dressed, smooth-talking Lawrence Bouchard last winter. But that was simply because she'd felt protective of Katy and knew that Lawrence was not the man for her. But when he'd eloped with Ellen, it had given Anna more reason to dislike him. Especially after spending time with Clara, who'd been devastated by the messy affair.

Even so, it was possible Anna had dismissed the brash young man too hastily when he'd asked for employment. Had she turned into a hard-boiled, heartless newspaperwoman? A female version of Mac, back in the day when he ruled this newspaper with an iron fist? But as for being mercenary . . . Well, she sure hoped that wasn't true. But perhaps she'd been playing a bit too close to the borders. And although it stung her pride to admit this to herself, she was grateful that Jim—her soon-to-be son-in-law—was bold enough to point out what could've become a serious blind spot.

Katy's reasons for going to the dress shop were twofold this morning. First, she wanted to spend some time with her grandmother and good friends. But she also wanted to make a couple of posters for tonight's dance. She hadn't told anyone of her idea—not even Jim—but it first occurred to her while waiting for the train at Union Station. After a brief conversation with a young woman who was a Red Cross volunteer, Katy had confided that she was on her way to Camp Lewis—or so she hoped—to marry a soldier. That's when the woman challenged Katy to start a Red Cross chapter in Sunset Cove—a challenge Katy had accepted.

"What are you making?" Ellen asked when she discovered Katy at work in the storage room.

"Signs." Katy held up the poster, waiting as Ellen read it.

"You don't want *any* wedding gifts?" Ellen sounded shocked. "You're asking people to donate to the Red Cross instead?"

"Jim and I won't be able to set up housekeeping until the war ends." Katy blew on the poster to help dry the red and blue paint. "In the meantime, Red Cross donations will provide much needed medical help to our wounded soldiers and actually save lives. It could even help the war to end sooner."

"So, you really don't want any wedding gifts?" Ellen looked skeptical.

"I'd rather have friends and family help the Red Cross." Katy smiled. "In fact, I plan to start a chapter here in Sunset Cove. Right after I return from our honeymoon."

"But I think my mom already got you a gift." Ellen seemed unwilling to let this go. "What about that?"

"Perhaps she can return it . . . or save it for someone else." Katy leaned down to start the second sign. Her plan was to post them in highly visible places at tonight's dance. Hopefully everyone would understand better than Ellen.

"Lawrence and I never got any wedding gifts either," Ellen said sadly. "And no wedding either."

Katy didn't know what to say.

"Even Lawrence's family seemed unhappy with us."

"That's too bad." Katy felt a wave of compassion. "It must've been hard on you."

"It was." She sniffed slightly. "And it still is."

Katy set down her paintbrush and gave her a hug. "I'm sorry, Ellen. I probably haven't been very understanding. I suppose I've been caught up in my own life." She stepped back and smiled. "I hope we can become good friends again."

Ellen blinked. "Really? You mean that?"

"Of course I do." Katy pointed to the poster. "And I want you to be the first one I invite to become a member of our brand-new Red Cross chapter."

"Thanks, I guess. . . ." Her brow creased. "But I don't think I'd make a very good nurse. I faint at the sight of blood."

Katy laughed. "You don't have to be a nurse to volunteer."

"Then what do we do?"

"Oh, lots of things." Katy tried to remember what the woman at Union Station had told her. "We'll knit socks and vests and scarves—things to keep soldiers warm in the trenches. And we'll roll bandages. And collect items the wounded soldiers need . . . and we'll have fundraisers to help hospitals."

"You were really good at raising money for

the mayor's campaign," Ellen conceded. "Those events were pretty fun."

"And you helped me, remember?"

Ellen brightened. "I did, didn't I?"

Katy got an idea. "How would you like to help me now?"

"Sure. What can I do?"

"For starters, you could make sure these posters get hung at the hotel before the dance starts. In the foyer so people see them when they enter."

"Sure, I can do that after work. Lawrence and I are still living in the hotel."

Now Katy waved a paintbrush toward a couple of canning jars that she'd painted red crosses on. "Perhaps you can handle this too?"

"What do you want me to do? Can peaches?"

Katy chuckled. "Those are for the Red Cross donations. Would you want to manage them at the wedding? So people know what they're there for . . . in case anyone wants to donate to the cause."

"Sure, I can do that." Ellen picked up a jar. "How about if I tie some red, white and blue ribbons around the tops to make them more decorative?"

"That's a wonderful idea. Thank you."

Ellen smiled. "Thanks for including me, Katy."

Katy smiled and then asked Ellen what she planned to wear to the dance and to the wedding and, suddenly, it was like old times. Both of them were carefree girls again, looking forward to the upcoming festivities.

Until moving back to Sunset Cove, Anna had never been one to attend dances. But in the past year, she'd gone to many. And she'd usually looked forward to it, probably in the hopes of dancing with Daniel. But Daniel was on the other side of the country tonight. Still, she reminded herself as she drove Mac's Runabout to the hotel, tonight was about Katy and Jim. And Anna would do whatever she could to make sure it was a wonderful, memorable evening.

"I hope Lucille hasn't worn herself out too much with tonight's dance," Mac said as Anna parked in front of the hotel. "She's getting too old for this sort of thing."

Anna laughed. "Well, don't tell her that. It may hurt her feelings."

"Looks like it'll be a good-sized crowd." Mac waved toward the main entrance, where a number of people were already gathered by the doors. "I hope Lucille saved me a chair on the sidelines."

"What? You're not going to dance tonight?" Anna teased as she waited for him to put on his hat and get his cane into place.

"I did promise one dance to Lucille, if my bum leg is up to it. But besides that, I just plan to be a spectator."

"And I'll be by your side, a fellow wallflower,"

229

she said lightly. The sounds of music and laughter greeted them as they went into the brightly lit hotel.

"The Red Cross posters that Katy was telling us about earlier." Mac pointed to the prominent signage. "Such a nice idea."

Before long, Anna and Mac were greeting friends and getting refreshments. The hotel restaurant, with tables and chairs pushed to the edges, made for an adequate dance floor, but it was definitely crowded—so much so that Anna was glad to take a seat on the sidelines with Mac.

"Don't they make a lovely couple," she mused as she watched Jim and Katy waltzing. Jim was still in uniform, and Katy was looking sweet in a soft pink dress.

"And so happy. And I'm happy for them." Mac's voice sounded husky. Anna glanced over to see him dab his eye with his handkerchief.

After he pocketed the handkerchief, she reached for his hand. "I'm so thankful that Katy and I came home," she said quietly. "None of this would've happened if we'd stayed away."

He looked into her eyes. "You girls have made me happier than I ever imagined possible, Anna. I hope you're happy too."

Anna forced a smile. "I'm happy."

"Not missing Daniel?"

She shrugged. "Of course I miss him. But I'm glad he's with his father."

"It was nice of him to send us that telegram today."

She nodded. "Yes, Katy appreciated the congratulations." She waved at Frank as he led his young wife into the room. Hopefully, Frank would see that Lawrence and Ellen were among the merrymakers out on the dance floor. No need for their surveillance tonight. Especially since Jim had gotten Lawrence to agree to another interview at the newspaper. He'd set it up with Anna for Thursday morning after the wedding.

"Looks like you're not going to be a wallflower after all." Mac tipped his head toward where Randall Douglas was strolling their way with a look of intent.

Anna concealed her surprise when Randall asked her to dance, but since they were old friends, she couldn't refuse him. "I'd expect you'd be dancing with Clara," she said as he led her around the crowded floor. So far she hadn't seen the two of them together once tonight.

"Clara has been helping Lucille." He smiled a bit too brightly. "Besides, why can't I dance with my old girl if I want to? I'm a free man, am I not?"

Something about the way he said this made her wonder. She'd assumed that Randall and Clara were getting close to announcing an engagement—perhaps even a summer wedding. Had something changed? And if so, perhaps she didn't

231

want to get caught in the middle of it. So when he asked for a second dance, Anna excused herself by saying she'd promised to sit with Mac. "Maybe later," she said a bit stiffly.

But when she got back to the sidelines, Mac was surrounded by his older friends, including the mayor and police chief and their wives, as well as Lucille. "You go have fun with the young people," Lucille urged Anna. "Leave us old folks here to gossip."

Although Anna wanted to protest this exile, she didn't want to make a scene. And so she went off in search of Clara, offering to help her with the refreshment table. As they tidied it up and refilled trays, Anna inquired about Randall. "Did you come together?"

Clara just shook her head. "No, not this time."

"Perhaps you'd like to go dance with him," Anna suggested.

Clara bristled. "Are you suggesting I should go ask him?"

"No, of course, not. But perhaps if he sees you're not busy, he'll ask you."

"I don't think so, Anna."

"Maybe I should go drop a hint—"

Clara, eyes filled with tears, turned and hurried toward the kitchen. Anna waved to Virginia, asking her to take over supervising the refreshments table. "I need to check on Clara." Anna found Clara by the kitchen sink, wiping her eyes with a handkerchief. "What's wrong?" Anna gently asked.

"Nothing." She sniffed. "And everything."

"Would you ladies like some coffee?" Sarah Rose held up a pot. She'd been helping in the kitchen.

"That sounds wonderful," Anna told her. "And would you mind going out to help Virginia with the refreshment table?"

"If you think no one will mind." Sarah looked a bit uncertain.

"If they do mind, they can take it up with me or Mac or Lucille or Katy or Jim." Anna held out a coffee cup as Sarah filled it.

"Thank you, Miss Anna." Sarah smiled as she filled the second cup. "I would enjoy seeing Miss Katy dancing with her soldier man."

"They make a lovely couple." Anna turned to Clara, nodding toward a worktable. "We're overdue for a chat, Clara." She placed the coffee cups on the table. "Please, tell me what's troubling you."

"Where do I even begin?" Clara picked up her coffee, taking a small sip.

"Wherever you like." Anna waited.

"I suppose it starts with my being worried for AJ. I just know he's about to go into battle. Perhaps he's already there. And, yes, I pray for him, but that doesn't keep me from worrying. But that's only the beginning, Anna. For the past week, Ellen has been pestering me for money." She looked upward. "I told her that staying in this hotel is too expensive. I even offered to share my apartment above the dress shop with them. But it seems that's not good enough. Finally, I told her that Lawrence needs to find work."

"You're right about that."

"But Ellen hasn't lightened up. I know Lawrence is pressuring her about some money-making business scheme. And Ellen keeps assuring me it's only a short-term loan. She claims Lawrence needs cash for an investment that will pay off within a couple of weeks. I do have money from the sale of the fishing business, but I don't feel good about risking it. And I'm afraid I've loaned them too much already."

"I agree." Anna nodded firmly. "You're wise to be cautious, Clara."

"That's exactly what Randall told me earlier today."

"You should listen to him." Anna considered telling Clara about Lawrence's rumored involvement with Bud and Fred and the possibility of the group smuggling illegal alcohol into Oregon for profit, but she truly hoped that Lawrence's "second chance" could change all that. Why worry Clara about it now?

Clara's chin quivered. "I'm sure you and Randall are both right. But I suppose I was just worn out and weary. And tonight I told Randall, in no uncertain terms, to mind his own business."

"Oh." Anna cringed. "That's not good." No wonder Randall seemed out of sorts this evening.

"Poor Randall. He's been nothing but good to me, and then I go and snap at him like that." She looked at Anna with teary eyes. "Sometimes, and I hate to say it, but sometimes I feel like I'm a second-class citizen in our town."

"I don't see why."

"Oh, you know why. Everyone knows why. First it's my husband and his . . . *troubles* . . . and then it's AJ and the—"

"But AJ is cleared and serving honorably in the army now."

Clara waved a hand. "Yes, yes, that's true. But then my Ellen goes off and marries that good-for-nothing Lawrence Bouchard."

"Perhaps Lawrence will get on track."

"Maybe, but I have my doubts. And then, here I am tonight, watching Katy and Jim . . . seeing how dear and happy they both are and how everyone in town has shown up to celebrate with them. And why not? They're an admirable and beloved couple. And I am truly happy for them. But then I compare them to Ellen and Lawrence . . . and well, it just doesn't seem fair. It hurts my mother's heart." Her eyes grew misty again.

"I've had moments like that too, when life didn't seem fair." Anna sighed. "All those years of trying to work in a man's world, trying to raise my daughter the best I could on my own but always feeling it wasn't good enough. Imagining that other people had it so much better, so much easier than Katy and me."

"Yes, you've confided that before. And I'm so grateful that you did. I suppose I forget your life has been rough too."

"I only tell you now so you'll know I understand."

"But you must admit your life has certainly improved since moving back here."

"Yes, that's true. . . ."

"And your future seems bright."

Anna nodded, but her thoughts went to Daniel again. How lonely she'd been since he'd left, how sad she'd be if he never returned. But she couldn't mention that now.

"Oh, I may be over-blowing the whole thing, Anna, but sometimes it feels as if my whole family and I are just plain cursed."

"You are *not* cursed, Clara. Look at how you're partnering with Lucille and Katy in the dress shop and what a success that has been. And even if Ellen and Lawrence have their struggles, I think things will be looking up for them." At least, she hoped so.

Clara didn't look convinced. She leaned in closer. "Can I trust you?"

"Of course."

"I'm worried. I've reason to become suspicious that Lawrence could be involved in, uh, *something*. . . ." She glanced around as if to ensure no one was eavesdropping. "Something like what Albert and AJ got into last summer. I hate to even say it aloud, but I'm afraid."

Anna took in a slow breath, carefully considering her response . . . weighing her words . . . then reminding herself that Clara was her old friend. "You could be right, Clara."

Clara's eyes grew wide. "Do you know something?"

Quietly, Anna confessed what little she knew, trying to play it down. "And it could be just a rumor," she assured her. "Nothing has come of it yet. We've been keeping an eye on the fellows."

"It could very well be true." Clara shuddered. "And I've heard there's been illegal activities in these parts again. I'm just thankful that AJ is far away from it. But I am worried for Ellen. I'd hate to think she was involved."

"Oh, I can't imagine Ellen involving herself in that. After all, she saw what AJ went through."

"But she's changed so much since marrying Lawrence. Sometimes I feel I don't even know her anymore."

"Still, I don't think she'd participate in illegal activities. But could she be aware . . . I mean, if Lawrence were involved? Is it possible she knows about something?" Anna wasn't sure if she was asking this as a friend . . . or a reporter. Maybe both.

"I honestly don't know. But I do know Ellen is desperately trying to get funds for Lawrence. And she hands over every penny she makes at the dress shop to him. She says they're saving for a men's clothing shop, but I'm not so sure. I certainly haven't seen Lawrence making any definite plans. I just wish the boy would get a real job."

"Well, Jim just spoke to him today about working for the newspaper." Anna hoped she wasn't saying too much. "Lawrence agreed to a job interview on Thursday."

"Do you think he really wants to work there?" Clara brightened. "What about you, Anna, would you hire him?"

"If he's willing to work hard, I will. The war is contributing to a shortage of manpower." Anna lowered her voice. "But stick to your guns, Clara. Do *not* loan him any money. I hate to say this, but it's possible the investment he has in mind is illegal. It's no secret that selling black-market alcohol is profitable. If you hand over money, you could be very sorry."

"I know. Thank you so much." Clara grasped Anna's hand. "And thank you for taking the time to talk to me tonight. I didn't realize how much I needed a friend."

"We *are* friends. Old friends."

"But we should go back out to the dance." Clara stood, smoothing the skirt of her pretty blue satin dress. "After all, this is your daughter's celebration. And tomorrow is her big day. You need to be out there to enjoy this with her."

"On one condition." Anna held up a forefinger. "Let me drop a little hint with Randall for you . . . that perhaps you'd like to dance with him after all."

Clara looked slightly embarrassed but did not object to the suggestion. And now with arms linked together, the two old friends returned to the festivities. But instead of feeling relieved like Clara appeared to be, Anna felt worried. Her suspicions about Lawrence Bouchard and his cohorts seemed legitimate. They would bear close watching in the next few days. But at least he and Ellen were here tonight. That was something.

CHAPTER 19

Katy felt like the luckiest girl in the world as her mother, grandmother, and Sarah Rose helped her to prepare for her wedding. "This is so much better than doing this alone." Katy tried to stand still as Sarah Rose buttoned the back of her dress and Lucille arranged her curls into place.

"Much more fun for everyone." Anna handed Katy her white satin slippers. "But we need to hurry, sweetheart. It's nearly eleven now."

"And I hear Randall's horn honking," Lucille said. "It was so nice of him to offer to transport you and Mac to the church in his fancy automobile."

"I can take it from here," Katy assured them. "You three get going so you can get to the church before me." She smiled at her mother. "And be careful with those pretty shoes while driving the Runabout."

The three women fussed a bit more, and Anna insisted on helping with the veil. But they finally departed, and Katy was alone in her room. As she slipped on her lacy gloves, she took a moment to examine her image in the cheval mirror. The dress was truly perfect. Delicate, graceful layers of creamy white lace, intricate embroidery . . . refined and sweet and beautiful. She remembered designing this dress last winter, thinking it would be a perfect wedding dress but never dreaming it would be hers. And only days ago, she'd been prepared to marry Jim in a Washington city hall while wearing her blue silk suit.

Hearing Randall's horn again, she went over to her window to pick up the flower arrangement that Bernice had brought upstairs earlier. It was a lovely arrangement of pale pink roses, delphinium, and sweet peas. She could ask for nothing better.

"Katy Girl!" Mac called up the stairs. "You're not going to be late for your own wedding, are you?"

"I'm coming, Grandfather," she called back happily and, with light feet, skipped down the stairs.

"Oh, my!" Mac's jaw dropped and his pale blue eyes grew wide. "You are as pretty as a picture, Katy."

"Thank you." She linked her hand into his good arm. "Lead the way."

Randall Douglas, looking refined in a pin-striped dark suit, opened the back door for them. "You look beautiful," he told Katy as he helped her and Mac get in.

"Oh, darling," Clara gushed from the front seat, "you really do look gorgeous."

"The dress turned out perfectly," Katy told her. "Thank you for helping with it."

Mac continued to hold Katy's hand as Randall drove them to the church. "Are you nervous?" he asked quietly.

"A little." She smiled. "But mostly I'm just happy."

The others chatted a bit, but their words seemed to float right over her, as if she were in a dream. But before long, Mac was leading her down the aisle of the church, and there, standing by Reverend Williamson, was her beloved. Jim looked strong and tall and incredibly handsome in his dress uniform, but it was his smile that warmed her heart. And then, gazing deeply into one another's eyes, they repeated their vows and exchanged rings and kissed. It was all perfect.

Finally, they turned around to face the crowd of friends and family packed into the church and, seeing their brightly smiling faces—and many still wiping their eyes—Katy was reminded of how much she loved this town that had embraced her over the past year. How sweet to have such a wonderful community surrounding her in this memorable moment of her life. She turned to Jim. "Doesn't it feel good to be home?"

"Home is where the heart is, darling." He kissed her again and, wearing huge smiles, they paraded down the aisle, accepting the congratulations and best wishes of their loved ones.

Anna had never seen Mac's house so filled with guests. The after-wedding luncheon was supposed to have been for family and close friends, but apparently they had more close friends than they realized. Still, it was fun seeing everyone supportive of the newlyweds.

"Do we have enough food?" Anna whispered to Bernice as she carried a fresh platter of roast beef out to the dining room where the buffet was laid out.

"It may be like the loaves and fishes." Bernice winked. "I've been praying for the Good Lord to provide."

Anna chuckled. "Well, let me know if we run low. If so, I'll call the hotel restaurant to see about some backup."

Fortunately, they didn't run low, and everyone seemed happy and well fed as the festivities wound down. "I think it's time you got ready for the train," Anna said quietly to Katy. "Need any help?"

"I'd love help." Katy beamed at her. "Thanks."

They excused themselves, and Anna followed her daughter upstairs, a bittersweet mixture of feelings coming over her as they went into Katy's room. On one hand, she was pleased and proud of her young, headstrong daughter. But on the other hand, it felt like the end of an era. As Anna unbuttoned Katy's dress, her eyes welled up again.

"Oh, Mother." Katy frowned. "I want you to be happy for me."

"I am happy for you." Anna reached for a handkerchief. "I guess I'm just feeling sorry for myself."

"Well, it's not like you're losing me." Katy slid off her pretty dress. "After all, I'll be back as soon as Jim returns to camp."

Anna dabbed her tears. "Yes, that's true. But you won't be my little girl anymore. You'll be *Mrs. Jim Stafford.*"

Katy hugged her. "I'll always be your little girl."

Anna smiled. "Yes, of course, you will." She helped Katy slip into the first layer of her traveling suit. It was a lovely green-blue that brought out the color of her eyes. "You were such a beautiful bride, dear. But you'll make an even more beautiful wife."

"I hope so."

As Anna helped Katy with her outfit, she attempted to give her some motherly advice but was relieved to find out that Ellen had already been disbursing her own "words of wisdom."

"Do you think Ellen and Lawrence are happy?" Anna asked as she watched Katy pin her hat into place.

"Not particularly." Katy adjusted the angle slightly. "But that's Lawrence's fault."

"Oh?" Anna picked up Katy's gloves, stroking the soft kid leather.

"Ellen is trying to make things work. But Lawrence sometimes acts like a spoiled brat." She reached for a glove. "But at least Ellen and I are friends again." Now Katy explained about giving Ellen charge of the Red Cross donations.

"Oh?" Anna tried not to look concerned.

"She was so happy that I entrusted her with it, Mother." Katy slipped on her other glove. "And she's agreed to be in my chapter. I plan to start it when I get back."

"That's nice. I want to be involved too." Anna hated to be suspicious of people, but the newspaperwoman in her couldn't help but question things. "Would you like me to take care of the Red Cross funds for you—I mean, after the luncheon wraps up?"

"No, I told Ellen to just deposit the money into the account I created at the bank. It will be safe there."

Anna just nodded.

"Goodness, it's later than I thought." Katy held up her watch pendant. "Jim and I should be headed for the train station by now."

They embraced, Anna fighting more tears, and then they hurried down the stairs and outside to where Jim was waiting and Randall was warming up his gleaming car. Wedding guests lined the walkway, tossing rice at the heads of the newly-weds and shouting out cheerful farewells and best wishes. And just like that, Jim and Katy got into the back of the car and everyone watched as they drove away.

"I hope they don't miss their train." Lucille looked concerned.

"I doubt that." Clara laughed. "Randall planned to make good time. That's why I decided to stay behind."

"Hopefully they won't get into a crash on the way," Mac said, his brow furrowed.

"Don't worry, Mac." Anna patted his shoulder. "They'll be just fine."

The guests were starting to trickle away now, thanking Mac and Anna and going their ways. Anna felt a rush of concern as she noticed Ellen and Lawrence coming out of the house. Ellen had her handbag and parasol, and Lawrence was carrying the two Red Cross jars that Katy had put together for donations. Both jars appeared to be stuffed with cash.

"Would you like me to take care of these for you?" Anna offered in a friendly tone.

"That's all right," Lawrence answered. "We'll get it to the bank on our way home."

"Oh, good." Anna nodded. "Looks as if Sunset Cove's Red Cross chapter will be off to a good start."

"It was so nice of Katy to do this," Ellen opened her parasol. "So generous."

"I plan to write a piece about our new Red Cross chapter for the newspaper," Anna said quickly. Perhaps the thought had only just occurred to her, but it was a good idea. "I'd like to know how much was donated to include in my article." She forced a cheery smile. "Will you let me know, Ellen? After you get back from the bank?"

"Sure." Ellen nodded eagerly. "I'll call you on the telephone later."

Feeling somewhat reassured, Anna told them goodbye and went into the house. Hopefully her suspicions were unfounded. But it couldn't hurt to be cautious when it came to Lawrence Bouchard.

Several friends, including Clara and Sarah Rose, had remained at the house to help Anna and Bernice with the cleanup. The women worked congenially together, putting the rooms back to rights, carrying dishes to the kitchen, and then washing them and putting things away.

"Well, the newlyweds must be on the train by now," Clara said as she dried the last plate a good while later.

"What a whirlwind we've had these past few days." Lucille sat down at the kitchen table.

"And we so appreciate all the help." Anna closed the china cabinet. "We couldn't have done this without everyone."

"It was such fun to see the whole thing," Sarah Rose hung a dishtowel on the rack. "I'm so glad I was here for it."

Anna filled the big copper kettle at the sink. "How about a cup of tea, everyone?"

"Here." Bernice took the kettle. "Let me take care of that. You ladies go sit down in the living room, and I'll bring it out to you."

"Lovely." Lucille took Anna's hand. "It's about time we relaxed a bit."

The group of women settled into the living room, chattering about the events of the last few days, commenting on the guests, the clothing, the food . . . but Anna was too distracted to pay attention. It had been a couple of hours since Ellen and Lawrence had left. The bank would be closing soon. Had the Red Cross deposit been made as promised? And if so, why hadn't Ellen called?

Anna was tempted to call the bank and ask but didn't want to overstep her bounds. And yet . . . what if Lawrence had absconded with the money? Katy would be crushed. Anna was about to go to the telephone when she heard it ringing. "I'll get it," she called out to Bernice, hurrying into the hallway to answer it.

"Oh, Anna, this is Ellen. I nearly forgot to call you. I'm so sorry. I suppose I was a bit distracted . . . and perhaps a little worn out. But no worries—the Red Cross deposit is at the bank.

And the total was $273.64. Can you believe it?"

"That's wonderful." Anna let out a relieved sigh. "What a lot of bandages and supplies and knitting wool that will buy."

"Katy should be pleased."

Anna thanked Ellen for taking care of the deposit and then, feeling as if a weighty load had just been lifted, she returned to her lady friends and tea. Yes, all in all, it had been a very good day.

The first few days of married life passed blissfully for Katy and Jim. Sometimes Katy was so happy she felt as if she were the lead actress in a romantic motion picture. From riding a ferry boat to Victoria, to taking in the scenic beauty of the Seattle area, to window shopping in the city, to dining at the finest restaurants . . . It felt like a delightful dream. Then she would pinch herself and remember that it was real—and that she should savor each moment with her dear, sweet husband.

But suddenly it was Sunday and it felt that her beautiful dream was coming to an abrupt end. And thanks to her bright idea, it was turning into a rather unsettling end—making her question her insistence on accompanying Jim back to his army camp. He'd tried to put her back onto the southbound train this morning, but she'd protested until he agreed to change her ticket and store her luggage for the three-ten train. It was simply because she wanted to spend every minute possible with him. And so they'd ridden the nearly empty train to Camp Lewis. But upon arrival there, she began to feel uneasy.

Witnessing the multitude of soldiers—or doughboys, as people were calling them—dressed in field uniforms and preparing to load the long train and seeing the wooden crates of ammunition and supplies stacked on the platform all proved a harsh reminder that a horrific war was being waged overseas. Oh, it wasn't that she'd forgotten about it, but she had managed to push it into the corners of her mind. But watching the young men loading boxcars and wondering how many of those soldiers would make it back cast a dark shadow on what had otherwise been a perfectly magical week.

Jim, oblivious to her concerns, seemed happy to be back in camp. He gave Katy a quick tour of Camp Lewis and introduced her to a few of his buddies. But careful to keep from interfering with the busy activities in preparation for war, he wrapped it up within an hour.

"This Washington location has proven ideal for training troops," he said as they stood outside the officers' quarters. "The weather conditions here are similar to the battlefronts where our men are headed." He chuckled. "Although I hear there's more mud over there. Hard to imagine that."

Katy shivered. Although it was mid-June, the sky was overcast, and a cool breeze insisted that her summer-weight dress wasn't warm enough. She could understand why Red Cross volunteers were so busily knitting woolen socks and scarves for soldiers. How would it feel to be cold and wet . . . and shot at?

"I've arranged for you to ride with General Proctor's wife back to Seattle." Jim handed Katy her train and baggage tickets. "They'll drop you at the train station, but you'll have to hurry to catch the three-ten to Portland." He peered into her eyes. "And you have everything arranged with your friend Rebecca there?"

"She promised to meet me and put me up for the night," she assured him. "No worries."

"By the time you get back to Sunset Cove, I'll probably be somewhere in Montana."

"Will you write to me before you ship out from the East Coast?"

"Of course." He touched her cheek. "You'll probably have several letters from me by then."

She smiled. "I'm so lucky to have married a writer." A honking horn made her jump, and soon Mrs. Proctor was urging Katy to tell Jim good-bye.

"Parting is such sweet sorrow," the older woman chimed at them. "Best to just get it over with." She chuckled. "Kiss the girl, soldier."

And so he did. And clinging tightly to his

251

woolen uniform jacket, Katy kissed him back . . . then reluctantly let him go. "I love you," she whispered.

"I love you too." He smiled. "Forever."

"Come on, darling girl," Mrs. Proctor called out. "We don't want you to miss your train." And then Katy was swept away and loaded into the back of the big black car. She turned to wave and then watch out the rear window as Jim, still waving, grew smaller and smaller. Would she ever see him again?

CHAPTER 20

On Monday morning Anna was surprised to discover that Lawrence Bouchard hadn't shown up for what was supposed to be his first day of work at the newspaper.

"Do you think he's even coming?" Frank asked her with a suspicious expression.

"He said he was." Anna sorted through the mail Virginia had just laid on her desk. "He seemed to earnestly want the job."

"Or was he just playing you?"

Anna looked up. "Playing me?"

"Saying what he thought you wanted to hear." Frank scowled.

"Oh, I don't think so. I explained that he'd have to work hard and prove himself. He seemed to accept that. I really think young Lawrence has decided to buckle down and get serious about work." She drummed her fingers on her desk, thinking. "I probably shouldn't divulge this because the news isn't out yet, but I know I can trust you to keep it under your hat."

Frank leaned forward with interest. "Yes?"

"Lawrence disclosed to me that his wife is expecting a baby, due to arrive around Christmastime. For that reason, he seemed serious about securing solid employment."

Frank pursed his lips. "Is that so?"

"You sound skeptical." Anna frowned. "Do you think Lawrence would make something like that up? Just to garner my sympathy?"

"I'm not suggesting that." He rubbed his chin, a hard-to-read look on his face, but she suspected skepticism, which made her feel strangely defensive of Lawrence.

"Because only last week, I noticed that Ellen appeared different," she declared. "She seemed fairly worn out after all the wedding activities. According to Lawrence, she hasn't told anyone yet—not even her mother. Apparently she wants Lawrence to be set with a steady job before she goes public with her condition. Can't say that I blame her for that."

"No . . . I can understand her concern." Wearing a serious expression, Frank sat down in the chair across from her desk. "I came in here to tell you that I was down at the docks yesterday. Just taking a stroll with the family. And I happened to notice that Bud Griggs's fishing boat was out."

"Yes?"

"Well, I didn't want to appear too curious about it yesterday since I had my wife and boys with me. But I stopped by there this morning to check.

Seems that Bud and Fred and someone else went fishing Friday morning."

"Someone else?" Anna felt a wave of concern and irritation. "You mean Lawrence Bouchard?"

"That'd be my guess."

"And the boat hasn't been back since?" Anna picked up a pencil, spinning it between her fingers.

Frank nodded grimly.

"Yes, but that's not so very odd. Boats are known to stay out for a few days. Maybe they're crabbing and—"

"In June?"

She sighed. "I suppose you're right to be suspicious. But what now? Have you mentioned anything to Chief Rollins yet?"

"I was about to but wanted to speak to you first, especially since you hired Bouchard. I didn't want to implicate him if he was here at work."

"I appreciate that."

"And I would've tipped you off last night, but you've been so busy with the wedding and all last week. Besides, I wasn't sure. I guess I'm still not."

She laid down the pencil. "We don't know for certain that Lawrence was the third person on that boat, but I know how to find out. I'm going to pay a visit to Kathleen's and speak to Ellen."

Frank stood. "Then I'll leave this in your hands. I've got a lot to get done today, especially

255

if you're still planning to leave early to welcome Katy home."

"That was my plan. We'll see now." She was already reaching for her hat. "I'll let you know what I find out."

As Anna walked down Main Street, she knew she'd have to be careful of what she said to Ellen. She didn't want to upset or worry her, but she did want to get to the bottom of this. And she wanted to do it without alarming anyone else. She would need to make a plan. To her relief, Ellen was working in the front of the dress shop.

"Good morning," Ellen said cheerfully. "Are you here to shop? We have some pretty new hats for the summer."

"I came for some stockings," she told Ellen. "I'm running low, and I've heard there will be an increased shortage of silk. I thought I should get a couple of pairs."

"A shortage of silk?" Ellen frowned.

"You know, because of the war." Anna followed Ellen to the cabinet where stockings were stored.

"Speaking of the war, I was thinking about Jim Stafford this morning. I assume he's on his way by now. At least that's what Katy told me. And she gets home today, doesn't she?"

"That's right. The afternoon train."

"That must've been sad for her." Ellen removed a box of stockings. "Telling her husband goodbye like that."

"I'm sure it was difficult." Anna took in a breath. "Speaking of husbands, I thought yours was coming in to work today."

"Today?" Ellen blinked. "But he's not due back from a deep-sea fishing trip until this afternoon."

"Oh, so he went fishing?" Anna tried to sound interested. "How long has he been gone?"

"Since Friday morning." Ellen's eyes twinkled. "To be honest, I've sort of enjoyed having this time to myself. Our hotel room feels a little crowded at times. It's lovely to just relax with a book, or take a nice long bath. Although I do look forward to having him back."

"Yes, I'm sure you do." Anna hid her disappointment. So Frank's assumptions had been right. Apparently, Lawrence had been playing her. Certainly, if he was out there running prohibited alcohol, which everyone knew could be a lucrative business, he would have no interest in working for the newspaper. And she would have no interest in employing him either.

It took awhile, but finally Ellen located two pairs of silk stockings and rang them up. Anna had to control herself from rushing her as she carefully wrapped them in white paper and tied the package with a string. "Thank you." Anna forced a smile and was about to go out when Lucille came in.

"Oh, Anna, you're just who I wanted to see. Do you have a minute?"

Anna wanted to say no but didn't want to draw attention, especially since a couple of women were examining the millinery section. So she let Lucille lead her into the back room where the seamstresses, including Clara and Sarah Rose, were at work. Naturally, this resulted in more greetings, inquiries as to Katy's arrival, and so on.

"That's what I wanted to ask," Lucille told Anna as she led her into the office in the back. "I know it's late notice, but I'd love to have you and Mac and Katy over for dinner tonight. I already told Sally about it and was about to call you. Would you mind?"

"Of course not. And I'm sure Katy would enjoy it too." Anna nodded. "But be sure to let Mac know so he can give Bernie and Mickey the night off."

"Oh, good." Lucille began to gush about how lovely the wedding festivities had been and how eager she was to hear about Katy's time in Seattle.

"If you'll excuse me, I have a lot to do today." Anna patted Lucille's shoulder. "It's very nice of you to plan an evening for us. I'll see you tonight." And without saying another word to anyone in the shop, she slipped out the back door, hurried down the alley, and went straight to the police station, only to learn that Chief Rollins was not there. His secretary offered to take a message, but Anna was unwilling to leave anything in writing.

"Do you know where he is or when he'll be back?"

"He's meeting with the hospital committee. I believe he's at your house, Anna."

"Oh, yes." Anna suddenly remembered Mac mentioning this yesterday. "I'll catch him there." So Anna hurried home and, after excusing herself for interrupting the hospital committee, she asked to speak to the chief in private.

In Mac's sitting room, Anna quickly relayed the news of possible rum-running. "I realize it's probably too late to get the coast guard down here in time," she said apologetically. "I only just learned of it this morning. But, according to Ellen, who thinks Lawrence is on a fishing trip, they're expected back this afternoon."

"Maybe they *are* on a fishing trip." The chief looked out over the ocean with a longing expression. "It's certainly been good weather for it. Makes me wish I was retired like I'd planned on. I'd be out there fishing myself."

"Do you really think a man like Lawrence Bouchard is fishing?" Anna demanded. "And has been since Friday?"

He chuckled. "Well, I doubt he's got on his fancy, citified clothes."

"I did see him buying some boots and a rain-coat."

The chief nodded. "I appreciate the tip, Anna. I'll look into it later in the day. Although I doubt they'd bring the boat to dock in broad daylight."

"Probably not. I can't imagine them unloading their contraband with a lot of folks around to see."

"Albert and his boys usually waited till late at night, after everyone was in bed." He frowned. "I suppose this means another sleepless night for me. I think I'm getting too old for this."

Anna felt sorry for the chief. She knew he'd planned to hang up his hat by now, but with losing who he'd thought was his right-hand man last winter and with so many other young men being drafted, it seemed Chief Rollins was stuck for the time being. "If it makes you feel any better, Frank and I will be doing surveillance tonight too."

"I suppose it makes a good news story." He sighed. "But another black eye for our town."

"At least you could be nipping this one in the bud," she said.

He nodded. "I'll send a couple of my men down to keep an eye on the docks for the rest of the day. But I do expect the real action—if there is any—won't be until much later. And I know I don't need to warn you to be careful tonight. I understand you want to get your story but keep a safe distance and don't get in our way."

She agreed to this, and while the chief used the

hallway telephone to call the station, she exited through the kitchen, tipping off Bernice about Lucille's dinner party plans tonight. "Let Mac know too," she called as she hurried out the back door.

Anna's mind raced as she headed back to the newspaper office. Almost there, something unsettling occurred to her. Lawrence Bouchard would've needed cash to purchase illegal alcohol outside of the Oregon borders, and everyone knew he was broke. Suddenly she remembered Katy's Red Cross money—the money Ellen had assured her she'd deposited. And no one besides Katy should have had the authority to withdraw it from the bank since she'd set up the account.

Instead of going to the newspaper office, Anna returned to the dress shop. Waiting for Ellen to finish helping the ladies with hats, Anna took her aside. "I'm sorry. I meant to ask you earlier if I could pick up the bank receipt for the Red Cross deposit and I completely forgot."

"Receipt?" Ellen looked blank.

"Yes, I need to give it to Katy so she can record it in her Red Cross bank book."

"Oh, well, I don't have a receipt. Lawrence must have it."

"Lawrence?"

"Yes. He made the deposit for me on Wednesday. I was so worn out after the wedding, he insisted I go home and rest." Ellen blushed. "He's very sweet like that, very protective of me."

"Yes, that's nice." Anna nodded, trying to conceal her distress as she moved toward the door. "I see."

"But I'll ask him for it this evening." Ellen smiled brightly.

"Yes, that'd be good. Have a lovely day, Ellen." Feeling rather sickened, Anna went outside. Lawrence had probably never deposited the Red Cross funds. How else could he have paid for the "fishing trip" and purchased the banned alcohol? This was turning out to be far worse than she'd expected. More than ever she wanted to get to the bottom of the whole, ugly mess. And even though it would hurt Ellen—and Anna knew it would—she wanted Lawrence to be caught red-handed and to suffer the consequences of his extreme selfishness and terrible choices. And once he was caught, it would become front-page news in the midweek paper. Lawrence Bouchard's name would be mud in Sunset Cove by Wednesday. But poor Ellen . . . How would she fare?

Anna asked Frank to meet with her right after lunch, and by one o'clock, she was telling him about her conversation with Chief Rollins and her suspicions about the Red Cross funds.

"I hate to say I told you so." Frank's smile didn't look happy.

"Yes, yes, I know. Now put everything else aside and mock up a story."

"I already started one," he confessed.

"Right. And hold room for it on the front page," she said. "And make the headline big. We need to shock this community with a strong warning that Sunset Cove is not a haven for crooks and—" She stopped at the sound of a knock on her office door. "I guess that's all for now."

Frank opened the door and to both of their stunned surprise, there stood Lawrence Bouchard with his hat in his hands. Dressed in a dirty canvas coat, he was unkempt and unshaven but smiling nervously. Anna was momentarily speechless but bursting with questions and hoping she could control her anger.

CHAPTER 21

"I apologize for the interruption," Lawrence Bouchard said politely. "And I'm sorry to show up looking like this, but I wanted to speak to you, Miss McDowell."

Anna exchanged glances with Frank. "And I'd like a few words with you as well, Mr. Bouchard," she said stiffly.

"I'll just go check on this story." Frank held up his notebook with a quizzical look. "And I'll speak to Chief Rollins about the matter we were just discussing."

"Thanks. Let me know what he says." Anna nodded to Lawrence. "Come in. And close the door." She waved to the empty chair across from her desk, waiting to speak until he sat. "What's going on?" she asked in flat tone.

He frowned down at his dirty clothes. "Well, as you may have surmised, I've been on a deep-sea fishing trip these past few days. I thought I'd be back in time for work today, but the fellows I went out with were reluctant to return before getting their catch."

"And did they get their catch?" She studied him closely.

"Unfortunately, they did not." He glumly shook his head. "I suppose I was bad luck."

"*Were* you?" She picked up a pencil, rolling it between her palms.

He shrugged. "Maybe. I mean the, uh, the fishing trip didn't exactly go smoothly."

For some reason she believed him. "Did anyone get hurt?"

"No. But Bud's boat is going to need some work."

"Oh." She wanted to say *good!* but wasn't ready to tip her hand just yet.

"I hope you won't hold it against me . . . I mean, for missing my first day of work. I promise I'll be here tomorrow, on time and dressed better than this." He held up his dirty hands with a scowl.

"So you still want this job?"

"Yes, of course. I told you I did."

She leaned forward, narrowing her eyes. "Then you better be straight with me. I have some tough questions, and I want honest answers. Do you understand?"

He sat up straighter then nodded. "Yes. Sure."

"For starters, you weren't really fishing, were you?"

"Well . . . we did do a little fishing."

"But that's not why you went out there, is it?"

He grimaced. "Well, no . . . not exactly."

She nodded, concealing her surprise that he'd been honest. "You were doing something more lucrative than fishing . . . something illegal . . . right?"

He barely nodded but said nothing.

"So you pretended to go fishing, but you made a run down to California. And there you picked up black-market alcohol to sell for profit here in Oregon."

"I guess you have it all figured out."

"Not completely." She drummed her pencil on her desk pad, planning her next question. "Wasn't anyone on the docks to meet you?"

"To meet me? Oh, you mean the police."

She nodded, waiting.

"Yes, a cop was there. He inspected our boat and gear and everything."

"And?"

"He didn't find anything."

"Nothing?" She felt her anger boiling up again.

"Because we didn't have any alcohol aboard."

"So you stashed it somewhere along the coastline? Dropped it offshore in crab pots with markers?"

"No, we sold it."

"Where?"

"Does it matter where?"

"Are you going to come clean with me or not?"

"We sold it in Coos Bay." He narrowed his

eyes. "But I swear if you repeat any of this, I will deny it."

"Then why are you confessing to me now?"

He shrugged. "I need the job . . . and I guess I thought I could trust you."

Well, this just made her madder. "Do not trust me, Lawrence. I'm a newspaperwoman and a law-abiding citizen."

"Yes, but you're fair."

"Fair?" She frowned. "The fair thing to do is turn you in right now."

"Are you going to do that?" He looked genuinely scared.

"Not until you answer my biggest question—and you better tell me the truth. You took the Red Cross money, didn't you?"

"No." He slowly shook his head with downcast eyes. "It's in the bank."

"Really?" She didn't believe him.

He looked directly at her. "I swear it's in there, Miss McDowell. Go check if you don't believe me."

"So you've just been to the bank." She pointed the pencil upward. "You just made a deposit into the Red Cross account to cover up the fact that you stole it last Wednesday?" He looked down at his dirty hands and nodded.

"I figured as much." She let out a disgusted sigh.

"If it makes you feel any better, I'm not proud

of what I did." His eyes seemed sad, but it could have been part of his guise.

"Then *why* did you do it?" she demanded.

"I was desperate. I needed cash—badly."

"That's no excuse. I've been desperate before, Lawrence." She told him about being alone in the big city with a new baby and an incarcerated husband. "I was frightened and alone and broke, but I never broke the law, and I never stole anything from anyone."

His eyes were wide. "Is that really true? I mean, about your husband being in prison and the baby and all?"

She nodded grimly. "And it looks like you want to put Ellen in the same position. And that just makes me—"

"I don't want that! I truly don't. I didn't realize it last week but I do now. It all came together for me out there on the ocean. I knew I'd made a bad mistake. That's why I unloaded the stuff in Coos Bay. Sure, I knew I could get more for it up here, but I just wanted to be rid of it. And to never do that again."

"That's the truth?"

"I swear it is, Miss McDowell."

"Does Ellen have any idea what you were up to?"

"Of course not. She thinks I was fishing."

Anna believed him. "Has Ellen told you everything about her dad and her brother?"

"I know her father died and that AJ is in the army."

"That's *all* you know?" Anna studied him closely. "Has no one told you about how and why Ellen's father died last fall or why AJ so eagerly enlisted last winter?"

"I know that AJ had some trouble with the law, but to tell the truth, I wasn't paying much attention to those things back then. And Ellen never spoke much of her family. She never wanted to."

"I can understand that, but it's hard to believe you haven't heard about this." Anna told him a shortened but dramatic version of last year's rum-running and the devastating consequences.

"I do remember the explosion at Charlie's and the insinuations that there were illegal activities up there. But I never had anything to do with any of it."

"And your friends?"

"You probably haven't noticed, but I don't have many friends in this town. I spend most of my time with Ellen."

"Bud and Fred?"

"I barely know them."

"You just spent four days with them."

"The worst four days of my life. If I could take it all back and do it differently, I would."

She didn't think he was lying but said nothing.

"I got terribly seasick on the first day out. I begged them just to leave me somewhere on land. But they wanted their cut of the money." He closed his eyes and shook his head as if reliving it. "It was terrible. I really wanted to die. I even considered just slipping off the boat to drown. But then I remembered Ellen and the baby. So I held it together until we met my connection in Crescent City. I paid for the alcohol and helped the guys load it onto the boat. But then I refused to go with them. I wanted to take a train back here. But they weren't having it."

"Why?"

"Because it had been my plan, and they weren't letting me off the hook. Bud actually whacked me on the head." He reached up to rub the back of his head. "When I woke up, we were out at sea again."

"This is quite a tale, Lawrence." Was he just reeling her in?

"I swear it's true. I still have a lump on my head. You can feel it if you don't believe me."

She waved her hand. "No thanks."

"So I told the guys we were going to sell the stuff in Coos Bay. I knew it wouldn't be as profitable farther north, but I didn't care—and I didn't tell them that. They were just glad to be paid off. By then I must've had my sea legs and coming by boat was the fastest way to get home. But as soon as Sunset Cove came into sight, about the same time as Fred's boat started to take on water, I informed my *fishing friends* that I was done with this. They weren't too pleased with me. I suppose I'd given them the impression I was going to start up a big rum-running business. But I'm out."

"You're sure about that?"

"I swear to you, Miss McDowell, I deeply regret what I did. It was incredibly stupid. I thought it was a smart way to make some quick money, but I wish I'd never done it."

"So did you make some quick money, Lawrence?"

He blew out a long sigh then nodded. "I guess so."

"But it's *dirty* money."

He shrugged. "I just wanted enough cash to get caught up some, and to put toward a retail business that could support Ellen and the baby. You know, to start a new life."

"You want to start a new life with dirty money?"

"I don't know." He looked back down at his lap.

"I honestly don't know what to make of you, Lawrence." The truth was, she felt a bit sorry for him. He looked so miserable and hopeless and dejected. But was he just playing her? "I'll admit I'm caught off guard by your confession. It seems a risky thing to tell me all this."

His eyes looked scared. "Are you going to report me to the police? Or put this in the newspaper? Because, if you do, I'll deny it. And there's no proof. The cop down at the docks can attest to that."

"What about the missing money that you replaced? Or the fact that I know all the details now?"

"Fine. You can tell everyone about it. But I'll just disappear. Hopefully everyone will forget about me by the time the baby is born . . . and Ellen won't suffer too much humiliation." His eyes actually looked misty as he pulled out a grubby bandana to wipe his nose.

Anna didn't know what to say. She closed her eyes and prayed a silent prayer, asking for wisdom.

"I guess I shouldn't have told you," he said in a husky voice. "I'm sure you think it's your responsibility to turn me—"

"Wait." She opened her eyes, holding up a hand. "I have an idea."

"An idea?" He frowned.

"What if you anonymously donate all your illegal profits to the hospital fund and the Red Cross fund?"

"What?" He looked confused.

"If you gave up that money, and if you promise to never do anything like this again, I won't go public with your story."

"*All* my money?" His eyes grew wide.

"All your illegally obtained money, Lawrence. Your dirty money."

Now he closed his eyes—tightly—looking as if a real battle were waging inside of him. Anna waited in silence, wondering if she was crazy to make this kind of offer to him. But then she remembered Wesley Kempton. Mac's protégé reporter had made bad choices too, involved himself with the wrong people. And she remembered her regrets for not having helped him more. And then it was too late. Perhaps it wasn't too late for Lawrence Bouchard.

"Well, what is your answer?" she pressed. "It's your choice. But be assured of this—if you insist on keeping your dirty money, I won't keep your story quiet. I will headline it on the front page. And you most assuredly will not have employment at this newspaper."

"You mean I could still have a job?" He looked hopeful.

"Only if you make this right and swear you'll never run black-market goods again—*ever.*"

She saw him swallow hard then nod. "I agree," he said solemnly. "Now, if you'll turn your back, I'll get out my money belt for you."

She turned her chair around, nervously listening to the rustle of clothing and belt buckle and still wondering if she were mistaken to partner in this wild plan. Wasn't this a bit like taking the law into her own hands? It actually felt like something Mac might do. And, strangely enough, she knew that he would approve.

"Here you go."

She spun her chair about in time to see him plunk a dirty white money belt onto her desk. "Oh my." She smiled as she picked up the heavy bag by its strap. "I don't know how much is in here, but it will help a lot of people, Lawrence. For Sunset Cove Hospital and for soldiers in the war overseas."

"I guess I should be glad about that." His tone was sullen.

"I have one more question."

"What?" He looked so downhearted she almost didn't want to ask.

"And it's important you tell me the truth." She explained the rumor she'd heard about embezzlement at his family's business in San Francisco. "What happened?"

His eyes flashed angrily. "It's a total lie."

"Please, explain."

He sank into the chair, just shaking his head. "I did not embezzle."

"Then why the rumor?"

With a sigh, he told her about an older employee in the family business who'd been jealous of Lawrence's increased responsibilities. "When I came home married, my father put me in charge of more responsibilities and considerably increased my salary. But to be honest, it was probably more than I was ready for. And Gerald Thompson knew it. I was doing the managerial job that should've been his, and he resented me—and my family. He was the one who took money and tried to pin it on me. At first my father believed Gerald, but my grandfather knew I was innocent. It got a little ugly. And my feelings got hurt. My grandfather encouraged me to leave and make a fresh start. He even gave me funds to help." Lawrence let out a long sad sigh. "Ellen and I didn't manage that money very well. That's why we wound up here . . . and nearly broke." He looked into her eyes. "And as hard as it is to admit that, it feels like a weight lifted too. And I swear it's the truth."

"I believe you." She nodded.

"And you could easily get your mother to verify it. She and Grandfather are on good terms."

"I know. But I don't think it's necessary. Thank you for your honesty."

He stood with what almost looked like a smile. "All I want now is to see Ellen . . . and to take a bath and burn these disgusting clothes."

"See you tomorrow morning," she said. "Don't be late."

Anna put the money belt into her briefcase, hiding it amidst papers and files. She'd have to concoct a safe plan to get it anonymously to the hospital and Red Cross, but she could think about that later. She had just sat back down to her typewriter when Frank returned, his face full of curiosity. But before he could question her, she asked if he'd seen Chief Rollins.

"Yes, and I told him you had Lawrence here at the newspaper."

"And what did the chief say?"

"Well, the cop who'd been down at the dock was back at the station. Apparently, there wasn't a shred of evidence on the boat. And, naturally, Fred and Bud claimed they'd been fishing. They even had a few fish to prove it."

"And the chief bought that?"

"Not much else he could do. Although he plans to keep an eye on those boys and their boat. And Lawrence too. And he wants to talk to you."

"Oh." She just nodded, wondering what she would say to the chief. She knew she couldn't lie.

"What did Lawrence say?" Frank looked eager.

"That he'd been fishing and hadn't enjoyed it much." She smiled. "He'd been dreadfully seasick a good deal of the time. He also said that Bud and Fred were not his friends. And that he never plans to go back out there with them again."

"That's all?" Frank frowned.

"That's all for now."

"What about the Red Cross money?" he demanded. "Where's that?"

"In the bank—safe and sound."

"Oh." He sounded disappointed.

"Now, if you'll excuse me, I need to go speak to the chief."

"And I've got work to do. Need to revive that previous story for the front page and a dozen other things."

"By the way, Lawrence will be in to work tomorrow." Her smile felt more like a smirk. "And I told him not to be late."

As Anna headed for the police station, she felt uneasy. She knew the chief deserved to hear the full story, and she intended to tell it to him. But what if he came down hard on Lawrence? He might even accuse her of aiding and abetting a criminal. And wasn't it true? Hadn't she just taken the law into her own hands? But as she walked through town, she prayed the chief would listen . . . and that he'd be understanding.

CHAPTER 22

After much shouting and arguing and pleading of Lawrence Bouchard's case by telling his whole sad story, the chief finally agreed that Anna's plan was acceptable. "To be honest, there's little we can do without proof anyway," he conceded. "And at least I know enough to have my men watch Bud and Fred. Does Bouchard think they'll try this again?"

"I think he's worried. It sounds like his buddies were pretty miffed at him for pulling the plug on the rum-running business."

"I just hope he means it. And I expect you to keep a close eye on him at the newspaper, Anna. And if anything fishy develops—if Bouchard suddenly decides to go fishing again—I expect you to come to me immediately."

"I think he's done with boats and fishing. His bout with seasickness probably helped to knock his criminal aspirations out of him."

"Well, we can all be thankful for that." He slowly shook his head, gazing over the stacks of bills that they'd counted together. "This will be most helpful in finishing off the hospital. And not bad for the Red Cross either." He pressed his forefinger to his lips. "But it will remain our secret."

She simply nodded. "And if you'll excuse me, it's about time for the afternoon train, and I promised to meet Katy."

"Give the sweet girl a hug from me." He shook Anna's hand, clasping it for a moment. "And thank you for coming to me with this. I know it wasn't easy."

"Oh, I figured we'd exchange some heated words." She smiled. "But I felt sure you'd do the right thing."

"Not everything is black and white when it comes to enforcing the law." He picked up the bills, put them into a desk drawer, and locked it. "The older I get, the more I realize there's more than one way to attain justice."

Anna knew that Katy was tired as they drove home from the station, but it seemed like more than that. Hopefully she wasn't coming down with something. "Are you feeling all right?" Anna asked as they pulled up to the carriage house where Mickey was already waiting, ready to unload the baggage.

"I suppose I'm feeling sorry for myself," Katy admitted.

"Oh?" Anna glanced at her daughter. Katy had

never been a person to indulge in self-pity. Not for long anyway.

"I haven't even been married a week . . . and now Jim is gone." Her eyes filled. "And I may never see him again."

"And then again, you may." Anna got out of the car, pausing to greet Mickey then waiting for Katy. She slipped an arm around her daughter's slender waist. "And that's what you need to keep telling yourself, Katy. You need to think he's coming back. He's coming back."

"But you know that many soldiers won't come back, Mother. You print those stories in the newspaper, listing the numbers of how many die . . . or get injured."

"Yes, that's true. But Jim seems like a survivor to me. I believe he'll come home. And that's what I'm praying for. Whenever you get worried for him, you need to realize that's just a reminder to pray."

"Do you think those prayers will really work?" Katy locked eyes with her.

"I do believe it. And that's where faith comes in." Anna opened the door to see Mac coming toward them. He embraced Katy, welcoming her home. After the sweet reunion, Katy excused herself to clean up for Lucille's dinner party.

"She seems different," Mac told Anna as they went to his sitting room where Bernice had already set out some tea things.

"She's married," Anna said lightly. "And I think she's worn out."

"Of course. She's done a lot of traveling. Hopefully she'll come back to her old lively self at dinnertime. I'd like to hear about Seattle. I was just reading up on it. Sounds like an interesting place."

Anna filled Mac in about Lawrence, but she told him a version similar to what she'd told Frank and, to her relief, it seemed he believed her. It wasn't that she liked deceiving him—she did not—but she knew it was in everyone's best interest to let the suspicions about Lawrence Bouchard sleep for now. But if he ever tried a stunt like that again, she was determined to shout it from the rooftops.

Katy continued to appear quieter than usual at dinner, but Anna attributed it to weariness and sadness. At least she came to life when she shared about the honeymoon in Seattle, describing the many sights, all they'd done and seen. And then she told them about Camp Lewis. "It was a huge place. Rows and rows of barracks. And soldiers preparing to leave the next morning. I can't shake the feeling," she said sadly, "that so many of them will never come home."

"Oh, darling." Lucille patted Katy's hand. "You must keep hope in your heart. Those patriotic young men are doing a wonderful thing, bravely serving their country like this. We, the ones who stay behind, must be equally brave."

"She's right," Mac told Katy. "It's our job to be supportive and to hope for the best. We can't fight over there, but we can do our part over here."

"I want to do my part too," Sarah Rose said quietly. Anna had been pleasantly surprised when she'd agreed to join them tonight. "If you think it's all right, Katy, I'd like to join your Red Cross chapter. I'm a good knitter."

"I know you are." Katy smiled at her. "You taught me to knit. And I'd be honored to have you join. Now we have three members. You and Ellen and me."

"And me too," Lucille assured her. "And Clara told me she wants to join."

"Which reminds me of something," Anna said, eagerly jumping in. "The Red Cross fund, Katy. You'll be shocked to learn how much was donated at your wedding." She told her the amount.

Katy's eyes lit up. "That much? How wonderful. I never would've guessed."

"That's not all," Anna looked around the table. "I just heard some good news that an anonymous donor has matched that number. Your Red Cross account now has nearly five-hundred and fifty dollars. Can you believe it?"

"That's amazing." Katy brightened considerably. "Oh, I can't wait to start having our chapter meetings. Think of all the good we can do with that much money. How exciting."

Mac beamed at Katy. "You make us all very proud, darling girl."

For the next few days, Katy tried to shake off the sadness that seemed to cling to her like the heavy fog bank over the ocean. But by the end of the week she received a cheerful letter from Jim, which definitely brightened her outlook. When she wrote back, she managed to keep her words light and uplifting too. She told him about her first Red Cross chapter meeting, how pleased she'd been that nineteen women had shown up, and added that Mac's house would not be a good place for them to meet and work. She told him how the ladies were excited and full of good ideas but that she was searching for a bigger place for them to meet. And she told him she loved him.

By late June, Katy had accumulated a small box of letters from Jim. He'd sent her one each day while traveling across the country but warned her she wouldn't receive letters while he was shipboard, though he'd continue to write daily. She too kept writing daily. She told him of securing the vacant second floor of the new hardware store for her chapter, and for a very reasonable amount of rent too. She described how her volunteer ladies were quickly equipping the room with worktables and chairs, two sewing machines, and a number of other useful items. And, as always, she told him she loved him and kept him continually in her prayers.

Katy knew from reading the newspapers—her family's and the *Oregonian* that Mac subscribed to—that US troops were starting to land in France. She knew that it was just a matter of time before Jim would be there too. But instead of giving into despair, she buried herself more than ever in work at the dress shop and in running her Red Cross chapter.

By midsummer, Kathleen's looked different. Due to the war, not only had fashion changed but materials were more limited as well. Anything previously imported was scarcer than hen's teeth, and as a result women's styles became more serious. Although Katy missed the old ruffles and ribbons and lace, she welcomed the war-influenced styles of women's clothes, including double-breasted jackets and wide lapels. The severity of design and dull colors seemed to match her general subdued mood. And her own designs, like so many dress designers around the world, began to adapt to a more military look.

Anna no longer felt overly worried for Katy. Oh, she knew her daughter was not her old usual cheerful self, but at least she was keeping herself busy. Not only was her dress shop prospering with the new wartime fashions, but Katy's Red Cross chapter was producing lots of useful items for soldiers. And Katy's first official fundraiser, a picnic and dance in the city park, had been a big success on Independence Day. Although Anna had attended the event to show support for the Red Cross, her heart had not been in it. Seeing couples happily dancing was a stark reminder that Daniel was far away. But then she'd spotted Katy working away on the sidelines. And instead of wearing her usual stylish attire of a feminine party dress, Katy had on a gray dress that, although fashionable, looked rather somber. It seemed that both mother and daughter were in a similar place.

"What on earth is that?" Anna asked Katy in mid-July. Her daughter was seated at the dining room table surrounded by a pile of papers.

"Letters." Katy grinned. "From Jim!"

"Oh my. Why so many?"

"He wrote one letter a day while on the ship then sent them all at once from England." Katy held up a page. "I think this is the most recent one. And—good news too—it looks like he'll remain in England for another month or two. And he may possibly be assigned a position as a war correspondent."

"Wouldn't that be a blessing!"

"Yes." Katy nodded eagerly. "I'm going to ask everyone to pray that happens." She dug through the pile. "Oh, and I almost forgot. There's a letter for you too, Mother."

Anna waited as Katy sorted through her mess of papers. "Here it is. Looks like it's from Doctor Daniel." She made a sly smile. "I'll bet he's been missing you."

Anna wasn't so sure about that, but eager to hear how he was doing, she opened it and began to read.

Katy was leaning forward. "What does it say?"

"Daniel is on his way back," Anna declared.

"That's wonderful."

"Yes, it is." Anna continued to skim the page. "And he wants to know if Sarah Rose will be available to help him again. Two or three days a week."

"That'd be fine. We don't have as much sewing work these days anyway. We already let one of our seamstresses go. And I'm sure Sarah would love to go back to working for him."

"Oh my. Listen to this." Anna wrinkled her nose. "Daniel is bringing his father with him."

"You mean Dr. Blowhard?"

"Katy." Anna sternly shook her head.

"You know I'd never say that to his face."

"But I can't disagree," Anna admitted. "And I'm sure Mac won't be too thrilled to learn his competition is back."

"Guess we better hide the shotgun." Katy chuckled.

"Maybe it'll motivate Mac to talk to your grandmother about their future together," Anna said quietly.

"Maybe we should drop some gentle hints." Katy gathered her letters, piling them into a box. "Give him a head start."

Anna nodded. "Mac seems to listen to you."

"I'll start nudging him." Katy stood. "When will the two doctors arrive? Does it say?"

Anna scanned down to the bottom. "Goodness, it says here that they expect to be here by Tuesday."

"That's only three days away." Katy paused by the door. "Maybe we should plan a welcome home dinner for them."

"Why don't you mention that to Mac?" Anna slid the letter back into its envelope, knowing she would carefully reread it later in private. "I promised to drop by your grandmother's this afternoon for tea. Care to join me?"

"No thanks. I said I'd be at the dress shop until closing today." Katy beamed at her. "And after that, I have a nice, long letter to write."

"Good for you." Anna was glad to see Katy smiling again. Hopefully Jim would get that journalist assignment. He'd never been amenable to the idea of fighting in the battles. Covering the war in the news would be a much better use of his talents. As she walked to Lucille's house, she silently prayed for Jim. Then, pausing by the bench that overlooked the ocean—a place she and Daniel had sat together on a number of occasions—Anna sat down and reread his letter more carefully.

He sounded as surprised as she felt that his father was willing to return to their little one-horse town. But it seemed his health condition was forcing him to slow down some, and the promise of fresh sea air and the companionship of his son was appealing. Or perhaps Daniel had simply caught him in a weak moment. Whatever the case, they would be leaving by train about now. She prayed they'd have a quiet, uneventful trip.

It warmed her heart to hear that Daniel was "greatly looking forward" to seeing her again—and that he'd signed his letter with *Love, Daniel.* Perhaps nothing between them had changed after all. She could only hope.

She put away the letter and headed to Lucille's house, where tea was already laid out. "I'm sorry I'm late." She explained about today's mail. "Katy was so excited to have finally heard from Jim again."

"Oh, that is good." Lucille poured tea. "I know she's been worried about him . . . not quite her old self. I hope this improves her disposition." She handed Anna her tea. "And what about your letter? How is the good doctor?"

"He's coming home," Anna said happily.

"Wonderful!"

"And bringing his father with him." Anna watched for her mother's response.

Lucille's pale brows arched. "That should be interesting."

"We haven't told Mac yet." Anna grimaced to imagine her father's reaction. "But I'm sure he'll have something to say about it."

Lucille chuckled. "Hopefully he'll go easy on poor JD."

"JD?"

"James Daniel." Lucille's eyes twinkled.

"Ah. So should I assume that you and, uh, *JD,* are still on friendly terms?"

"He's written me a couple of nice letters." Lucille reached for a cookie. "But I never expected to see him here again."

"Well, they should be here by Tuesday. Katy thinks we should have a welcome home dinner for them, but I'm not sure Mac will—"

"Oh, Anna, please, let me host it."

Anna shrugged. "That's probably a good plan. Although I'm not sure Mac will want to come."

"If I invite him, he'll come."

They chatted a bit more and then Lucille inquired about Lawrence Bouchard. "I've been meaning to ask, how is it working out for him at the newspaper, Anna?"

"He seems to be pulling his weight." Anna

sensed more to Lucille's question. "Why do you ask? Is anything wrong?"

"No, no . . . I don't think so. But Ellen is hard to read sometimes. She's been rather hard to get along with of late. Clara claims it's due to her delicate condition. And we've all suggested that she should consider giving up her job. Of course, she won't hear of it. Don't repeat it, but I think she's concerned about finances. And, well, I wondered about Lawrence. . . ."

Anna still wasn't sure what Lucille was insinuating. "Lawrence's salary isn't great, but it should be enough to support them if they live frugally. Especially now that they have that apartment over the coffee shop."

"I'm not sure Ellen knows how to live frugally." Lucille shook her head.

"Maybe Clara should talk to her."

"Ellen doesn't listen much to her mother."

"Perhaps she'd listen to you," Anna suggested.

"I'll see what I can do."

"And if you should hear of anything that sounds the least bit shady regarding Lawrence— for instance, a weekend fishing trip—please, let me know."

"Well, that's one of the things I wanted to talk to you about today." Lucille frowned. "I wasn't sure I should say anything . . . I could be wrong about this, and I don't like to spread idle gossip."

"What is it? Have you reason to suspect something?" Anna felt a rush of alarm. Had she missed something?

"Well, I just happened to see Lawrence in a rather animated conversation with a couple of rough-looking men yesterday afternoon. It aroused my curiosity."

Anna asked her to describe the men, who sounded disturbingly like Bud and Fred. "I can't believe he would associate with those thugs again." Anna scowled. "He gave me his word."

"To be fair, it didn't seem he wanted to speak with them. It was almost as if they'd cornered him. He did look uncomfortable, Anna. Do you suppose they could be blackmailing him?"

"I guess that's possible. Maybe I'll ask him about it on Monday. At least he'll know that I'm aware he's been in contact with his *fishy* friends." But now Anna felt very uneasy. What if Lawrence were out on the ocean with those lowlife rum-runners right now? Surely he wouldn't be that stupid. Just the same, she asked to borrow Lucille's phone to call Frank at home, but when no one answered Anna decided to conduct her own investigation. Thanking Lucille for tea and excusing herself, Anna headed straight down to the docks only to discover that Bud's boat was nowhere to be seen. She found a fisherman mending a net and inquired.

"Bud just got his boat out of dry dock a few days ago." The old guy rubbed his chin. "He and Fred took it yesterday afternoon to test it out. Haven't seen 'em back yet. Reckon they're fishing."

She asked if anyone else was with them, but he didn't seem to know. She considered paying Ellen a visit but didn't want to upset her. And maybe she was overreacting. Perhaps she should just sit tight until Monday and ask Lawrence himself—if he showed up. And, if he didn't show, she would start looking for his replacement.

Chapter 23

To Anna's relief, Lawrence reported for work on Monday as usual. And when she questioned him, he assured her that he had no interest in doing *anything* with Bud and Fred. "They pressured me to go out with them," he confessed. "But I emphatically told them no, and that I like my job here and am done with them."

"Glad to hear it." She believed him.

"They sure weren't." He grimly shook his head. "But I'm sticking to my guns, Miss McDowell. I gave you my word, and I plan to keep it."

"Glad to hear that too." She pursed her lips. "Perhaps it's time to tip off Chief Rollins to keep a closer eye on those two." She reached for her phone then paused. "And this gives me an idea for my midweek editorial. I think it's high time to remind the good citizens of Sunset Cove that rum-running is still a problem along our coastline. And with the coast guard's involvement in the war and watching for U-boats, everyone else needs to keep their eyes and ears open too."

"Makes sense." He paused by the door. "I

wonder if I could ask you something, Miss McDowell?"

"Of course." She waited.

"Well, I know I need to prove myself here. And I hope I've been doing that. But I was thinking that I may make a good investigative reporter. I know that Frank's been doing that, but he's got his family responsibilities on weekends and evenings. So if you ever need a backup guy, especially if Frank is busy, I'd be glad to give it a go."

"That's not a bad idea, Lawrence. I'll keep that in mind next time there's an after-hours story to follow up."

After he left, she called Chief Rollins, sharing how Bud and Fred had "taken up fishing" again. "May pay to do some closer surveillance now that Bud's boat's running. Just in case they're bringing in something besides fish." He thanked her for the tip, and she set to writing a hard-hitting anti-rum-running opinion piece.

Anna borrowed the Runabout on Tuesday afternoon, leaving work a little early to surprise Daniel and his father by picking them up from the afternoon train. As she drove to the station, she wondered if they would actually be on it. After all, there'd been no word from Daniel since the last letter, and it was possible they'd changed their travel plans or stopped somewhere along the way. But when the train pulled into the station, she spotted Daniel in the coach car. Waving with enthusiasm, she hurried up to meet them.

"I could hardly believe my eyes," Daniel said as he swept her up into a big hug.

"I thought you may like a ride." She greeted his father, noticing that he looked worn out with dark circles beneath his eyes. "I hope you had a good trip."

"A *long* trip," he said dourly. "Is anything farther away from Boston than Sunset Cove?"

"China?" Daniel teased as he set their bags onto the luggage cart.

His father just grunted, and Anna took his arm. "Well, I'm glad you decided to return to our little hamlet. I know that my mother is eager to see you again."

"Lucille?" he said more gently. "How is she?"

"She's fit as a fiddle. Helping Katy to run the dress shop seems to keep her youthful." As Anna slowly walked the older man to the car, she filled him in a bit on the recent goings-on in town. "Our Red Cross chapter is doing a fabulous job. Especially considering we're such a small town."

As Daniel made arrangements to have their luggage delivered, Anna helped his father into the front of the little Runabout, tucking a warm blanket over his legs. "We're having a rather cool day," she said.

"I don't mind the cool air," he told her. "It was

unbearably hot for most of the trip. I almost feel like I can breathe again."

"All set," Daniel announced as he joined them.

"Why don't you drive?" she suggested. "I'll sit in the rumble-seat." And before he could protest, she hurried to get settled. The truth was she was already feeling a bit uncomfortable around Daniel's father. They'd never gotten along too well during his last visit, which she suspected was related to her involvement with his son. And now she was worried she'd run out of conversation before she got them to Daniel's place. She still had no idea how long Daniel or his father planned to stay in Sunset Cove, but she hoped this was more than just a visit . . . and not just Daniel's opportunity to shut down his medical practice.

It didn't take long to reach Daniel's apartment, but Anna didn't want to stick around long enough to watch the old man slowly climbing the stairs to the second floor. Already he seemed out of breath. But at least his son was a physician. "I'll talk to you later," she called out to them. "Welcome home." And without much ado, she drove away. She still had a dozen questions for Daniel but knew they'd have to wait.

Anna was barely in the house when she heard the phone ringing. "I'll get it," she called out as she rushed for the hallway phone. To her surprise, it was Daniel calling to thank her for the ride.

"I assume you and your father made it safely up the stairs."

"Believe me, it wasn't easy. And now I realize we'll need to find another place to live as soon as possible. There's no way Dad can make it up and down those stairs. Do you know of any houses for rent in town? Or better yet, anything for sale?"

"For sale?" she asked with interest. "Does that mean you plan to stick around?"

"Of course I do. That's why I brought Dad with me. We're going to make Sunset Cove our home. I thought I said as much in my letter."

"You may have insinuated it, but I suppose I wasn't certain." She felt a happy wave of relief. "Hey, I did hear that the Henderson house is going to be for sale."

"The Henderson house?"

"It's a large brick house on the corner of Third and Pacifica. I'm sure you've seen it before. Two stories, big front porch with white columns."

"Oh, yes, that does sound familiar. Maybe I'll walk over there and have a look."

"That's about a mile from you," she told him. "How about if I give you a ride?"

"That'd be great."

"And, if you like, we can swing by the hospital on our way. I'm sure you'll enjoy seeing the progress."

"Perfect."

Before long they were parked in front of the hospital site. Anna was pleased to see that Daniel seemed suitably impressed. "I can't believe how much got done while I was gone. At this rate I wouldn't be surprised if they finished by early next year."

"Probably sooner. Mac told me they hope to open in late November."

"Even better."

Next they went to the vacated house and, once again, Daniel seemed impressed. "It's bigger than I imagined."

"Do you think it's too big?" Anna asked as they stood on the wide front porch.

"Not at all. Do you think anyone would care if we went around and peeked in the windows?"

"I don't see why. It's obviously unoccupied."

So they walked around, looking in windows and trying to get a feel for the property. "That downstairs bedroom would be perfect for Dad," Daniel said as they returned to the front porch. "And it looks like there may be enough space to convert that parlor and dining room into an office and temporary clinic."

"Temporary?"

"Until the hospital is finished."

"Oh, yes. Of course." Anna felt silly for imagining that he was going to leave again . . . and yet, she didn't know.

Daniel peered up the road they'd just come down. "And it's handy to the hospital too. I could walk to work."

"That's true." Anna wanted to ask if he could afford this house, but that felt intrusive. Besides, they didn't know the price anyway.

They were just preparing to leave when another car pulled up and Mr. Henderson got out. "Neighbor called me," he said as he approached them. "Said someone was poking around my place. Can I help you?"

Daniel shook his hand, explaining his need for a house. "This looks like just the ticket." He asked the price, and Mr. Henderson told him a figure that didn't even seem to faze Daniel. "Any chance we can look inside?"

"You bet." Mr. Henderson grinned as he produced a key. "I'll open it up, and you youngins can snoop around as much as you like." He winked at Daniel. "I think you two could be right comfortable here. Me and the wife lived happily here for more'n fifty years. But she passed away . . . about three years ago . . . and I'd just been rattling around by myself. Last spring my daughter Lizzie insisted I move in with them, and now it's time to sell the place. Too big for Lizzie and her husband. Too big for me."

Daniel stepped aside to let Anna enter. She could feel her cheeks blushing as she went into the musty smelling house. Naturally, Mr. Henderson had assumed they planned to marry and live here. Part of her liked that idea, and another part of her felt concerned that there may soon be a rumor circulating through town.

They walked through the downstairs rooms, and it seemed Daniel was right. The parlor and dining room were large enough to become a temporary doctor's office. "And I could have my private office in here." He pointed to a small den-like room. Next they peeked into the bedroom in back, a bathroom that looked like it had been recently added, and a kitchen that appeared in need of a good cleaning and coat of paint. Upstairs were three more bedrooms and another recently added bathroom.

"These bedrooms could even double as patients' rooms," Daniel said with enthusiasm. "Until the hospital is finished."

"What did you think of the price?" she asked tentatively.

"Seems fair to me. Considerably less than what my dad and I had budgeted for our house."

"Oh, that's good." Of course, Daniel's father was helping him. And, although it was reassuring, it was also disappointing. For a brief dreamy moment, Anna had imagined herself and Daniel as blissful newlyweds, living in this house, happily ever after. She'd nearly forgotten about Daniel's ailing father. Perhaps she needed to give up on any illusions of romance, at least for the time being.

"Well, I should get back to my dad." Daniel checked his watch. "I promised to be gone less than an hour. He's having a nap, and then we'll have an early dinner."

"Do you need to go by the store?" she asked as they got back into the car.

"No. I sent Sarah Rose a telegram from a train stop yesterday, asking her to stock my kitchen. She got everything ready for us."

"I knew she was organizing your office."

"Well, that woman's efficient. Not only did she get my office in order, she tidied my apartment, aired it out, and put out clean linens and even fresh flowers."

"Sarah Rose is a wonder." Anna felt guilty for having a flash of jealousy. Sarah Rose was probably a more gifted homemaker than Anna could ever hope to be.

"I want to ask her if she'll consider working full-time for my dad and me—mostly in the office but partly housekeeping too. Do you think Katy will mind?"

"Probably not. Thanks to the war, business has slowed down at the dress shop."

"And it seems my business has picked up. Sarah Rose already had calls from patients and made some appointments."

"Well, here you are," Anna proclaimed as she stopped in front of his office.

"Do you mind if I send Sarah Rose down to ride home with you?"

"Not at all."

"She told me that she's been walking to and from work unaccompanied lately. She seems unconcerned, especially since it's summer and she goes home in daylight. But I'm not so sure. What do you think?"

"I don't know. I understand she wants independence, but Katy mentioned some mean comments that were made recently. It's probably best to be cautious."

"Well, I'll send her down." He grinned. "Thanks for your help this afternoon, Anna. I haven't even had much chance to say how glad I am to see you. I hope we can take a beach walk together in the next day or two. I have lots to tell you."

Anna's heart warmed. Maybe it wasn't time to give up after all.

Before long, Sarah hopped into the car. "Thank you for giving me a ride," she said. "I put in a long day on my feet, and I appreciate it."

"And Dr. Daniel appreciates all you did to welcome him and his father home."

"He asked me to work full-time for him."

"Would you like to do that? Or would it be hard to give up the dress shop?"

"I would gladly work full-time for the doctor." Sarah sighed. "Sometimes I feel out of place at the dress shop."

"Oh." Anna nodded. "Well, I know that the doctors would be lucky to have you, Sarah Rose." She told her about the large house they just looked at. "Especially if they buy it and move there. You would definitely have your hands full."

"That sounds wonderful."

Although Anna was glad for Sarah Rose, she still felt a little out of sorts. Oh, she knew this longing to set up housekeeping for Daniel was silly. After all, she could barely cook, clean, or anything else it took to run an efficient home. Yet a part of her wanted to try. Perhaps she would ask Bernice to give her some lessons or tips. Or perhaps she should stick with what she knew— newspaper work.

For the next few days, Anna stopped by Daniel's office after work. Her excuse was to escort Sarah Rose home, but she really just wanted to see Daniel. Unfortunately, he was extremely busy—not only with his medical practice, since word had quickly gotten around that the doctor was back, but also because he and his father had successfully purchased the Henderson house. Obviously, he had much to do in preparation for their move the following week.

"What a gorgeous day," Anna declared as she and Sarah strolled toward home. They'd taken the long way to enjoy the perfect weather.

"Town seems quite busy," Sarah said as they waited for some noisy vehicles to pass by before they crossed the street.

"From now until August, we'll have a lot of tourists," Anna told her. "Folks who are fleeing the inland heat love to spend time at the beach this time of year. Much more now than what I remember from my childhood. I'm sure the train and use of automobiles has contributed to that."

"I've been indoors all day, so I didn't notice the extra people."

"I'm sure you've been busy, preparing for the move."

"Yes. Besides the office work, I've been trying to get everything packed and ready to move. I'm almost done."

"Sounds like a big job."

"Dr. JD helped some." Sarah chuckled. "Or he *thought* he helped. And I didn't tell him otherwise."

"How is the old guy doing?"

"It depends. Sometimes he seems hale and hearty, full of opinions about everything and anything no matter who's listening. Other times, he's quiet and moody. Almost like he's sulking. I sometimes imagine him as an overgrown child. But I would never say as much."

"I can see that." Anna chuckled. "It must be quite an adjustment for him."

"I suppose it is. . . ."

Anna glanced at Sarah Rose. "I'm sure you can relate. It's been a big adjustment for you too, but you seem to have adapted nicely." She smiled. "I'm proud of how well you've settled in here."

"I do love living near the sea like this." Sarah gazed out toward the ocean. "That makes up for a lot."

"Do you ever miss your friends back in Portland?"

"Yes, I suppose I do."

"Do you ever think you'd like to go back there?"

Sarah sighed. "I'm not sure, Miss Anna. Sometimes I think I would. But then I don't know. But I have saved up some money . . . just in case."

"Good for you. No matter what you do or where you live, it's good to have savings . . . ." Anna's voice trailed off. Up ahead were a couple of familiar figures, and the way they were striding directly toward them set off an alarm inside of her. "Let's double back that way," she quietly told Sarah. "I nearly forgot that tonight is Lucille's dinner party. I need to get home and—"

"What have we here?" Fred Jones stepped right in front of them, blocking the sidewalk.

"Excuse us," Anna said stiffly, locking her arm into Sarah's and trying to go around.

"Don't be in such a hurry." Bud stepped in front of her.

"Yeah, we're just being friendly." Fred narrowed his eyes at Anna, not looking the least bit congenial.

"Come on," Anna told Sarah, tugging her toward the street. "Let's go this way."

"Not yet." Fred grabbed her arm. "Not until you hear what I have to say, Miss Lady Editor."

"What?" she demanded, glancing around to see if anyone was watching, hoping for a kind intervention.

"Some folks don't like the lies you print in that newspaper," Fred growled. "And some folks don't like you acting like you run this town." Now he pointed at Sarah Rose. "And some folks don't like the trash you've brought—"

"That's enough!" Anna shouted at them. "Now get out of our way." With her arm still linked with Sarah's, she tugged her toward the street and pushed past the ruffians. As she and Sarah hurried away, the thugs made a few more nasty comments. "Just ignore the ignorant beasts," Anna hissed at Sarah.

"Believe me, I do," she said in a solemn way that suggested this was not new to her. Naturally, that only aggravated Anna more. She certainly did not intend to ignore the monsters. Not completely, anyway. First, she would report this ugly incident to Chief Rollins. Sure, there was probably nothing he could do about it, but she wanted him to know. After that, she would seek out the power of the pen and express her disgust in a public forum that circulated biweekly.

CHAPTER 24

B y Saturday morning, Anna knew that Mac was in a foul mood. For that matter, she didn't feel overly cheerful herself at the breakfast table. It wasn't that last night's dinner party at Lucille's had been a complete fiasco, but it did seem that Daniel's father intended to make life difficult for everyone. Well, perhaps not everyone . . . not for Lucille. But he seemed intent on tormenting Mac and Anna.

Sometimes it seemed that the elder doctor personally blamed Anna for Daniel's decision to remain in Sunset Cove. Anna had looked forward to some alone time with Daniel last night, but even that had proven brief. And when Anna realized that Daniel was completely preoccupied with his upcoming move and new accommodations, she knew it was pointless to attempt to compete with all that. As a result, she'd called it a night early in the evening. Apparently, Mac had done the same.

"Well, at least Daniel is getting his father

settled in," Anna said without much enthusiasm. "That may help matters."

"Humph." Mac growled. "Sounded to me more like JD is getting settled into Lucille's house right now."

"That's only while the movers get furnishings put into place, Grandpa." Katy laid down her napkin. "It's a lot of work to make a move like that. And I think it's very nice of Sarah Rose to help them with it."

"She's in the doctor's employ," Mac said dourly. "Before long they'll take over everything. Maybe they'd like to steal Bernice and Mickey too."

"Don't be ridiculous, Mac. And I agree with Katy. It was kind of Sarah to offer to help with this. She already put in a long week."

"Perhaps she should go back to work with Katy," Mac said. "I doubt that JD will treat her with much respect over there."

"What did you expect?" Anna refilled her coffee cup.

"You're both wrong about that," Katy declared. "Sarah told me herself that the older doctor treats her just the same as he treats anyone else."

"Meaning he acts like an imperious blowhard with her too." Mac scowled darkly, and Anna couldn't help but laugh.

"Well, if you two happy rays of sunshine will excuse me, I promised to open the dress shop this morning." Katy stood with a half-smile. "Hopefully you'll both be in better spirits by dinnertime."

"I suppose we do seem a little down in the mouth," Anna confessed to Mac after Katy left.

"Well, I know why I'm grumbling, but what's bothering you?" He pushed aside his coffee with a softer expression.

She shrugged. "I guess I'm a little worn out. It was a long, busy week."

"So you say." His brow creased with suspicion. "More likely you're resenting that intruder just as much as I am."

"What?" She feigned innocence.

"Don't try to kid me. *JD*—as he insists we call him—seems determined to take over everything in Sunset Cove. From the hospital project to Lucille and even Daniel. Don't tell me that's not aggravating you, Anna."

She smiled. "I suppose I'm a bit bothered. But not nearly as much as you. Honestly, do you think Lucille could prefer JD's company to yours?" She stood up, going over to kiss his cheek. "Especially since you're such a sweet and kind and congenial fellow." She chuckled.

"Flattery will get you nowhere." But at least his face brightened.

"Don't let him get to you, Mac."

"You better believe I won't." He slowly stood. "In fact, I'm going to invite Lucille over here for dinner tonight. Just the four of us. Like a family."

"Don't waste a minute," she teased, "I can just imagine JD is probably making plans with her right now. Better get on the telephone quick."

"I'll do better than that," he declared. "I'll go over in person."

Anna couldn't help but chuckle as he hurried to grab his hat, making a beeline for the front door. At least he hadn't taken any firearms with him. Although she felt sorry for him, she thought that in some ways, Mac's troubles were more easily solved than her own. If Mac really pleaded his case with Lucille—or offered her a ring—he could probably seal the deal. But Anna knew it wouldn't be so simple with her when it came to Daniel's father. JD seemed to have cut off all ties to Boston. The cantankerous old man was here to stay. And he and Daniel had become, it seemed, a package deal. She wondered if she'd ever get any time with Daniel without his father nearby.

Anna picked up the newspaper Mac had just tossed aside. She usually read the *Oregonian* from front to back on Saturdays but had hoped for something more interesting now that Daniel was back. But, knowing he'd be busy moving into his new house, she knew it was futile to hope for anything more.

She was surprised to see that today's headlines were not about the war but something else. She'd already heard about the racial unrest in various parts of the country. In fact, she'd run the full story about the lynching crimes in Texas and Tennessee and the riot in Saint Louis a few weeks ago. She figured it was a message the citizens of Sunset Cove needed to hear.

But today's news was interesting. It seemed the National Association for the Advancement of Colored People had staged a "silent parade" in New York City to protest the recent string of racist crimes in the South. Anna had written a piece on the start-up of the NAACP back at the *Oregonian* several years ago. She remembered her dismay at discovering her story buried deep within the newspaper. In comparison, it felt like progress to see this news on the front page today.

And now she was determined not only to reprint this story but to write an accompanying editorial. Without naming names, she would mention yesterday's little incident of nastiness aimed at Sarah Rose and herself. People deserved to know about these local injustices, and as a newspaper-woman she felt a responsibility to shine a light into the dark, shameful corners. Besides, it was a good way to distract readers from the grim war stories that just seemed to keep coming.

Katy and Clara were the only ones working at Kathleen's Dress Shop on Saturday morning, but thanks to the tourists and a pleasant sunny day, the shop was busier than expected. Women from out of town were shopping for summer hats, swimming costumes, and a variety of random things. Some items they had and some items were simply hard to get. But Katy started a list of things they might want to begin stocking.

"Goodness, that was an interesting rush we just had," Clara said as they straightened the millinery section. "But at least we made some good sales."

"Yes, but some of those women had such high expectations for our little shop." Katy sighed, tucking a stray curl back behind an ear. "It wore me out."

"You're starting to sound like my daughter," Clara teased. "Everything seems to wear Ellen out these days. I'm glad she has the day off today."

"Yes, well, that's because she's expecting." Katy adjusted the blue ribbons on a pale straw sunhat before returning it to the stand.

"True enough. Plus, she's overwhelmed with setting up housekeeping in their little apartment." Clara secured an ostrich feather on a felt hat.

"I offered to help her," Katy said, "but she refused. She didn't even want me to visit her."

"That's because she's embarrassed," Clara said quietly. "Their place is . . . well, it's rather shabby and rundown."

"But can't she fix it up? What about wallpaper and paint and—"

"I'm sure you could do those things, Katy. You

have that creative ability to make anything you touch prettier. But Ellen isn't like that."

"Yes, she'd rather buy something ready-made than attempt to create it herself." Katy frowned. "But I wish she'd let me help her. I actually think it would be fun. And it'll be a long time before I get the chance to create a home for Jim and me."

"Have you heard from Jim recently?"

"Yes." Katy smiled. "Thankfully, he was still in England. They've begun testing him as a war correspondent. Although he warned me I may get fewer letters from him as a result. But I wrote back saying that was fine. I'd prefer he remain behind the battle lines, writing about the war, rather than smack in the middle of it."

Clara nodded grimly. "Like AJ."

"Oh . . . yes." Katy put a hand on Clara's shoulder. "I guess I forgot. When did you last hear from him?"

"He wrote me right before they shipped out to France. Nothing since. I can only assume he's there right now. Probably little time to write home." Clara's voice trembled slightly.

"I'm sure AJ is a good, strong soldier," Katy assured her. "That young man always had a lot of energy, a lot of get up and go."

"Even when he was going the wrong way." Clara smiled sadly.

"Yes, but aren't you thankful he straightened

that out? And now you can be very proud of him, Clara."

"I am. And Rand keeps reminding me of those very same things. It's true that AJ is a fighter and a survivor. Besides having grown up working on the fishing boats, all those other things he went through . . . well, I'm sure they've made him tougher."

Lucille entered the shop now. "I'm here, ladies. Sorry to be a bit late, but I had two gentlemen callers this morning." She chuckled as she unpinned her hat.

"Grandfather and JD?" Katy asked.

"Of course."

"Hopefully not simultaneously," Clara said.

"Unfortunately, JD was already there when Mac showed up." Lucille shook her head. "It did get rather interesting."

"What was JD doing there?" Clara asked.

"Daniel dropped him by to visit. Apparently he's moving into his new house this weekend and needed a safe, quiet place to leave his father."

"I'll bet it wasn't very quiet after Mac arrived," Katy teased.

Lucille laughed and told the story of how the two men immediately got into a ridiculous argument over the length of the beach. "Of course, JD didn't stand a chance against your grandfather on that subject," she told Katy. "But that didn't stop him from blustering."

"Did you leave them like that?" Katy suddenly felt defensive of her grandfather being stuck with Daniel's contrary father like that. Plus, it may not be good for his health.

"No, no." Lucille shook her head. "Mac stormed off home, and JD settled down with a book." She pointed to Katy as the bell on the door jingled to signal customers. "I know you opened up this morning. Perhaps you should take your lunch break now."

Katy didn't argue this. Although she wasn't hungry, she did want a break. She hadn't slept well last night, and although it was early in the afternoon, she had no interest in popping into the Red Cross office where she knew a number of volunteers were probably hard at work. Instead, she decided to pay Ellen a visit. Maybe Clara was right—perhaps Katy should simply force her way in and attempt to help. At the very least, she'd get to see the apartment . . . and she might even give Ellen some suggestions for prettying it up. That could be fun.

She just hoped that Lawrence wouldn't be there. Even though he seemed to have made some positive changes recently, she still wasn't that comfortable around him. She wasn't even sure what she'd say if he answered the door, but to her relief, it was Ellen. Although she looked rather frumpy and unstylish in a housedress and slippers. But at least she didn't seem to mind letting Katy into their rather lackluster abode.

"Sorry to burst in on you uninvited." Katy forced a cheery smile.

"Well, here it is in all its glory." Ellen waved a hand into the tiny living room with an even tinier kitchen off to one side. "Welcome."

"Are you alone?" Katy asked quietly.

"Yes. Lawrence is spending the afternoon with Frank Anderson." Ellen led her into the gloomy space, pointing to a sagging divan. "They're fishing off the dock while keeping an eye on a couple of suspicious characters that your mother wants watched."

"Interesting." Katy peeled off her gloves and looked around. "Well, it must be nice having your own place, Ellen. Instead of the hotel."

"Well, I suppose it's quieter. And it's a lot cheaper." Ellen frowned. "But it's ugly as sin, don't you think?"

"You could fix it up." Katy already had several ideas percolating but didn't want to be pushy. She knew how she could overwhelm people at times. But beyond that, she just didn't feel that energetic today.

"How is that even possible?" Ellen asked in a flat tone with narrowed eyes.

Katy studied her for a moment. "Do you really want to know or are you simply being con—"

"I'm sorry." Ellen sighed. "I didn't mean to snap at you. It's just that this place looks completely hopeless to me. I don't even want to clean it. What's the point? But I am curious, Katy, what would you do to make it better?"

Katy stood and slowly walked around. "Well, for starters, I'd bring in some pretty fabric for color. Maybe make some cushions. Perhaps make a slipcover for the divan." She fingered the dull grayed curtains blocking the only window. "These are about to fall apart. What about some nice white chintz to let some light into here?"

Ellen slowly stood with a frown. "Goodness, I hadn't even noticed how grimy that window is."

"Simply a good washing of the window and the curtains would brighten it up."

"But that would just show how horrible this place looks."

"Not if these walls were painted a nice, bright, cheerful color. Perhaps a pale robin's egg blue." She wandered over to the tiny attached kitchen. "And maybe a buttery yellow on these cabinets. Or some charming wallpaper. It wouldn't take much to make a world of difference here, Ellen. During the summertime, Sarah Rose and I used to do little projects like this in our apartment in Portland. My mother would come home and be so surprised."

"That's nice. But I don't know how to paint or hang wallpaper." Ellen patted her slightly rounded midsection. "And to be honest, I just don't have the energy. I come home from work and don't feel like doing a thing." She pointed to the dirty breakfast dishes still in the stained porcelain sink. "As you can see, I'm a slovenly housekeeper."

"How about if I help?" Without waiting for a response, Katy checked the teakettle for hot water then tied on an apron and rolled up her sleeves. While Ellen sat at the tiny kitchen table, Katy began to scrub dishes. One by one, she handed them to Ellen to dry, and she continued to make suggestions for how the apartment could be fixed up. By the time she finished, Ellen seemed to be improved in spirit. And Katy felt better too.

"I think this apartment could be very attractive." Katy hung the apron back on the hook. "And if you want, I'd like to help you do it. Maybe we could have a little work party."

"Really?" Ellen looked hopeful.

"Sure. It would be fun." Katy leaned onto a kitchen chair, suddenly feeling a little dizzy or woozy or whatever it was that seemed to catch her off guard at times lately.

"Katy?" Ellen stood, putting an arm around her shoulders to steady her. "Are you okay?" She pulled out a kitchen chair. "Sit down."

Katy shrugged as she sat. "Sure. I just get these lightheaded spells sometimes." She took in a slow deep breath. "Takes me a minute to get my bearings."

Ellen sat across from her, studying her. "Does your stomach get easily upset?"

"I don't know. I haven't had much appetite lately. I barely touched breakfast this morning. Just dry toast and juice."

Ellen nodded. "And do you feel tired a lot?"

Katy nodded. "If I lay down for a nap right now, I'll bet I could sleep for a couple of hours."

"Katy McDowell." Ellen's eyes opened wide. "Do you know what I think?"

"Huh?" Katy frowned. "What do you—"

"I'll bet a week's worth of wages you're expecting a baby."

Katy blinked. "No, no, I don't think so."

"How do you know?"

"Well, I, uh, I don't know. But I can't imagine . . . I mean, our honeymoon was so short and—"

"Don't kid yourself, Katy. You're a married woman. It's a real possibility. Plus, you have all the symptoms." Ellen stood. "Wouldn't it be great?"

"I, uh, I don't know." Katy felt her head spinning even more now. Pregnant? No, no, no . . . This was not how her life was meant to go. She was a modern woman, destined to be a famous fashion designer. And Jim was going to take her to France after the war. A baby did not fit into this picture.

Ellen was counting on her fingers now. "I estimate your baby would be due around April.

Oh, this is so exciting, Katy. My baby will be about six months old by then. They can be friends, and we'll be mommies together. I'm so happy."

"Don't get too happy." Katy stood. "Because I'm pretty sure you're mistaken, Ellen. I truly don't think I could be pregnant. I really don't."

Ellen stood too, placing her hands on her hips with a disgruntled expression. "Well, you had a honeymoon, didn't you?"

"Of course." Katy nervously smoothed her skirt.

"You need to make an appointment with Dr. Hollister," Ellen persisted. "Because if you're not pregnant, something else must be wrong. Forgive me for saying so, but you haven't been yourself lately. My mother thinks it's because you miss Jim, but I suspect it's something more."

"Yes, well, I'll keep this in mind." Katy retrieved her gloves and purse from the divan. "And I'll be seeing you, Ellen."

"Thanks for helping with the dishes."

"No problem." Katy reached for the doorknob, eager to escape this dusty, frumpy, forlorn place.

"Do you still want to help with our apartment?" Ellen looked hopeful.

"Sure." Katy nodded without enthusiasm. "I said I would, and I will." Then, feeling flustered and worried, she said goodbye and hurried for home. Her only plan was to take a nice long nap.

Maybe she'd sleep until dinnertime. Maybe even later. And she would attempt to forget all that Ellen had just told her. Ellen had to be mistaken. Katy felt certain she could *not* be pregnant. It would just be all wrong. She wasn't ready for a baby. Jim was too far away. And Katy was too young. It was all too much . . . too impossible . . . and far too soon.

CHAPTER 25

Katy told no one, not even her mother, about Ellen's wild prediction regarding Katy's possible maternal condition. Really, it was preposterous. For the next two weeks, she not only managed to convince Ellen she was dead wrong, but she convinced herself as well. To further drive home this point, Katy managed to put forth a convincing image of her old energetic and optimistic self.

Part of her vigorous façade included a concerted effort to renovate Ellen and Lawrence's sad little apartment. To this end, Katy and Lucille hosted a belated wedding shower for Ellen. It was a fun time for everyone, and Ellen was deeply touched by the unexpected female attention and thrilled by the thoughtful gifts aimed specifically at prettifying her home.

Of course, Katy's efforts had been a twofold ploy. Both to improve her friend's forlorn abode as well as to distract Ellen from the disappointment over the news that Katy would not be playing mommy with her after all. At least, that was what Katy had been telling herself. And now that she'd accomplished her challenging feat of transforming the apartment, she felt satisfied.

"I think this finishes it off." Katy stepped back to admire the oil painting she'd just hung above the recently slip-covered divan. It was a seascape she'd done almost a year ago. "I hope you don't mind that this picture is a loan," she told Ellen. "But it's kind of special to me, and I haven't been doing much painting lately. Of course, the other two paintings are yours to keep forever, if you want them. Although it won't hurt my feelings if you don't."

"Of course I want them." Ellen went over to study the fruit bowl still-life that Katy had hung behind the little table in the kitchen. "They add a real touch of class to the place." Now she hugged Katy. "I can't believe how wonderful everything looks now. Thank you so much!"

"I can hardly remember what it used to be like." Katy straightened the floral cloth on the table.

"I don't *want* to remember. It made me feel so hopeless and miserable." She grinned at Katy. "But you're like a magic fairy."

Katy laughed. "Don't forget I had help." She patted a recently painted kitchen cabinet door, looking so fresh and clean in buttery yellow. "And Lawrence did a great job painting. If the newspaper job doesn't work out, he could probably get hired as a painter."

"Lawrence loves working at the paper. Frank has really taken him under his wing. Did you see that Lawrence even had an article in Saturday's paper?"

"Yes. Even Mac admits he has good potential as a reporter."

"Oh, it'll make him so happy to hear that."

Katy checked her pendant watch, surprised to see that it was after four. "Speaking of Mac, I need to get the Runabout back home."

"Is Mac driving again?"

"No, no. But I don't like to keep the car out too long. Don't like to worry him." As she picked up her borrowed toolbox, Katy felt guilty for concocting this lie. She hated to lie to anyone, but she needed an excuse to leave right now. "Anyway, I hope you and Lawrence enjoy all this."

"We definitely will. Although I still don't know where we'll put the baby." Ellen patted her rounded midsection. "But we still have more than three months to figure that one out."

"Babies are small," Katy said. "Shouldn't take up too much room." Eager to escape more baby talk, she opened the door, bade her friend goodbye, and hurried out to the car. Grandfather didn't give a hill of beans how long she kept the car, but she wanted to drop it at the house . . . before she went for her doctor's appointment. She did not want the Runabout parked conspicuously out in front of the building that everyone knew also housed Dr. Daniel's medical practice. Katy had made the appointment a few days ago, asking Sarah Rose for the last appointment of the day in the hopes she wouldn't run into anyone she knew or who knew her. Naturally, Sarah Rose had been curious as to the nature of the appointment, but Katy had disclosed nothing. She'd even asked Sarah to keep the appointment quiet, which she appeared to have done.

As Katy walked through the front door of the doctor's office, she felt a cold rush of nerves. By now, despite her denial to Ellen, she knew it was a real possibility she was expecting a child. But she also knew, from reading a motherhood book, that she could be mistaken. She hoped she was mistaken.

"Good afternoon, Miss Katy." Sarah Rose came over from behind the reception desk to greet her.

"Hello, Sarah Rose." Katy forced a smile. "Are you enjoying your work here? I've barely seen you at home the last couple of weeks. I'm sure they must be keeping you busy."

"Oh, they surely have. But I do enjoy my work here. Very fulfilling."

"Mother told me you may be moving over here, that there's a spare room for you. I suppose that means I won't see much of you anymore." Katy frowned.

"That's true." Sarah nodded. "But it would be

rather convenient for me. Although I'd miss you . . . and my ocean view too."

"Then you should stay with us," Katy insisted.

"Thank you, honey. I appreciate that." Sarah reached out to clasp Katy's hand, looking intently into her eyes. "How are you doing?"

"I, uh, I'm actually feeling quite well considering. . . ." Katy grimaced, worried she'd given away too much. "But I still want to talk—"

"Don't worry, honey. I *understand.*" Sarah placed her forefinger to her lips, speaking softly. "Your secret is safe with me."

"My *secret?*" Katy blinked. "Wh—what do you mean?"

Sarah's eyes lit up. "Oh, I'm not suggesting anything, but I do have eyes . . . and my own thoughts. And if I'm right, well, I'm so very, very happy for you. Everyone will be. Especially your dear sweet Jim."

Katy was speechless. Was it that obvious?

"Mrs. Lewis?" Dr. Daniel stuck his head out of a doorway. "Oh, I see my next patient is here."

"Yes, she just arrived." Sarah squeezed Katy's hand. "Everything's going to be just fine, honey. Don't you worry a bit."

Katy hoped Sarah Rose was right as she went into the examining room and sat down across from Dr. Daniel. "I'll get straight to it," she declared with brave resolve. "Although I do hope that I'm wrong, I realize it's possible that I'm not. And Ellen seemed fairly certain of it, as does Sarah Rose, which is a bit disconcerting."

"Certain of what?" He learned forward with interest.

"It's just that, well, I . . ." She felt tears well in her eyes as she twisted her wedding ring around and around. "I can hardly bring myself to say the words, Doctor. But I—I'm afraid . . . You see, it's possible that I am with child."

"Why, that's delightful news, Katy. Congratulations."

The tears spilled down her cheeks. "But I—I don't want to have a baby. Not yet anyway. It's too soon. I—I'm not ready."

With concerned eyes, he slid his chair closer to hers, taking her hand in a fatherly way. "It's not unusual for you to feel like this, Katy," he said gently. "Many young women are caught off guard with their first pregnancy. And most new mothers feel unprepared . . . at first. It's a perfectly natural reaction."

Katy bit into her lower lip. It wasn't only that she felt unprepared, it was that she felt unwilling. She did not *want* a baby! But to say those words . . . well, it sounded so terribly wrong.

"But you'll soon see as time passes and you get further along in your pregnancy that your feelings will change. Even my most reluctant mothers reach the place where they want nothing more than to hold their baby in their arms. In fact, they become downright impatient about it. Trust me, Katy, I've been down this road a lot."

"I'm sure you have, but the truth is that I—I don't want to go down this road."

His smile faded slightly. "I do understand. It's a shock right now. Especially for a young woman with the sort of big dreams and plans that you have. But a baby doesn't have to change any of that. Not really. There are ways to manage and—"

"You can't be serious." She retrieved a hanky from her purse, blotting her damp cheeks. "A baby will change *everything*. And not for the better either. I just know it."

"I'm sure it seems like that right now. But give yourself time and you'll—"

"But is there any chance I'm *not* pregnant?" she blurted. "That's really why I came to see you today. I was hoping you could tell me I'm wrong. I'd be so grateful to be wrong, Doctor. Is there even the slightest chance? I've read about how women can mistakenly assume—"

"Yes, well, anything is possible." He reached for a clipboard. "Let's officially begin this consultation." He began to ask a number of questions. The first ones were similar to what Ellen had asked, but then he moved on to more personal and somewhat embarrassing questions for a newlywed woman. She tried to maintain her composure, but her cheeks grew flush as she honestly answered. To her relief, he barely seemed to acknowledge her discomfort, simply nodding and jotting down notes.

After that was done, he listened to her heart and breathing and checked a few other things then finally smiled with a sigh. "Well, Katy, it is my professional opinion that you are in excellent health, and I have no reason to doubt you're expecting your firstborn child. Congratulations."

"You're absolutely certain of this?"

"As certain as I can be. Based on what you've told me, I'm fairly convinced that you're pregnant. But don't worry, just give yourself time . . . and you'll see that I'm right." Now he began to talk to her about diet and exercise and what to do to ensure a healthy baby. He handed her a booklet with an ink drawing of a mother and baby on the cover. "This should help you, but if you have any questions, feel free to ask me."

The lump in her throat grew harder, and her tears came even more freely than before. "I—I had other plans," she sobbed. "I wanted a career. Jim was going to take me to—to Paris to study design and—" She could no longer talk because the tears were choking her.

"Your body is going through a lot of changes, Katy. And sometimes that affects your emotions too. It's possibly the reason you're so upset right now. But trust me, you won't always feel like this. You'll have your ups and downs, but in time, you will probably be happy as a clam. I'm sure of it." He made what seemed a forced smile.

Katy firmly shook her head, wiping her nose. She didn't think she would ever be happy again. It seemed impossible.

"And Jim will be so happy to hear about this. Imagine his joy." He tipped his head to one side. "But I suggest you wait to tell him. In fact, you may wish to wait to tell anyone. Well, except for your mother. You will need her support."

"Wait?" She looked up with blurry eyes. "Why wait?"

"Well, during the first three months of pregnancy . . . things can change. A mother-to-be can be disappointed and—"

"What do you mean 'disappointed?' " she asked.

"Statistically, more mothers lose their babies in the first few months than later on. But you shouldn't worry. It's statistically rare. Especially in a young, healthy mother. Just the same, I usually advise my patients to wait until they're past that stage before they tell everyone." He shrugged. "Although my patients don't always take my advice."

"So are you saying there's still a chance I may, uh, lose this baby?" She felt horrible for even asking this question, but she wanted to know.

"You're healthy and young." His expression grew slightly grim. "I see no reason why you'd have any trouble with your pregnancy."

Her tears streamed down again. "I—I'm sorry. I didn't mean to sound like that. It's—it's not that I want to lose this baby. I don't. After all, it's Jim's child too. But I'm just so—so confused. I don't even know how to think at the moment."

He studied her as she blew her nose. "Do you consider yourself to be a strong, modern woman, Katy?"

She nodded vigorously. "Yes. Absolutely. Of course."

"How about your mother? Is she a strong, modern woman as well?"

Katy considered this. Sometimes she thought her mother was a bit old-fashioned and stodgy, but that probably wasn't fair. "I suppose she is . . . in her own way."

"Of course she is. Your mother has worked in a man's world as an editor for years. She runs a newspaper. She raised her daughter on her own. I would say that's quite strong and modern."

"Yes, I suppose you're right."

"So I have no doubt that you can manage a child and your career goals, Katy. Just like your mother has done. She's set you a fine example."

She barely nodded. "Yes, I suppose she has."

"And your mother will stand by you during your pregnancy. I know she will."

"Yes, I have no doubt of that."

"As will the rest of your family and friends." He smiled. "You're fortunate to have so many loving people around. Even with your husband overseas, you won't be alone. Not like your mother was." His eyes grew sad.

"That's true," she conceded.

"And imagine how thrilled Jim will be when you finally do tell him the good news. Can't you just see him bragging about it to his army buddies? And did you know that married men with children have a better chance of making it safely home from war?"

"I hadn't heard that, but I suppose it makes sense," she said woodenly. "Probably gives them something to fight harder for . . . a will to survive." Now if only she had that same kind of will.

"So you are actually helping your husband. Not only by bearing his child, but by offering him more incentive to remain safe. Who knows, maybe this war will end soon. Jim may be home in time to welcome his baby."

She couldn't help but let out a groan. It was all too much . . . too soon.

"Here's what I recommend for you, Katy. Don't give your condition much thought for the time being. Just go about your regular life. Be sure to eat properly and get enough rest. But don't think about your pregnancy for now. Your emotions should level out in a month or two. And I'll bet you'll be feeling just fine by autumn." He grinned. "Speaking of autumn, you haven't even asked me about your due date. That's usually one of the first questions I get."

"Oh, yes . . . When is the due date?" She feigned interest.

He glanced at the clipboard again. "By my calculations it should be here around mid-April. A spring baby. Won't that be nice?"

"Yes. Thank you." She nodded mechanically. "And I'd appreciate it if you didn't mention this to anyone . . . particularly my mother."

"Trust me, everything said in this room is strictly confidential." He frowned. "Won't you want to tell your mother?"

"It's not that I want to keep it from her, but I like your idea of not saying anything for a while . . . your suggestion of just going about my usual life. I think I can do that." She took in a deep breath. "At least I'll try."

"Good for you." He glanced at the clock on the wall.

"Oh, I'm sorry. You should be closed by now. Well, no worries. I'll be on my way. And I'm sure I'll be just fine. Sorry for my emotional outburst."

"No need to apologize. And, really, if you need to talk again, please, feel free."

She stood, picking up her purse. "If I hurry, I can walk home with Sarah. And, by the way, please don't tell her either. Although she already suspects."

"I wouldn't be surprised. She has a good sense about these things."

"Well, thank you." She forced a smile. "And I'm sure you're right that I'll feel better before long. I'm not usually an overly emotional person."

"It's just a part of the package." He opened the door for her. "But things will improve, probably faster than you expect. I promise."

As Katy went out to the reception area, which appeared vacated now, she wondered how he could promise something like that. "Sarah Rose?" She poked her head into a sitting room, hoping to spy her old friend.

"Mrs. Lewis went home." The older Dr. Hollister glared up from his easy chair with a sour expression.

"Oh, I'm sorry to disturb you."

"I'm used to it. This place is like Grand Central Station."

"Yes, I suppose it can get busy." Katy backed away.

"People coming and going all day long and sometimes in the middle of the night too. Can't wait until that doggone hospital gets finished." He picked up his newspaper. "As I said, Mrs. Lewis is not here. She left our dinner in the oven as usual then took off. I keep telling Daniel that we need a live-in housekeeper. Not one who comes and goes."

"Well, it sounds like Sarah Rose is considering that," Katy assured him. "But I hope you know she's much more than just a housekeeper." She paused in the doorway to lock eyes with him, ready to lecture him on the fine qualities of her old friend.

"Yes, yes." He stuck his head back into his paper. "So I've heard."

"Goodnight, Dr. Hollister." Without saying another word, she turned on her heel and hurried out. Old curmudgeon. How did Dr. Daniel put up with him? As she walked home, her heart went out to Sarah Rose. Having to work for such an old grump couldn't be much fun. Maybe Katy should entice her back to the dress shop. Perhaps with a raise. After all, Katy would probably need extra help . . . especially if she were going to have a baby by next spring. Not that she planned to think about that now—or anytime soon.

CHAPTER 26

Anna had just joined Mac at the dinner table when Katy rushed in, her eyes wide with worry. "Has anyone seen Sarah Rose?" she demanded.

"Not since this morning," Anna said. "What's—"

"Bernice said she didn't come down to get her dinner. And I just checked her room. She's not there. And it looks like she hasn't been there."

"Where could she be?" Mac rubbed his chin. "Perhaps she stopped by Lucille's?"

"Or Clara's?" Anna suggested, although she doubted this.

"I'll call them both." Katy headed for the telephone.

"That's odd." Anna laid her napkin back on the table. "It's not like Sarah Rose to go off anywhere. Not without saying something."

Mac grimly shook his head. "What about those articles you've been running in the paper lately, Anna?"

"Which articles?"

"For starters, the one about those demonstrations back East."

"You mean the NAACP protesters? Are you suggesting our newspaper does not support the fourteenth amendment?"

"Don't be silly, Anna. You know I support equal rights."

"Then are you suggesting the good citizens of Sunset Cove have no right to be informed in regard to racial tensions in other parts of the country?"

"Of course they do. That's not my point. What if you've created racial tensions in *this* part of the country?"

"What?" Anna could barely conceal her indignation.

"It's possible you've said too much, Anna."

"Too much?" she demanded.

"There's such a thing as caution."

Anna could hardly believe her ears. "Caution in a newspaper? I thought it was our responsibility to print the truth, Mac."

"Yes, yes . . . but it's also our responsibility to do it *responsibly.*"

"Responsibly?" She frowned. "What are you—"

"What about that op-ed piece you ran about racial discrimination a week or so ago?" he asked. "Was *that* responsible?"

"After the way those thugs treated Sarah and

me? You don't think that was responsible?" She felt her temper rising.

"I'm not sure."

"I can't believe you, Mac. Are you actually suggesting I shouldn't have written that piece?"

"I'm saying it may've stirred folks up unnecessarily, Anna. I almost mentioned it at the time, but I hoped this business would just run its course."

"Run its course?" Anna pounded an angry fist on the table, making the glassware rattle. "Meaning we should keep quiet and bury our heads in the sand about racial inequality? The same way folks did about women's suffrage for so many years? You can't be serious."

"I *am* serious. Those pieces you wrote were like poking a hornet's nest."

She considered this. What if Mac was right? She had wanted to stir up the good citizens, not provoke the rabble rousers.

"For Sarah Rose's sake, I was concerned, Anna."

"Oh . . ." She nodded with a glimmer of realization.

"Remember what I told you about my friend Ben."

"Big Ben," she said slowly. "Yes, I remember that . . . now."

"No one has seen Sarah Rose," Katy announced as she returned to the dining room. "Not Lucille or Clara or even Ellen."

"Oh dear." Anna stood. "What about Daniel?" she said suddenly. "She's probably there, Katy. She was getting ready to move over there and—"

"She's not there," Katy declared.

"You called him to check?" Mac pushed himself to his feet.

"No, but I know she's not there." Katy bit her lip.

"How can you know that if you didn't call him?" Anna questioned.

"Because I was there," Katy said. "I wanted to walk Sarah Rose home, but she'd already left. And now I just know something is wrong."

"I'm calling Chief Rollins." Mac grabbed his cane.

"Should I hold off on dinner?" Bernice asked with a worried expression.

"Yes. Keep it warm for us," Mac called at her. "We need to put out a search for Sarah Rose."

Anna followed him to the telephone. "Tell the chief to keep an eye out for those fishing thugs, Fred and Bud. He'll know what I mean by that."

"Let's go look for her," Katy told Anna. "It's still light out. Maybe she went for a walk on the beach."

"By herself?" Anna demanded as she shoved on her hat and grabbed a cardigan.

"I don't know. Maybe . . ."

"I don't think she's down there," Anna said as they went outside. "I have another plan. You run down to Lucille's and borrow her telephone. First call Lawrence Bouchard and explain the situation. Tell him to contact Frank and for them to meet me down at the docks. I'll hurry down there and start looking around. In the meantime, I want you to call anyone and everyone you can think of who might be sympathetic to Sarah Rose, including Daniel. Ask our friends to be on the lookout for her. The more eyes we have on this, the sooner we can resolve it."

"I'm on it." Katy started for Lucille's but then turned. "But should you go down to the docks by yourself?"

"Don't worry. I'll drive the Runabout. And it's still light out. And I'm sure there'll be other fisherman about. Just make sure Lawrence and Frank get down there as soon as possible." Anna waved to Katy and hurried to the carriage house to get Mac's vehicle.

As she drove down to the docks, Anna felt a mixture of guilt and worry. Was this her fault for printing those controversial pieces in the paper? She had never meant to put Sarah Rose at risk. Just the opposite. She'd hoped to garner sympathy for Sarah's difficult situation. But now this. Was she to blame? Was Sarah in danger?

Anna parked next to the docks and got out, peering up and down, trying to see if Bud's boat was anywhere in sight. A few fishermen were loitering around the docks, but she wasn't sure how helpful they would be. Some of them were probably on friendly terms with Bud and Fred. And perhaps not so much with a female editor in chief of the local newspaper. Still, what could she do?

Acting braver than she felt, she strode down there and, approaching a pair of younger fishermen, inquired about Sarah Rose. The response she got was not encouraging. Not so much because they gave her no information, but because of their obvious lack of interest or concern for Sarah Rose—and their derogatory comments.

"I'm surprised," she firmly told them. "My daughter is a member of your younger generation, and she's quite modern. I thought perhaps you were as well. But it seems she holds more progressive ideas than you fellows. Perhaps not everyone realizes that we are living in the twentieth century." Without saying another word, she turned around and headed down to where an older fisherman was mending a net. She politely greeted him then asked about whether he'd noticed Bud Griggs's boat going out today.

"Yep." He nodded. "Not too long ago." He glanced at the western sky as if gauging the sunlight. "Reckon it was about six o'clock they took off. Must be planning to go out a ways. Probably stay out until tomorrow or longer."

"Was it only Bud and Fred?" she asked eagerly. "Or did someone else go with them?"

"Can't say. Never saw 'em board the boat. Just heard the motor start up and looked up in time to see 'em leave."

"Anna!"

She glanced down the dock to see Daniel waving and hurrying toward her. She quickly filled him in on what little she'd learned, unconcerned that the older fisherman was listening.

"You think they took Sarah Rose out on the boat?" Daniel asked with a furrowed brow.

"I'm afraid that's a real possibility." She reminded him of the unfortunate encounter she and Sarah Rose had experienced with Fred and Bud.

"You talkin' about that colored woman?" the fisherman asked with a scowl.

"Yes. That's Sarah Rose." Anna nodded eagerly. "Have you seen her today?"

"Nope. But may be better if she were gone." His tone was belligerent. "Sunset Cove's no place for the likes of her."

"Sarah Rose is a good person," Anna said hotly. "It's too bad you don't understand—"

"Come on," Daniel grabbed her by the arm. "Don't waste time here, Anna. I see the *Lucky Lady* just coming in to dock. Maybe Captain Rex will give us some help."

The old fisherman laughed. "Don't count on it."

"Never mind him," Daniel said quietly as he led Anna down the dock.

"Oh, he just makes me so angry," she declared, hurrying to keep up.

"Here comes more help." Daniel waved to a group of men coming down the dock steps. They paused to talk to Lawrence, Frank, and Randall, exchanging what little information they had.

"How about if I call the coast guard?" Lawrence offered. "I know what that boat looks like, inside and out. I'll tell them everything I know about Bud and Fred too."

"Thanks," Anna told him. "Sounds like they've been out for about an hour, so it's possible they could be heading past a station before too long."

"I'll let Chief Rollins know about this," Randall said. "I noticed him and a couple of cops getting into cars. I'm guessing they're headed down here too."

"And we're going to talk to Captain Rex right now," Daniel said. "Maybe he'll be willing to take his boat out again to look around."

"I'll come with you," Frank offered. "It's a nice evening for a boat trip."

"Tell the chief to get some of his men down here fast," Daniel yelled to Randall. "If we get the *Lucky Lady* to go out, we'll need backup on board."

● ● ●

It was about eight-thirty by the time the *Lucky Lady*, with a crew of policemen and a few other volunteers, was ready to go out looking for Bud Griggs's boat. A part of Anna wished she could go too, but she knew that Captain Rex didn't want a female on board, and she was so grateful he was willing to go after several days of fishing that she simply waved from the dock, wishing them well. She was glad that Daniel had offered to go with them. Hopefully Sarah Rose would not be in need of medical attention when and if they found her, but at least he would be ready.

The dock was surprisingly busy for this time of the evening. Anna knew it was because many people had been notified, probably by Katy, that Sarah Rose was missing—most likely abducted—and they'd come out with a willingness to help find her. Although it was encouraging, Anna hoped it wasn't a lost cause. She hated to consider it, but her worst fear was that Fred and Bud could've simply tossed Sarah Rose overboard.

"A group of high school kids are combing the beach," Katy told Anna as they walked up to the car. "And Clara organized the Red Cross women to walk through town, asking everyone and anyone if they saw anything."

"That's good."

"And the mayor is driving Grandfather around

to look on the north end of town," Katy continued to explain as they got into the car. "Randall and Lawrence are driving around the south end of town."

"It's wonderful how much everyone is helping," Anna said quietly as they got into the car. "I just hope it's not too little too late."

"But why, Mother?" Katy's voice cracked. "Why would anyone want to hurt her like this?"

"Partly because of her skin color," Anna said in a flat tone. "You know that, Katy. But also partly because of me."

"You?" Katy looked at Anna with fearful eyes. "Why is that?"

Anna reminded her of the pieces that she'd printed in the paper. "Mac suggested that I poked a hornet's nest."

"But that was after those two lowlifes threatened you and Sarah Rose. Surely, you don't blame yourself for that."

"I don't know." Anna slowly shook her head. "Maybe I shouldn't have been so vocal in the newspaper. Maybe I did aggravate them." Anna almost mentioned how she'd also thwarted the two crooks in their rum-running schemes by helping Lawrence Bouchard to reform. But that was a secret.

Anna drove the Runabout up to the hospital building site, which had a good vantage point over the ocean. They got out and looked over the horizon. Although the sun had just set, the sky was still light enough to spot the *Lucky Lady* making its way out to sea. Because they suspected the coast guard boat from up north would be heading this way before long, Captain Rex had decided to head south.

"It'll be like finding a needle in a haystack," Anna said glumly. "Look how much ocean there is . . . how small the *Lucky Lady* is looking already."

"Maybe we should pray for her, Mother," Katy said quietly.

"You're right." Anna nodded. And so, standing there by the hospital building, which looked close to completion, Katy and Anna prayed. They'd just said amen when a breeze picked up off the ocean, and Anna noticed Katy starting to shiver. "You don't have on warm enough clothes." Anna put her arm around her. "Let's get you inside."

Back in the Runabout, Anna handed Katy the car blanket. "I'd suggest we drive around and look for Sarah Rose, but I feel fairly certain that she's been kidnapped by Bud and Fred. It's the only thing that makes sense."

"Plus there are lots of people already out looking for her," Katy said. "Maybe some of us should be near a telephone . . . just in case."

"Yes. Good thinking. If Sarah Rose isn't with Bud and Fred, she may try to call us." Anna headed the Runabout toward home. When they got there, the house was quiet. Bernice left a note saying that dinner was in the oven and that she and Mickey were out looking for Sarah Rose, and it didn't appear that Mac was back yet.

"I don't feel hungry," Anna told Katy. "But maybe we should eat something."

They sat at the kitchen table, poking at the somewhat dried-out dinner and not talking. Finally, Katy broke the silence.

"It's my fault, Mother."

"What is your fault?" Anna set down her fork.

"If any harm has come to Sarah Rose. I'm the one who asked her to come to Sunset Cove. You told me not to and—"

"It's not your fault," Anna firmly told her. "Sarah Rose is a grown woman. She made her own choice. And I warned her about what she was getting into. She knew the situation here, and yet she chose to remain."

"She loved living by the ocean," Katy said sadly. "Even when she was planning to move down to the doctor's office to help the Hollisters, she said she'd miss the view from her room."

"So, you see, you can't blame yourself. If we're going to blame anyone, we should blame me." Anna felt close to tears. "Mac was right. I never should've put those pieces in the paper."

"But you did that in defense of Sarah Rose, Mother. Because you love her."

"I know, but if that stirred those men up—and

if anything has happened to Sarah—I'll feel like—"

"Let's both promise not to blame ourselves," Katy said. "We need to keep hoping for the best. And to keep praying for her."

"You're right." Anna nodded. "When did you become so grown up, Katy?"

Katy sighed. "I don't know. It seems to have happened rather quickly. A little too quickly."

Anna squeezed Katy's hand. "Well, being a married woman has probably helped that some. But you've always been mature for your age. No denying that."

"Mother?" Katy looked at Anna, her eyes glistening with tears. "I need to tell you something."

"What is it?" Anna studied her daughter, worried that she was about to hear some more bad news. She hoped nothing had happened to Jim.

"I'm going to have a baby."

Anna was too stunned to speak. She wanted to ask how this happened—except of course she knew how. But Katy wasn't even eighteen yet. And she'd always wanted to be an independent and modern woman. She'd wanted a career . . . and so many other things. How could this be?

CHAPTER 27

After recovering from her shock, Anna stood up and threw her arms around Katy. "Oh, dear, dear Katy, I'm so glad." She hugged her daughter tightly. "Congratulations. This is wonderful." She held Katy back, looking into her now teary eyes.

"Really?" Katy reached for her handkerchief. "You mean that?"

"Of course I do. It's just that you took me by surprise. And, of course, I'm still worried for Sarah so—"

"Oh, dear, I suppose that was bad timing on my part. I'm sorry." Katy wiped her eyes.

"No, I think it's good timing. I needed a bit of happy news just now. And honestly, I couldn't be more pleased. A baby! This is so exciting."

"Is that the truth or are you just trying to make me feel better?"

"Feel better?" Anna blinked. "I should think you'd be over the moon about this. And think of Jim. He'll be ecstatic to hear he's going to be a daddy."

"I hope so."

"But you seem sad, Katy. Are you feeling all right?" Anna sat down again, looking closely at her daughter. "I'd noticed you seemed different lately, but I thought perhaps you were simply tired or missing Jim."

"Both of the above." Katy sighed. "But I'm fine. Even Doctor Daniel says I'm in excellent health."

"So he knows about this?" Anna felt a bit of jealousy.

"Yes. I had an appointment this afternoon." Katy looked sheepish. "I specifically asked him not to tell you."

"Not to tell me?" Now Anna was hurt.

"I didn't want to tell anyone," she confessed. "Not even Jim. But I think Sarah Rose figured it out. . . ." Katy let out a sob. "I wanted to walk home with her from the doctor's office. But she'd already gone. Those nasty men must've grabbed her then. If only I'd ended my appointment sooner, maybe I could've—"

"Remember you said we weren't going to blame ourselves," Anna said.

"Oh, Mother, what if they've done something horrible to her?"

Anna closed her eyes and pursed her lips. She'd worked at the *Oregonian* long enough to know this was a possibility. Bigots who hated people for their skin color had few if any scruples.

"We're not going to worry, Katy. We're going to pray for her instead."

"I know what I'll do." Katy stood up. "I'm going to call Reverend Williamson and then everyone I can think of, and I'll ask them to meet at the church to pray for Sarah Rose. The Red Cross ladies and Clara and Ellen and Grandmother and anyone else who is willing to go."

Before Anna could question this, Katy was on the telephone. By nine o'clock, the church was partially filled with mostly women and a few older men. Reverend Williamson spoke briefly then led them in a prayer vigil that lasted nearly to midnight.

"That was an encouraging show of people," Anna said as she drove herself and Katy home.

"I hope God was listening." Katy's voice was weary.

"I'm sure he was." Anna pulled up in front of the darkened house. Hopefully Mac had gone to bed by now. She'd left him a note explaining their plans but asked him not to wait up.

They tiptoed up the stairs, pausing on the landing, where Anna hugged Katy again. "I'm still so happy to know about the baby, Katy," she whispered. "It's like a bright ray of sunshine in the midst of a dark threatening storm."

"I don't know if I'll be able to sleep much tonight." Katy yawned.

"You need your rest. Tell you what—if you

promise to try to sleep, I'll keep my ears perked in case the telephone rings."

"And promise you'll wake me up if you hear any news?" she asked. "Good or bad?"

"I will," Anna reluctantly agreed. "And I'll keep praying. You and your baby need a good night's sleep. All right?"

Katy nodded. "Thanks."

As Anna went into her room, she felt an overwhelming wave of deep sadness wash over her. Really, what was the likelihood that they would ever see Sarah Rose again? The thugs who took her out tonight would make sure that never happened. There'd be too much to lose if their crimes were brought to light. And without evidence of their offenses, people could only make assumptions and accusations . . . but the law's hands would be tied.

Despite all the sincere prayers spoken tonight, justice seemed an impossible dream. Sarah's fate had probably been sealed the moment she'd been abducted. Poor, dear Sarah Rose. It sickened Anna to think of it. How she had loved the sea . . . and that the sea would probably be her demise. So unfair . . . so maddening. Still, as promised, Anna prayed for Sarah's welfare and for the men out on the *Lucky Lady* looking for her.

The breakfast table was glum the following morning. No one had slept well, no one had an appetite, and no one had heard anything about Sarah Rose. But, according to Lawrence, who'd called earlier, the *Lucky Lady* was still at sea. Because it was Saturday, Anna had no plans to go to the newspaper office, and Katy, because she was worn out and worried, decided to spend the day at home as well. As they finished up breakfast, the conversation was almost nonexistent.

Anna had suggested that Katy tell Mac the baby news earlier this morning, but Katy had firmly said no and that she wasn't ready to go public yet. Anna hoped that it wasn't because of her hesitant reaction yesterday. Certainly, she'd been shocked and was, in fact, still getting used to the idea. But she thought this news might cheer Mac some. Still, it was Katy's news, and Anna didn't plan to steal her thunder.

As Anna set down her coffee cup, the doorbell rang, and she leapt to her feet. Hoping it would be Sarah Rose, Anna eagerly ran to open the door, concealing her dismay to see it was a pressman from the paper. "What is it, Leroy?" she asked anxiously. "Is there trouble at the newspaper?"

"Nope. But Henry just noticed this letter. Someone must've slipped it under the front door after closing hours yesterday. Thought you'd want to see it."

She took the letter, thanked Leroy, and closed the door.

"What is it?" Katy asked eagerly.

"I don't know." Walking back to the dining room, Anna tore open the envelope to remove a barely legible note with so many misspellings it was a challenge to decipher.

"It's from Fred and Bud," she told Mac and Katy. "Our kidnappers."

"You're kidding." Katy sat back down. "What does it say?"

"Do those scoundrels expect ransom money?" Mac asked angrily.

"I'm not sure . . ." She skimmed the poorly written letter. "But this is clearly some retribution for recent pieces in the paper."

"I told you," Mac said dourly.

"So that's why they kidnapped her?" Katy was incredulous. "Just because of views in the newspaper?"

"What about ransom money?" Mac demanded. "What does it say about that?"

Anna pointed to the bottom of the letter. "They want five thousand dollars in small bills."

"Those dirty rotten crooks," Mac growled, shaking his cane. "I'd like to take my cane to the backs of both of them."

"What else does it say, Mother?"

"They warn me not to contact the police as well as give instructions for dropping off the money." Anna had intentionally left one piece of the letter out. The demand that Anna dismiss

Lawrence Bouchard from the newspaper. Probably so he could return to rum-running with them. They'd obviously enjoyed the easy money but were apparently clueless as to how to pull it off themselves. But did they honestly think their half-baked scheme would work? That no one would know?

"That's the most ludicrous thing I've ever heard," Mac declared. "Those scoundrels are complete imbeciles."

"But it does mean that Sarah is probably alive," Katy said hopefully.

"Yes, it seems that way." Anna slowly shook her head. "But how in the world they think they can get away with this mystifies me. I suspect this whole thing is as much to punish me as anything else." She felt a pang of guilt for running those pieces in the paper.

"What about their demands not to notify the police?" Katy asked.

"That bell can't be un-rung," Mac said wryly. "Those numbskulls probably had no idea that half of Sunset Cove would be out looking for Sarah Rose by now."

"But will they hurt her because of that?" Katy sounded worried again.

"Hard to say," Anna told her. "But I'm guessing they'll want that money. How can they get it without keeping Sarah alive?"

"What do they say about the money?" Mac

asked. "Did they plan to exchange Sarah Rose for the money?"

"All they say is to drop the cash on the west side of Little Rock Island . . . today."

"That's just north of the lighthouse," Mac said. "Only accessible by boat and only at high tide."

"What do we do?" Anna asked Mac.

"Good question." He rubbed his chin. "Since the police are already involved, I think we need to notify the chief. He needs to see that letter."

"I'll call him right now." As Anna headed for the phone, she had no qualms about sharing this letter with Chief Rollins, but she hoped they could keep it safe from other prying eyes—for Lawrence's sake. So far they'd been able to keep his involvement with Fred and Bud a secret. And Lawrence had made such a good turnaround, she hoped to keep it that way.

By the time Anna finished talking to the chief, Mac had started putting together a plan. "I'll call Wally and ask him to take us out in his new fishing boat. She's a honey with a good strong engine." He held up a tide table. "Tide will be high again by two this afternoon." He peered out the window. "Looks like a nice calm sea too."

"But who will go out on Wally's boat?" Anna asked. "And what about the police?"

"Naturally, we'll need some officials around," Mac explained. "But they'll have to move in later so as not to scare off our crooks. I'll go out on the boat with Wally, and I'll take a carpet bag—and make it look like it's full of money. And then I'll—"

"No, you will not," Anna declared. She could just imagine Mac stumbling over the slippery wet rocks with his cane, trying to hand over a bag of fake money.

"Why the dickens not?" he demanded. "I've gone out in the boat with Wally before. I most certainly am going."

"Well then I'm going too," Anna insisted. "After all, the ransom letter was sent to me. I have every right to go. Besides, it'll make a good story for the front page next week."

Now the argument began. Mac was determined to protect Anna, and Anna argued about the logistics until Katy got into the debate, demanding to go along too. "This is absolutely crazy," Anna told them both. "I don't think any of us should go. For all we know, it's a set up. Why should we even trust the kidnappers?" Of course, this was simply her attempt to throw off Mac and Katy. Neither of them had any business going out in a boat in pursuit of a pair of unpredictable criminals.

"Then what are we going to do?" Katy asked.

"I'm taking the letter to Chief Rollins." Anna pulled on her cardigan. "He'll help us concoct a good plan." She put on her hat. "I'll let you know as soon as it's all figured out." Anna didn't tell them that she'd already convinced Chief Rollins that she should be the one to deliver the ransom package. And she'd even suggested they use real money in case the thugs refused to turn over Sarah without it. And although the chief said he wanted to think about it, she figured he'd see the sensibility of her plan.

To save time, she drove the Runabout to the police station, and there she and the chief went round and round over a plan that finally seemed plausible. Since Mac had already called the mayor, getting him to agree to using his new fishing boat for the mission, Chief Rollins agreed to let Mac go. "But you'll do as I say," the chief told Mac over the telephone. "And like it or not, I'm putting Anna in charge. They wrote the letter to her. So you let her handle this thing." They exchanged a few more words then the chief hung up and turned back to Anna. "I won't pretend this isn't dangerous, Anna. But you've shown me you have a clear head before. I'll count on you having one today too." He frowned. "But what I want to know is how do you always get yourself in the middle of these messes? You're supposed to report the news, not make it."

She gave him a half-smile. "I don't really know. Mostly I just want to ensure Sarah Rose gets safely home. And I feel that a woman handling these negotiations will be less intimidating than a man." At least, she hoped so.

"I'd ask you to carry a firearm . . . but I'm worried that may make things even more dangerous. However, I'm going to ask Wally to take a rifle with him. Just in case."

Anna cringed inwardly. "Well, at least he's a good shot."

"And I've already called the coast guard station in Bandon. They'll send a flag message to the cutter when it passes by. To send it back up here."

"What about the *Lucky Lady*?" Anna asked with concern, mostly for Daniel. "Any way to get word to that boat?"

"I expect the coast guard caught up with them. I'd think they'd have turned around back by now." He reached for his phone. "I'm going to call Wally and nail down the plan for his boat." He glanced at the clock. "He'll probably want to leave the dock around one. You want to meet him down there?"

She nodded. "Sounds good."

"And I'll have a bag ready for you. We won't have the full five thousand. But we'll make it look like it. Good thing they specified small bills."

She thanked him and excused herself and, wishing that the *Lucky Lady* might've returned to Sunset Cove, she drove down to the docks to check. But the big fishing boat was still at sea. And now, feeling concerned for Daniel's dad, she stopped by the house. After knocking loudly for a couple of minutes, she felt more worried. What if the stress of being alone had taken a toll on the old man's heart? Checking the door, she saw it was unlocked. "Hello?" she yelled into the house. "Anyone home?"

Not hearing a response, she let herself inside. "Dr. Hollister?" she called out. "Are you here?" She found the old doctor still in his dressing gown, looking very unsettled, in the living room. "I'm sorry to intrude," she told him. "But I wanted to check to see if you're all right." She sat down beside him on the sofa. "Are you well?"

"Where's Daniel?" he demanded.

"Didn't he tell you he was going out on the boat?"

"No. No one told me anything. I'm here by myself. There's nothing to eat." He glared at her. "Where the devil is Sarah Rose?"

"You didn't hear?"

"Hear what?" he growled. "Where is everyone? What is going on?"

"Let me see if I can find you something to eat." She removed her hat and gloves. "And then I'll explain." She hurried to the kitchen to find a well-stocked pantry and icebox. Was that silly old man really incapable of finding food for himself? What if he were alone for a week— would he starve? She put on the teapot and began to cook some bacon and eggs. Anna wasn't a great cook, but she knew how to get by. And breakfasts had always been her specialty. Before long, she carried a loaded tray out to where he was still sitting hunched over like a stone on the sofa.

"Here you go." She set the tray on the table in front of him and poured him a cup of tea. "While you eat, I'll explain what's going on." So she told him about Sarah Rose and how she'd been abducted and how Daniel had gone out on the fishing boat in case they needed medical assistance.

He paused with his fork in midair. "I knew this was a barbaric backwoods sort of town. I never should've agreed to move here with Daniel. No good will come of it."

"I don't agree." She poured herself a cup of tea. "This town needs a good doctor. And we're building a hospital to prove it. That's just some of the good that will come of it."

"Humph." He forked into his eggs. "Building a hospital for a bunch of small-town bumpkins. A place to treat ruffians, kidnappers, rum-runners, and fishermen. Harrumph."

Anna took in a slow breath. "The people of Sunset Cove are good people." Now she told him about how many folks had been helping to look for Sarah Rose and about the prayer vigil last night. And how, even today, the chief and she were putting together a plan to rescue Sarah Rose.

"What kind of plan?" he demanded.

Deciding it couldn't hurt to humor the old curmudgeon, she explained about the ransom letter and how she and Wally and Mac would go out to make the exchange. "We'll leave around one." She checked her pocket watch to see it was almost eleven. "So if you'll excuse me, I have things to attend to. I hope Daniel will be home before long. Or, if you like, I could ask Katy to come by and keep you company."

"Wait a minute, young lady." He held up a finger. "Are you telling me that *you* are going out on a fishing boat to meet up with the hoodlums that kidnapped Sarah Rose?"

"That's exactly what I'm telling you." She stood.

"Well, I can't say that I approve." He scowled.

"I don't expect you to approve," she told him. "I'm sure you wouldn't approve of many things I've done or plan to do."

"You are a very stubborn woman."

"Thank you. I'll take that as a compliment." She smiled. "In my business, it helps to be stubborn."

"What about Daniel?" he demanded.

"What about Daniel?" she repeated in a softer tone.

"What does he think of you gallivanting about in a boat, trying to catch some crooks and—"

"I am not trying to catch any crooks," she

363

clarified. "I'm only trying to get Sarah Rose safely home. I should think you'd appreciate that." She pointed to the tray of half-eaten food. "At least you'll have someone here to keep you from starving."

"I don't know what my son sees in a woman like you." He narrowed his eyes at her. "I suppose you've never heard that a woman's place is in the home."

"I know you're fond of my mother, Dr. Hollister, but perhaps Lucille never told you about how she left my father and me when I was a small child? So, no, I suppose I never did hear that a *woman's place is in the home.* I think a woman's place is wherever she feels most at home. Whether it's a newspaper office, a dress shop, or even a smelly old fishing boat." She forced a smile as she put on her hat. "Perhaps a woman's place may sometimes be in a home. But for me, that home would have to be filled with love and kindness and acceptance." She tugged on her gloves. "Excuse me."

She controlled herself from stomping out of the living room or from slamming the front door. But she was definitely irritated at the old grump. He never even thanked her for making breakfast. As much as she loved Daniel, she wasn't sure she'd ever be able to accept a package deal that included his father. Her "place" would never be in a home where that old curmudgeon ruled supreme.

CHAPTER 28

A s Wally piloted his boat through the mouth of the jetty, Anna spotted a large fishing boat approaching from the south. "Mac," she called out. "That looks like the *Lucky Lady* out there."

"Sure does," he confirmed somberly. "Passing like ships in the night."

"I wish we could tell them what we're doing," she said.

"No time for that," Wally called over his shoulder. "We're already cutting it close if we want to make it by two."

"That's right," Mac said.

"And we'll need to get in and out as quickly as possible. Before the tide starts to turn on us. Otherwise we'll get stuck on the rocks."

Even so, Anna waved to the big boat, imagining Daniel looking out from the bow, although it was probably too far away for anyone to see her. And being that she was dressed in men's clothes, including a pair of Wally's smelly old fishing waders, Daniel probably never would've recognized her anyway. Besides, they didn't need the *Lucky Lady* to follow them to the rendezvous. That would ruin everything.

She looked up at the clear blue sky. "Such a beautiful day," she said in attempt to keep her nerves at bay. "Too bad this isn't a pleasure cruise."

Mac scowled. "I still hate the idea of you taking the money to those nasty scoundrels, Anna. What if they decide to hold you hostage too?"

"Why would they do that when I'm handing over the money?"

"For more money?"

"If that happens, I'll make them understand it's a one-time payment and there's no more money."

"But these crooks are dumber than rocks, Anna. Who knows what they may pull?"

"We're covered, Mac. I already told you that the chief has an excellent secondary plan. I'm sure they're already in place by now."

"Those plans could fail too. What then?"

"It's a dependable plan, Mac." To reassure herself as much as him, she went over it all again. "While Fred and Bud are distracted with our boat's arrival on the west side, the coast guard and state police will be silently rowing over from the lighthouse. They'll come up on the east side of the island. While I keep our kidnappers' attention with my carpet bag of cash, stumbling along on the rocky surface, making it look like I could accidentally drop the money bag, the police will silently creep up from behind."

"Yeah, yeah." Mac nodded with a grim expression. "I know, I know. But if anything goes wrong, Wally has his rifle. Right, Wally?"

"You bet." Wally nodded firmly. "Old Betsy is loaded and ready to go."

"And don't forget Wally won the turkey shoot last fall," Anna reassured Mac.

"I even took some practice shots this morning," Wally said.

Anna really hoped this mess wouldn't be resolved with gunfire. As the boat bounced over the gently rolling waves, she bowed her head, silently praying for God's help . . . praying that she would successfully play her role . . . and praying for Sarah Rose's safe recovery.

Anna's mouth felt dry as paper as Little Rock Island came into view. From her vantage point it looked deserted, but that didn't mean they weren't already there, possibly watching them approach from behind one of the jutting rocks. According to Wally, the island was only about a hundred feet wide and, because of the rocky shore, he wouldn't be able to get his boat right next to it. His plan was to drop anchor at a safe distance and then Anna would have to climb over the side and wade up to the tiny island. She hoped she wouldn't lose her footing. Although Fred and Bud would probably risk themselves to rescue the money bag, they'd probably be glad to leave her behind to drown.

"Drop anchor," Wally yelled to Mac as he put the motor in reverse, maneuvering as close as he safely could to the island.

Anna went over to help Mac with the ropes but was impressed to see that, even with his bum arm, he was managing just fine. "You get ready to go," he gruffly told Anna. "And be careful."

She kissed his stubbly cheek, realizing he hadn't shaved today. "I'll be careful, Mac. You too. And say a prayer." She picked up the carpet bag, looping the strap over her shoulder, then slung one leg over the side.

"I've got your back, Anna," Wally said from the helm. "But be safe."

"I will." She slowly eased herself into the roiling water, trying to find something firm to plant her feet on. When she felt the rocks through the sole of the boots, the water was nearly to the waist of the waders. Holding the money bag over her head, she struggled to keep her balance, slowly working her way to the edge of the island and then crawling up the rocks like a crab until she finally made it to the somewhat flatter surface on top. Pausing to catch her breath, she looked up to see two familiar figures standing in the center of the island—and looking way too pleased with themselves.

Chief Rollins had warned her to maintain a balance between inner confidence and the appearance of an outward fear. "So that the thugs don't suspect anything." But as she continued toward them, she realized she didn't need to pretend terror—her hands already trembled so much that the carpet bag was shaking as she held it out in front of her. "Here it is," she yelled loudly, like the chief had told her to do. "It's all here." She cringed to see they were armed—Fred with what looked like a sawed-off shotgun and Bud with a gleaming pistol.

"Bring it to us," Fred yelled sharply. "And make it fast."

She took a step then feigned a stumble. The chief had encouraged her to drag out her approach to them for as long as possible. This would give the lawmen more time to get into position.

"Come on," Bud said sharply. "Hurry it up!"

She continued to stumble toward them, trying to act the helpless woman and thinking it was only partially an act. "I—I'm coming," she said breathlessly.

"You're not Miss All High and Mighty now, are you?" Fred taunted.

"Move it!" Bud yelled.

"I'm trying. It's hard to walk in these waders." She shifted the bag to her other shoulder and stumbled over a rock, falling down on her knees and moaning in real pain. Finally she was there, looking right into their greedy faces as Bud grabbed the bag from her. "Where's Sarah Rose?" Anna asked.

"Not so fast." Bud opened the bag, looking inside and even digging a bit through the mounds of loose bills. Hopefully not deeply enough to discover it wasn't all cash.

"It's all there," she gruffly told them. "Where is Sarah Rose?"

"Why should we tell you where she is?" Fred used a derogatory term. "Why do you even care? Trash like her don't belong in Sunset Cove anyway."

Anna locked eyes with him. "I doubt that you'll be welcome in Sunset Cove anymore either. Not after this."

"We got bigger fish to fry than Sunset Cove," Bud snapped.

"Well, you better honor your word about Sarah Rose," Anna told him. "Or else I'll make sure your story is printed in every newspaper in this country, complete with your pictures. I'll make sure you can't go anywhere without being recognized."

Bud's eyes widened as if he'd never considered the power of the press.

"I mean it. And there are good folks out there who would turn you guys in to the law. So unless you tell me where Sarah Rose is—*right now*—

you'll be big news all up and down the coast by tomorrow morning."

"She's in a cave." Bud snapped the bag closed. "On Osprey Point."

"Who you got in the boat out there?" Fred asked with suspicious eyes.

"My father and Mayor Wally."

Fred snickered. "Brought a couple of old men with you, huh? That was smart."

She glared at them, biting her tongue lest she say something that would ruin everything. "Sarah Rose had better be all right," she snapped.

"Oh yeah, she's all right." Fred laughed in a mean way. "She's just fine."

Anna couldn't stand any more and so she turned and, without stumbling once, hurried back toward the boat. It wasn't that she thought they'd shoot her in the back, although she wasn't too sure about that, but the chief had warned her to get away as quickly as possible. As she scrambled down the rocks and into the water, she heard men's voices yelling.

"Hurry," Mac called, tossing her a rope that he and Wally both tugged on to pull her back into the boat. She tumbled to the deck and turned to Wally. "Let's get out of here."

"Get that anchor up," Wally yelled as he revved the engine.

As Anna scrambled over to help Mac pull up the anchor, they heard the popping sounds of what must've been gunshots. Then Wally gunned the engine and the boat took off, leaving Little Rock Island in its wake. After they were a safe distance away, Wally slowed down and they all looked back. Although they could see nothing from their position, they heard a few more rounds of gunshots. Anna closed her eyes, hoping and praying that none of the lawmen were hit . . . and praying that this ordeal would soon be over.

"Do you know where Osprey Point is?" she asked Wally and Mac.

"Yeah, it's just up north a ways," Wally said. "Good fishing spot."

"Maybe five or six miles," Mac added. "Why?"

"They said Sarah Rose is there," she told them. "In a cave."

"Is she okay?" Wally asked with a furrowed brow.

"I hope so," Anna said grimly. "I really, really hope so."

It took about an hour to locate the cave where Sarah Rose was curled up in a dark corner. Her hands and feet were bound, and she was shivering from the damp cold. While Wally cut the cords to free her hands, Anna threw the blanket she'd brought over her and helped her to sip water from the canteen. "I'm so sorry this happened to you," she said as she hugged the trembling woman close, hoping to warm her. "Are you all right? Can you walk?"

"I—I think so," Sarah said in a husky voice.

The three of them helped Sarah into the boat and there, wrapped in blankets and with Anna by her side, they headed back to Sunset Cove. Anna held Sarah close as the boat bumped over the waves, but Sarah's eyes were closed. Whether it was from exhaustion or pain or both, Anna wasn't sure, but she wished Wally could push his boat faster. It seemed to take forever to get home.

A small group of folks were gathered on the docks as Wally guided his boat into the slip. Before they began to disembark, Daniel, Frank, and Lawrence rushed up to the boat and Daniel climbed aboard. "How is she?" he quietly asked Anna.

"I'm not sure," Anna whispered back. "She's been through a lot."

"We'll take her to my house," Daniel told Anna. "In case she needs any medical treatment." He called out to Frank and Lawrence to help him, and they carried her up to where Randall's big car was waiting.

"You're shivering," Mac told Anna as they walked up to his car. "Are you all right and able to drive?"

"Yes," she assured him. "Just cold and wet."

By the time they got home, her teeth were chattering. She peeled off the waders on the back porch then hurried inside to where Katy and Bernice were anxiously waiting.

"You look like a drowned rat," Bernice said. "Let's get you upstairs and out of those wet—"

"I'll go run a hot bath," Katy said, running ahead of them.

Before long Anna was soaking in a bubbly, steaming tub. Katy brought her a hot cup of tea and insisted on hearing the full story of Sarah Rose's rescue.

"How did she seem? Was she hurt at all?" Katy asked as Anna pulled on her dressing gown.

"I'm not sure," Anna confessed. "I know she was exhausted. But at least she's in Daniel's care now."

"I'm going over to check on her," Katy declared.

"We'll go together," Anna said as Bernice brought a food tray into her room.

"Not until you eat this." Bernice gave her a no-nonsense look as she pointed at the food. "You barely touched breakfast and you never had a bite of lunch. Now sit down while this soup is still hot."

Anna submitted, eating as much as she could. "Katy," she said as she finished the soup. "Why don't you ask Bernice to put something together to take over to Sarah? I doubt the two doctors will have much of anything to eat."

Katy picked up the food tray. "I'll go help

Bernie pack a basket while you get dressed. Then I'll drive us over there."

Just as they were getting ready to leave, the phone rang and Anna ran to answer it. To her relief, it was Chief Rollins, reporting that none of the lawmen had been injured in the exchange of gunfire on Little Rock Island. "But the kidnappers were wounded. Not mortally. Apparently they were well enough to be sent directly to the state pen, and since the whole thing happened outside of our jurisdiction, their trial and sentencing will be handled by the state."

"Well, that's good to know."

"How are you?" he asked. "We sure appreciate your help in getting them apprehended like that.

She assured him that she was fine and on her way to check on Sarah Rose.

"Well, be sure to let me know how she's faring so I can pass this on to the prosecuting attorney," he said. "And maybe you and I can meet up tomorrow after church, and I'll fill you in on the full story for the newspaper."

"She's resting upstairs," Daniel told Anna while Katy took the food basket into the kitchen.

"Can I see her now?" Anna asked.

"Yes, of course. I'm sure she'll be glad to see you."

"Is she okay?" Anna asked quietly.

"I'm sure they were pretty rough with her. She had bruises and abrasions and was chilled from exposure, plus the shock of the ordeal. But no broken bones."

"Well, I'll go check on her. And Katy has some hot soup to bring up, if that's okay."

"That's perfectly fine." Daniel gave her a small smile. "And when you're done, I'd sure love to hear about what happened. I didn't ask Sarah Rose for any details. I felt she was too traumatized to tell me much. And I told her that I want her to rest up so, even if she feels like getting out of bed, remind her of doctor's orders."

Anna nodded. "If she's sleeping, I won't disturb her."

"And she's in the room at the end of the hall," he called as she hurried upstairs.

Anna was relieved to find Sarah sitting up in bed and looking a bit more like her normal self. "How are you feeling?" Anna asked as she scooted a chair next to her bed.

"Worn out." Sarah sighed. "But grateful to be alive."

"I'm grateful for that too. We were so worried about you." Anna took her hand. "Katy's downstairs heating some chicken soup for you."

"Dr. Daniel made me drink tea and honey."

"Well, you need some real nourishment too." Now Anna filled in Sarah about the fate of her kidnappers. "The chief said they weren't seriously wounded. They're probably in the state pen by now."

"I'm glad they weren't killed."

Anna was surprised. "Really? You didn't wish them dead after what they did?"

"No . . . We're supposed to forgive our enemies."

Anna pursed her lips. Truth be told, she wouldn't have felt disappointed if both of those brutal hooligans were dead.

"And we're supposed to pray for those who persecute us."

"Well, Sarah Rose, you are a better Christian than I am." Anna paused as Katy came into the room with the soup.

"I'm so happy to see you." Katy beamed down on her. "I hope you're hungry."

"That does smell good." Sarah Rose smiled.

"Here, take my chair," Anna told Katy. "I need to talk to Daniel anyway." She gently patted Sarah's shoulder. "You're an inspiration, my friend." Then feeling slightly guilty for her un-Christlike attitude toward Fred and Bud, Anna went back downstairs to fill in Daniel about today's rescue mission.

Katy set Sarah's empty bowl onto the bedside table and then sighed. "Sarah Rose, I feel like I owe you a great big apology."

"Whatever for?" Sarah dabbed her mouth with the napkin.

"For asking you to come to Sunset Cove." Katy slowly shook her head. "I never dreamed something like this would happen when I invited you here. But afterward . . . well, my grandfather and mother warned me it could be dangerous for you." Katy felt her eyes filling. "I'm so—so sorry."

"Oh, dear girl." Sarah reached over for Katy's hand, clasping it firmly between the two of hers. "What happened to me was not your fault. It was an act of pure hatred. And all you've ever shown me was love. Don't blame yourself."

"But you could've been killed, and if you had, it would've been my—"

"I was not killed, Miss Katy. Thanks be to God, I'm here and alive."

"You must've been so frightened."

Sarah slowly nodded. "Yes, that's true. I was frightened at first. But then I prayed . . . and I realized that the worst that could happen was they would kill me, but then I'd be with my baby, and my Abe, and my parents, and all my other loved ones in heaven . . . and that I'd be free . . . free from the woes of this world."

Katy tried to absorb this. Oh, she knew that Sarah Rose's life had been hard and filled with loss, but Katy didn't usually think about such things. And Sarah didn't usually complain about

378

much of anything. "Well, your faith amazes me," Katy admitted, "but I wouldn't blame you if you didn't want to live in Sunset Cove after what happened to you."

"To be honest, I had similar thoughts. While I was shivering in that cave, I did wonder if I'd been mistaken to move here. Those men kept telling me I didn't belong in these parts." Sarah's eyes filled with tears. "Maybe they were right about that. I'm not saying that folks in Sunset Cove aren't good folks. But maybe they're not *my* folks."

"I think you're wrong about that," Katy insisted. "If you'd seen how everyone came together when you went missing . . ." Now she described in detail all that had taken place, from the town-wide hunt and the boats that went out, to the prayer vigil at the church until midnight, to the Red Cross ladies. "Almost everyone here was concerned for you."

"They did all that . . . just for me?" Sarah looked truly astonished.

"Yes. All that for you." Katy nodded firmly. "It seems you've a lot of friends in Sunset Cove."

"I just never knew that." Sarah shook her head. "Never knew that at all."

"Well, that's probably because people here don't always act that friendly," Katy said. "But when they heard what happened to you, they showed their support."

For a while, Sarah Rose said nothing. Then she looked at Katy with teary eyes. "The other thing I was thinking when I was in that cave was that if I ever escaped, I would go back to Portland."

"Oh?" Katy's heart sank. "Is that what you really want? I mean, I would understand it . . . but I'd sure miss you. More than you know."

"I'd miss you too." Sarah wiped her eyes with the napkin. "But if what you say is true—if I really have some friends in Sunset Cove—well then, I guess I'd like to stay."

Katy hugged her. "You're a brave woman, Sarah Rose. I'm proud to have you for my friend."

Her dark eyes twinkled. "And I want to be here when you have your baby, Miss Katy."

Katy smiled. "So you really did know, then?"

Sarah Rose nodded. "I think I knew even before you came to see Dr. Daniel. Don't forget that I helped raise you. And, if I can, I'd like to help with your baby too."

Katy felt a tinge of concern. Was it wrong to encourage Sarah to remain in Sunset Cove like this? Especially considering all she'd just been through. But then Katy remembered that Sarah Rose, not unlike Katy's mother and grandmother, was a strong-minded and independent woman. If she were inclined to remain in this town, no one—not even the likes of those horrid men who'd kidnapped her—would be able to dissuade her.

CHAPTER 29

Even though Katy wasn't quite three months along in her pregnancy, she decided not to keep it secret any longer. Perhaps it was from hearing of Sarah Rose's brush with death, or perhaps Dr. Daniel had been right about having a change in heart, but somehow Katy had reached the place where she realized a baby was something to celebrate. And suddenly, she no longer cared who knew about it.

But before telling anyone else, she wrote a long, cheery letter to Jim. She knew he'd probably hoot and holler and dance with joy when he read about his impending fatherhood—and that alone made her happy. But as her news spread among friends and around town, she discovered how much fun it was to receive congratulations and well wishes.

Naturally, Ellen was thrilled and slightly smug since she'd been the first one to suspect it in the first place. "My baby will be about six months old when yours is born," she told Katy as they decorated the Grange building for the upcoming Harvest Dance. This event was planned to be a fundraiser for the Red Cross. With US soldiers participating on the battlefield, the need for supplies was growing daily.

"Yes, you'll be an old and wise and experienced mother by then," Katy teased. "I'll have to come to you for your sage advice."

"What if I have a boy and you have a girl, Katy? They could fall in love and get married someday."

Katy laughed. "Good grief, Ellen, you're already planning your child's life."

"Why not?" Ellen patted her rounded midsection. "Someone has to think of these things."

As Katy tied off a piece of orange crepe paper, she noticed a uniformed soldier entering the building. For a brief instant, only seeing his dark silhouette in the doorway, she thought it was Jim and nearly shrieked with delight. But as the man came closer, she realized it was Ellen's husband. "Ellen, look!" she exclaimed, pointing toward the door. "What is he doing dressed like—"

"Lawrence!" Ellen dropped the roll of crepe paper, sending a tail of orange across the floor. "What on earth are you doing in that—?"

"Surprise!" He came over to hug her.

"What is going on?" Ellen demanded. "I thought you took the train to Salem to follow up that story on the kidnapping, but you come home looking like—"

"That's right. And I got my information. Then

I stopped by the recruitment headquarters. They gave me a physical and, well, here I—"

"But you told me you weren't eligible for the draft. You said your feet were—"

"Turned out I was wrong," he told her. "My mother told me that when I was an adolescent . . . and I never questioned her. Apparently she was misinformed."

"But you've always been opposed to war, Lawrence," Ellen reminded him. "Remember when you told me that you'd rather cut off your right arm than go over there to—"

"I've changed, Ellen." He nodded to Katy. "I'm going over there to help your husband."

"Help my husband?" Katy frowned to imagine Lawrence attempting to help Jim.

"Well, I won't actually help Jim personally. But I'm going over there to do my part."

Now Ellen started to cry. "But, Lawrence, you promised to—"

"Hush, hush." With his arm around Ellen, he made their excuses to Katy then led his sobbing wife out of the building.

Left on her own to finish the decorations, which were nearly done anyway, Katy just shook her head in wonder. Lawrence's feet were not flat after all. Go figure. And Lawrence was no longer a conscientious objector. Katy would have to write a new letter to Jim about this interesting new development. He'd be sure to get a good laugh over it. But she hoped it would turn out well for Lawrence. Somehow, she'd never imagined him, the stylishly dressed city boy, as a soldier.

As Katy drove the Runabout home, she stopped by the new hospital. She knew they were just over a week away from the grand opening and that Sarah Rose had been spending a lot of time working there. Since the front doors were unlocked, Katy decided to go inside and take a little look around. She was just past the reception area when she spied Sarah Rose in what looked like a private office. "Hello," she called out. "Is it okay if I look around?"

"Of course." Sarah came over to greet her. "I'll give you the grand tour, if you like. I've told you to come by anytime I'm here." She pointed to the opened door behind her. "That's Dr. Daniel's office. I was just getting his files set up. We hope to move fully in here by early next week."

"And will you have the grand opening then?"

"No, that won't be until the following weekend. We've still got furnishings to be delivered, and the painters aren't quite done. Dr. Daniel wants everything in picture-perfect place for the grand opening. It's scheduled for the first Saturday of November." She led Katy down a hallway, showing her a patients' ward that looked fairly well outfitted. "Of course, if we had some kind of medical emergency, the patient could be treated in here. But generally speaking, we're not advertising that the hospital is open just yet." She led Katy through another ward and then past several unfurnished patients' rooms and finally upstairs. "As you probably know, some of this second floor will remain unfinished at first." She pointed to a corridor that was blocked. "That won't get done until more funds come in. Of course, we won't really need all that space anyway. Not at first."

"Everything is so much better than what Dr. Daniel had before. It's all modern and clean and nice." Katy stood in a room with a view of the ocean. "Maybe when I have my baby, I'll get to stay here."

Sarah Rose chuckled. "We'll see about that."

"It's wonderful," Katy said as they went back down the stairs. "You must be excited to be a part of it."

Sarah let out a long sigh. "I hope I'll continue to have a part in it."

"Why wouldn't you?"

"Oh, I don't know." Sarah lowered her voice. "There's been some talk. Maybe I'm not a good fit here."

Katy felt her temper rising. "You mean because of—"

"Hush, hush." Sarah Rose nodded to where the older Dr. Hollister was coming their way. "Not now."

They paused to greet him. "What do you think of our new facility?" he asked Katy in an authoritative tone.

"It's impressive."

"Humph. If you think this is impressive, I wonder what you'd say about the hospital I left behind in Boston. Now that was a fine hospital indeed."

"I'd say that if I were in need of a hospital, it would be a very long trip to Boston." She suppressed the urge to giggle.

He just shook his head and walked away.

"Is *he* the problem?" Katy asked Sarah when she knew he was out of earshot.

She barely nodded. "He doesn't think I'm capable."

"Well, that's ridiculous."

She shrugged. "I don't know. Maybe he's right."

"What does Dr. Daniel have to say about this?"

Sarah pursed her lips.

"I can't believe he wouldn't back you in this, Sarah."

"It's not only that." She grimly shook her head. "I can't really say anything though. Not yet."

Katy wanted to pursue this further, but the older doctor was coming back their way, watching them with a hawk-like gaze that made Katy feel like an errant school girl. "Well, I suppose I should let you get back to your work," she told Sarah.

"Yes, I hoped to get that file cabinet all set up before quitting time today." Sarah's smile looked stiff. "And please, don't worry about what I said. Maybe I can explain it all later."

As Katy drove home, she wondered why Sarah was being so mysterious. More than that, she wondered why Dr. Hollister was acting so bossy. After all, the hospital was for the people of Sunset Cove. And although Dr. Daniel was in charge, that didn't mean his opinionated father should have a say in how it was run or about whether or not Sarah Rose should be involved. That just irked Katy.

Although Daniel had been busy with his practice and then even busier getting the hospital set up these past several weeks, he'd made room in his busy schedule to spend time with Anna. But usually only once or twice a week. Although, with the hospital's grand opening scheduled for tomorrow, Anna hoped they'd be able to spend a bit more time together in the upcoming weeks. From what she'd seen during her preview hospital tour on Thursday, everything was pretty much in place. And tomorrow's paper would not only contain a reminder of the grand opening but a comprehensive article about the modern improvements the new facility offered. Anna suspected everyone in town would go to see it.

As Anna walked home, she was tempted to swing by Daniel's house. But ever since Sarah Rose had permanently moved there—to help with housework as well as at the hospital—Anna no longer had an excuse to stop by after work. She missed her walks with Sarah almost as much as she missed her "random" encounters with Daniel. But being this was Friday, and Anna's work week was done, she decided to stop by and catch up just for the fun of it. She hoped they wouldn't still be working at the hospital.

"Welcome," Daniel said as he met her on the front porch. "I'm the only one here at the moment. Sarah Rose and my father are both still at the hospital." He grinned. "But perhaps you came to see me."

Anna felt both pleased and embarrassed. "I'm not sure who I came to see. I've been missing my walks with Sarah Rose. . . ." She smiled shyly. "And I haven't seen you for several days as well."

"Well, come on in and see how the house has changed." He held open the front door. "Now that I've relocated my office and examining room to the hospital, it's more like a house than a business." He led her through what used to be the reception area but now resembled a well-furnished parlor. "See, it's like a real house now."

"Very nice." Despite the improvements, the place no longer had the friendly feeling she remembered from the first day she and Daniel had walked through it . . . on that day when she'd allowed herself to imagine living there as husband and wife.

"My father had some of his furnishings shipped from Boston." He walked her through the living and dining rooms now. "As you can see, some of the pieces are a bit large and grand for this house, but the price was right." He grinned. "And it makes my father happy."

"Really?" Anna felt her brows arch. "Your father is happy?"

"Well, as happy as he can be . . . considering."

Now Anna felt guilty. "Yes, I'm sure this transition has taken its toll on him. But now that he's been here a few months, I hope he's feeling more situated. And with the hospital nearly done, it seems that life should be settling down some . . . for all of you."

"I hope it'll settle down. But tomorrow's the big day. I only came home to get some vases. Some people have sent flowers for the grand opening, but we had nothing to put them in. Want to help me carry them back up there?"

"I'd be glad to." She followed him into the kitchen, waiting as he hunted around in cupboards and the pantry.

"Sarah Rose assured me that we have some, but she didn't mention where."

"Let me help you look." Anna opened a storage

cabinet. "Aha." She pointed to where various-sized vases were on a high shelf.

Daniel reached to take them down. "You carry this crystal one. It looks like it may be precious. I assume these came with Father's things. And I'll carry these matching blue vases. They'll look nice on the reception desk."

Loaded with their vases, they headed for the hospital. "You must be feeling very good about everything," Anna said as they walked up the hill. "The hospital turning out so well and even a bit ahead of schedule."

"To be honest, I've been having some rather mixed feelings about the whole thing."

"Really?" Anna was surprised. "Hasn't it turned out as you'd hoped? Not as well equipped as the hospital in Boston that your father is so fond of, I know, but . . ."

"No, no, that's not it."

"Are you concerned about not having enough medical staff? Mac mentioned something about that to me the other day."

"My father is actually working on that for me. He's written to some nursing schools and whatnot."

"Oh." Anna nodded. "Katy mentioned something about Sarah Rose. She seemed concerned that you may not have need of her at the new hospital. I hope that's not true."

"Sarah Rose still has a job with me," he

declared. "She's a top-notch office manager, and I hope she'll continue for as long as she likes. Although I'm concerned she'll be doing too much in keeping house for us and working full-time at the hospital. I told her she may have to make a choice about that."

"Oh, that's good to hear." They were nearly at the hospital now, and Anna could tell that something was bothering Daniel. She hoped it didn't have anything to do with her or their relationship.

"How do you feel about arranging flowers?" Daniel asked as they went inside.

"Well, I'm not as talented as my artistic daughter, but I think I can hold my own."

He set the blue vases on the reception desk, next to a couple of floral boxes. "Well, if you have time and don't mind, I'd appreciate it. I need to take care of some things upstairs. Then, as a thank you, perhaps you'd allow me to take you to dinner tonight."

She smiled. "I'd love that."

So as he went upstairs, she worked on the flowers . . . finally getting them, she hoped, just right. She set the two blue vases on either ends of the reception desk and then walked around with the larger crystal vase, trying to find a good place to set it. Finally, she decided on the big round coffee table in the waiting area. If Daniel didn't like it, he could certainly move it.

"Oh, my, that does look pretty," Sarah Rose said. She held a box of what looked like information brochures, pausing to arrange some on the table. "Everything seems to be falling right into place."

"How are you doing?" Anna asked her. "I'm sure you've been busy."

"Yes, but I like being busy." Sarah laid some more brochures on the reception desk.

"Will you continue to work here at the hospital?" Anna asked. "Daniel sounds as if he hopes you will."

"I'd like to." Sarah frowned slightly. "We've been discussing it."

"Oh . . . I see." Anna remembered how Katy had hinted that Sarah had seemed mysterious.

"There you are, Anna." Daniel joined them. "The flowers look perfect. Thank you." He smiled at Sarah. "Unless there's anything else you think I should attend to, I promised to take my flower arranger to dinner. Will you let my father know?"

"Yes." She put the brochure box behind the reception desk. "I think he's getting ready to leave. And the janitors promised to lock up after they finish the floors upstairs."

"Good. You and Father should walk home together," Daniel told her. "And tomorrow will be a busy day for all of us." He turned to Anna. "Ready to go?"

"Whenever you are." They told Sarah goodbye and went back outside where it was already getting dusky. "I love these autumn evenings," she said as they strolled toward town. "The weather has been so nice and mild."

"Even my father has admitted that our West Coast climate is a bit more pleasant than Boston's." He linked her arm into his. "If you can believe that."

She laughed. "Well, I must say that's nice to hear. He's not usually complimentary about Sunset Cove."

"Give him time." Daniel paused to gaze out to the ocean where the last traces of a sunset were still coloring the sky with shades of plum and amber.

"Very pretty." Anna nodded toward the horizon. "A good boding for tomorrow's grand opening, don't you think?"

"I hope so." He turned them back toward town. "Anna, I want to talk to you about something. A couple of somethings."

"Oh?" Anna detected something in his tone again—almost as if he were the bearer of some kind of bad news.

"But first, I want to compliment you on the newspaper during the last month. It's really first rate. Very impressive."

"Well, thank you. That's nice to hear."

"Your war coverage is excellent. You don't

print anything sensational, and yet you don't play it down either. It's just right."

"Thank you very much. Sometimes it does feel like a balancing act."

"That piece last week about the mustard gas . . . I know it must've been hard to write about that hideous sort of warfare. But it's something Americans, even out here in Sunset Cove, should be aware of, I think."

"I made sure to put it in the midweek edition." She sighed. "And I didn't include all the details. It was too gruesome."

"You included enough. Not everyone needs to know how excruciating it can be. As a physician, I'm interested. But even I find the effects appalling. And I wonder about treatments for the internal and external bleeding. Or how to make a patient comfortable during a slow and painful death."

"It's so horribly inhumane." Anna shuddered.

"Yes, and I'm sorry to go on about it. But reading that article helped me to reach a conclusion. That's why I'm so grateful you wrote it."

"What sort of conclusion?" She felt her spirits sinking.

"I'm enlisting as an army doctor, Anna. I've already sent them a telegram."

"What?" Anna felt slightly sick. "But what about the hospital? Your future here?"

"You know the numbers of injured soldiers.

You've printed it in the newspaper. They add up more each day. By the minute and the hour. And you know those poor men desperately need good medical attention. More than anyone here in Sunset Cove."

"Yes, of course." She nodded grimly. "And I can't say this hasn't crossed my mind. But I suppose I hoped . . . selfishly . . . that the hospital would keep you here."

"The hospital is wonderful. I won't deny its lure. But I would feel guilty if I remained here." He turned to look into her face under the street-lamp. "You do understand that, don't you?"

"Of course." She forced a smile. "I wouldn't expect you to do anything else, Daniel. I'm proud of you for wanting to go over there. And, you're right, they desperately need you. More than Sunset Cove."

"I didn't want to make this announcement until after the grand opening," he confessed. "I've told Sarah Rose because I know this affects her."

"Meaning she won't have a job?"

"I'm not sure." He paused in front of the hotel restaurant. "I'd like to ask my father to take over as chief of staff. I know he can be an old curmudgeon. At least that's how it's been out here. But I sometimes wonder if that's just because he feels old and useless. If he had some responsibilities—"

"What about his health? His heart?"

"He actually seems to be improving. I just gave him a checkup on Monday, and he's definitely doing better. I've been crediting the clean sea air, but whatever it is, he is improving."

"Does he even want the job?"

"I haven't mentioned it to him yet. Not specifically anyway. For the time being, he's fairly content with his role as an assisting physician. Especially since he'd given up on practicing medicine again. I think a little more responsibility could give him a new lease on life. Anyway, I hope so."

"Well, then this is probably a good thing." She paused as they went into the hotel, waiting to be seated at a table in the restaurant.

"I want to keep all this under wraps for the time being."

"Yes, of course." Anna wondered why he was telling her all this. Perhaps he just needed someone to talk to. "I won't say a word to anyone."

After they were seated, Daniel turned to her. "There's something else I want to talk to you about, Anna. I'm not sure if this is the best time and place, but for some reason I feel I can't put it off any longer."

"Oh?" She studied him closely as she peeled off her gloves, suddenly feeling very nervous and self-conscious.

"Originally, I had planned to do this after the grand opening. But after sending that telegram and knowing that time is running short, I don't want to wait." He reached for her hand, holding it in his. "Anna McDowell, would you do me the honor of becoming my wife?"

She felt her eyes getting wide and, for a moment, couldn't speak.

"I know this probably seems sudden. But I think you know how I feel about you." He glanced around as if to ensure no one was watching or listening. "I have loved you for a long time. We've had our ups and downs and challenges, but I just don't want to head off to war without knowing that you'll be here waiting for me." He squeezed her hand. "Please, Anna, tell me your answer."

"Yes," she said quietly. "I would love to marry you, Daniel."

His face broke into a huge smile and then, despite the other diners, he leaned over and kissed her. "Thank you."

She felt her face growing warm. "I—I just hardly know what to say. I'm so stunned. I felt certain you were going to tell me some other bit of bad news. I didn't expect this."

"I'm sorry to have blindsided you." He patted her hand. "Thank you for not turning me down."

She laughed. "You should have had no worries on that account."

"I know we'll have a lot to figure out. And I

don't want to get married until *after* the war ends. I think that's only fair to you."

Anna wasn't so sure, but she didn't want to press him on this.

"And maybe by then it'll be easier to work out the details. I realize we both have our careers. But we've discussed it before, and I think we can figure it all out." The edges of his eyes crinkled with his smile. "Together. We'll work it out together, Anna."

"And perhaps this war won't last too much longer," she said quietly. "Now that our American soldiers are over there helping. Perhaps it won't be so very long until you come home."

"And it'll be reassuring to know I have you waiting for me here. Someone very lovely to come home to."

Anna smiled. "I'll be here . . . waiting for you." *And praying,* she thought, *for your safe return.*

Center Point Large Print
600 Brooks Road / PO Box 1
Thorndike, ME 04986-0001 USA

(207) 568-3717

US & Canada:
1 800 929-9108
www.centerpointlargeprint.com